About the A

Though born in America of Uk
Hayes came to England after obta ... egree from Rutgers University and then an MA in Washington D.C. Intending to continue her studies for a short time in London, she instead married an Englishman and stayed permanently, raising four children and settling in the Devon countryside. Besides being a poet and a short story writer, whose work has been published in numerous magazines, she has in the past been employed as a university lecturer in English literature, as a social worker in the Harlem area of New York City, as a yoga instructor, as a co-ordinator for basic education, and as a teacher of deaf adolescents. In the past few years she has spent time in rural France, where she finds the atmosphere and tranquillity conducive to her writing.

Summer Poem

Karen Hayes

POCKET BOOKS
New York London Toronto Sydney Tokyo Singapore

First published in Great Britain by Simon & Schuster Ltd, 1993
A Paramount Communications Company

Simon & Schuster Ltd
West Garden Place
Kendal Street
London W2 2AQ

Simon & Schuster of Australia Pty Ltd
Sydney

A CIP catalogue record for this book is available from the British Library.

ISBN 0-671-85209-4

Printed in Great Britain by HarperCollins
Manufacturing, Glasgow

For Julia, Jacki, Adrian, Jeremy - and Nigel, their father

Chapter One

The ferry churns towards France but Hester resolutely faces England. What does she want with France now, with its fine wines and its excitable people and the smell of herbs in the clear quiet countryside? She wants England, her own country, her own space. She wants to hold on to the tranquillity she is only just beginning to find there.

There's no tranquillity here: it's May Bank Holiday and the boat is heaving with those who, unlike Hester, have actually chosen to go to France. They come laden with children and packed lunches and paperback novels with covers as glossy as enamel. They all seem to be wearing bright shiny track suits and brilliant white trainers, and in spite of the rather dubious rolling of the ferry, everyone seems to be extraordinarily merry. It makes Hester feel dour in her long cord skirt the colour of rusty nails and her long suede boots as dark and grey as winter. 'Cast not a clout ere May is out,' her mother used to say: strange how Hester laughed at that once.

She is not normally a dour person, and wonders why she is feeling this way now. As she watches Plymouth fade in the overcast distance she is aware of all her assets: life and health and the absence, now, of responsibilities. Or so it seemed, before the phone call that put her on this wretchedly overcrowded holiday ferry.

The feckless sun wanders lazily out from under the clouds and Hester's fellow passengers perk up even more, stripping off outer layers to reveal flamboyant T-shirts of various colours and sizes. She takes off her baggy cardigan, Joseph-like with its many hues, and feels satisfyingly sombre in her black cotton T-shirt. She is, after all, a poet – she is expected to be downbeat on occasion.

After a time England, like all things, recedes; the boat ploughs on through grey and frizzy waters and everyone except the stalwarts puts their jumpers back on and goes inside, to the bars and cinema and the cafeteria and restaurant. Hester stays out on the deck a bit longer, watching for dolphins. They are never there when you are looking; they sneak up on you unexpectedly, like illness or snowdrops, she thinks sadly. Once many years ago, leaving the man she loved and staring at this same sea, she saw six dolphins leaping in and out of the water, playing with the ferry boat like children with a raft, diving under it, coming out the other side, following along, racing, soaring like swallows in the air and then down under, into the deep water. It should have been magic but their uninhibited joy only reminded Hester of what she was losing.

Later she wrote a poem about it. It was a sad little piece, and she finds herself wishing that the dolphins will come back for her again now, all these years later, so that she can write a happier poem about them. But the sea is grim and empty; she stares at it for a long time, seeing nothing. Finally she gathers herself and goes back inside.

Hester wanders aimlessly around the boat for a time, looking in the duty-free shop but not buying anything, checking out the tiny newsagents where she purchases *Le Monde*, and finally settling in a relatively peaceful area at the front of the boat off the main bar, a small room with only a few tables and some comfortable cushioned chairs. On two sides there are windows overlooking the sea, which would have made the room light and sunny if the sky wasn't beginning to turn the colour of mussels. Hester settles herself in a corner near a window and takes out a paperback, a novel she has been trying to read for months. Of course she has several collections of poetry with her, for she can never go far without that – but she decides against them now. Poetry is for more peaceful moments, when one is able to contemplate, to go into oneself like a little animal burrowing into its nest. This heaving mass of sea and sound and teeming people is hardly conducive to serenity.

The room is fairly quiet, compared to the rest of the boat. There is a loudspeaker that pipes in music from the bar, but it's not loud or intrusive, mostly innocuous folk music in both languages. Every now and again the music is interrupted by an announcement, first in French and then in melodious, heavily-accented English: *'If the boat sinks, you will go to the appropriate deck. Captain Lamont and his crew join in wishing you a pleasant journey. We are on English time.'* And so on.

The room is gradually filling, as people wander in from the sunless decks. A Frenchman with a beard lights a Gauloise but is politely asked to leave by a steward; this is a No Smoking area. Hester is relieved: the smell is too evocative for her at the moment. Two English couples settle at the table opposite; the women are both wearing tight white trousers and high-heeled shoes, and their hair is as permed and fluffy as a well-cared-for poodle. 'Jim'll get us drinks, won't you Jimmy?' says the woman with apricot hair as she takes out a small mirror from her handbag and tweaks a curl or two around. She nudges the compact, muscular man in a bright blue and yellow shell suit next to her, frowning slightly at him. 'All right then? You'll get us the drinks?'

'The usual for me, Jimmy, only make it a tall one, lots of ginger,' says the other woman, unbuttoning the top button of her sunny yellow see-through blouse. 'All this hanging around for hours in the car waiting to get on the boat has made me hot and sweaty.' She pouts cutely, undoing yet another button and revealing the lacy bits of a black bra coyly camouflaging a healthy cleavage. On the yellow blouse, pinned over her right nipple is a badge: *40 Today*. She looks terribly pleased with herself, smiling up at Jimmy, fanning her cleavage delicately with the open collar of her thin blouse. Such confidence, at forty, Hester thinks. When I was that age I trembled with children, a husband, a job – a house too big to handle . . . dreams which were beginning to surface. Eighteen years later and I am finished with all that, she concludes rather smugly, then remembers the phone call of the previous evening and swears mildly under her breath.

Turning away from *40 Today*, Hester opens her novel. The boat is now not only rolling but bobbing about like a kite with the string cut, seemingly out of control, though Hester tells herself rather uneasily that she has the utmost faith in Captain Lamont and his crew. There is definitely a storm at sea. With a sigh she gives up all attempts to read and looks out of the window, wondering if she will be sick, for it is years since she has been on a ferry. Outside, everything is grey and brown and foamy, like dirty soapsuds. She thinks of the dolphins and envies them, safe beneath all this turbulence.

Looking away from the window and around the room, Hester notices that her fellow passengers are not as boisterous as they were earlier; *40 Today* looks quite pasty and seems to be blaming her husband – a tall, corpulent moustached man in a green track suit – for this sudden change in the weather. He takes no notice, just lays his head down on the table as if he too were ill, though he notices Hester watching him and conspiratorially winks at her. She turns away quickly, amused, and looks towards the other side of the now crowded room.

There, sitting alone at a small table, his back towards her, a man with white-grey hair, slightly long and curling over his collar, takes a flask out of his old canvas rucksack. Hester watches him admiringly, wishing she had had the foresight to bring a flask rather than fighting the queues for the tasteless tea sold on the ferry.

She stares at him absent-mindedly, envying the tea. From where she sits she can just see his hands, one holding the cup, the other resting on a slight book that is lying on the table. She can see nothing else, yet suddenly she is wary, alert: all the hairs on her body are prickling. And yet she doesn't know why . . . A strong sense of *déjà vu* envelops her. And then the man moves his hand to put away the flask and there it is – the book. Hester recognizes it instantly. The cover is adorned with an abstract of old empty glass bottles, covered with cobwebs, the colours deep green and brown and black, reflecting the darkness, the loss and pain contained in the poems inside. For it is Hester's book, of course, her first collection of poetry. And even as she recognizes it, she is still unaware of the identity of the man holding it. Her mind refuses to remember, for it has kept a tight rein on her emotions for years now.

But her body knows. Her body has already acknowledged what her mind will not accept since she first noticed the man, saw those hands pouring the tea, cradling the cup in a gesture as familiar to her as those her own hands make. Her body reacts before her mind comprehends: it stiffens, the pulses race – it senses danger. She watches him pick up her book of poetry, turn the pages, and suddenly her mind explodes in a firework of recognition. 'Alex,' she says softly. '*Alex.*'

As if hearing her whisper, the man turns, glances around. Hester wants to look away but she can't. She has to see his face, has to find out whether her mind is playing tricks – if the man who turns to her will have a stranger's face, nothing to do with Alex. But it isn't a stranger. He's older, of course, and his face is thinner, but it's still Alex.

And then he sees her. For a moment his body tenses the way hers did, and she can tell his mind also refuses to take in what his eyes are telling him. Like Hester, it takes a moment. Perhaps he won't recognize me, she thinks. It is eight years and I too have grown older.

But he does, he does. The room has grown strangely quiet. The piped music has stopped, the passengers – queasy with the pitching of the ferry – are now drowsy and still. Outside, the sea foams and rain pushes darkly against the portholes. Alex's eyes meet Hester's and, in shock, they acknowledge each other.

Neither of them moves. The acknowledgement was a slight, almost imperceptible nodding of the head on his part: the merest parting of the lips on hers. It is not too late, she thinks wildly, not too late to withdraw my eyes, glaze over, turn back to my book, pretend I haven't recognized him. Maybe he'll be glad of this reprieve, able to turn away, too, look out to sea, convince himself that I am only a ghost – an aging woman who fleetingly reminded him of someone he once loved.

But neither of them turns away: neither has enough wit to dissemble, though both, for a fleeting, painful moment, have every inclination to do so. And then Alex does an endearing thing. He rolls his eyes skyward, smiling faintly in a gesture that was once a kind of a code between them – a message that said, 'Oh God, everything is out of hand again, everything is conspiring against us, but it's okay, love, we'll survive. Somehow we'll survive, against all the odds.'

It makes Hester smile, as it always did; reassures her, as it always did – and shaking her head in shock and disbelief, she stands up and runs to him, and then he's up and running too across the rolling, pitching boat and they meet halfway, hugging and clinging to each other with such obvious emotion that even *40 Today* turns a bleary eye up from her sickbag to glare at them balefully.

They don't notice – not anyone, not anything. Time slides back gracefully like a silk scarf on fine hair, lost before one knows it is slipping away. They cling, though it is too late now. They cling as if they were tying the knot harder, forgetting it loosened and unravelled all those years ago. Hester and Alex hold each other as tightly as they did the day they said *au revoir*, not knowing then that it was really goodbye.

And then, before they can disentangle, before they remember where they are now and the years that have passed, the boat makes a sudden plunge and they fall over, still holding on to each other. They are flung in a most undignified manner on to the table of *40 Today* and her Jolly Green Giant of a husband, and everywhere glasses tumble on to the floor and there is a great deal of activity as waiters clear the débris while the passengers, fighting nausea, slump deeper into their seats.

Hester and Alex extricate themselves with fulsome apologies and Alex collects his rucksack, moving over to Hester's table by the window.

'God, Hester, I don't believe—'

'Alex, this is, I don't know—'

They pause. Having stared intensely at each other for a few moments, they now awkwardly turn away, suddenly looking with great concentration out of the window.

'Terrible storm.'

'I know. The sea is quite fierce.'

'Look at those breakers.'

'Lucky dolphins.'

'What?'

'You know – dolphins.'

'Oh.'

'I mean, they're luckier than us. We're on top of the sea, they're safe underneath.'

'Ah. Yes, I see.'

'Listen to the wind—'

'Must be gale force.'

They talk in this inane manner for a few more moments, pondering what gale force this storm could be, as if it mattered, as if anything mattered right now except for their finding each other like this. But they both understand; they are collecting themselves, trying to regain the composure both have lost from this bizarre encounter.

So Hester says, to keep up the inconsequential chatter, 'Alex, are you going to be sick? How are your sea legs?'

'Oh, I'm never sick on boats. Love them, love them,' he replies happily, smiling suddenly and expectantly like a child, as if you are meant to share in his smile, to return it. So that hasn't changed in him, Hester thinks as she smiles back. Nor have his flecked tiger eyes – a curious green and gold colour with thick black lashes that look oddly young amidst the wrinkles on his face: they are exactly as she remembers. But his hair . . . Hester admits to herself that she is shocked by how that is changed. Where once it was dark, almost black, it is now all salty and white, like the sea churning and foaming outside. This is strangely disconcerting to her and she finds she has to look away from him.

'What about you? You don't like boats,' Alex says, his face suddenly concerned, tragic almost in his artless worry about her. He always did have a wonderfully expressive face, Hester remembers. She used to feel he should have been an actor, until she began to truly know him and to see that the emotions his face reflected were his own genuine feelings, and that it was impossible for him to express anything that wasn't.

He is looking at her now with real concern, so she says reassuringly, 'I took a tablet, I'm sure I'll be fine.'

They have exhausted the weather, so they are forced to be quiet and regard each other. Alex speaks first.

'So much to say, Hester. So many years to cross.'

'I know. I don't know how to begin.'

'Nor I. You're still lovely.'

'Oh, bullshit, Alex!'

'And you still swear in a very un-English manner. Good.'

'Like you I've grown older,' Hester says caustically. 'I have wrinkles around my eyes like the marks of birds walking in the snow . . .'

'That's from one of the poems in that first collection of yours, *Empty Bottles*. I've just been re-reading it – brilliant stuff. Yes, you do have some wrinkles around your eyes. They suit you.'

'Thanks,' Hester says, sardonic.

'Why isn't your hair grey? I'm terribly jealous. I know – you touch it up!'

'Don't be daft, of course it's got some grey, only you can't tell because of the plait.'

'Hardly any – I can see by all the wispy bits that have come out. I like your hair like that, the long plait down your back. You look like a lady poet.'

Hester smiles. It used to be a joke between them, when she was struggling to write poetry that no one wanted to publish. Alex would say, 'At least you *look* like a lady poet,' admiring her strings of beads and silky Indian scarves and the dangly earrings that used to get caught up in her dark thick tangly hair when they made love wildly like gypsies in abandoned barns, or fields of hay surrounded by high, dark hedgerows.

'You mean I'm neither a lady nor a poet,' Hester would reply laughingly, half-naked either in sun or rain. The weather never bothered them much, though Hester blushes now to think of it.

'Not at this moment, you're not,' Alex would reply. 'Not a lady nor a poet, thank God for that.' And he would carry on making love to her even when the ground was white with frost, or the skies leaked with drizzle, or the wind bellowed above them.

God, thinks Hester, how impetuous we were then, and we didn't even have the excuse of being young. She feels faintly embarrassed, and wonders if Alex feels the same.

The boat gives another lurch as they sit silently, remembering. All around them everyone is still. Most people have curled up in coats and jumpers on the floor and those who remain upright are motionless, eyes on the erratic horizon. Alex and Hester both look out at the foaming, churning sea and then, simultaneously, back at each other.

And then it all bubbles up; there is so much to say that they begin speaking together – where are you living, what are you doing now, how did you come to be on this boat. . . ?

What has happened to your life? is what they are really saying. *Where has it gone while I wasn't around? Where are you now,* who *are you now?*

But Alex says it first. 'Are you still married, Hester? Still with Martin?'

'You haven't heard?' Hester replies, searching his eyes.

'I've not heard anything about you or your family for years.'

'Martin died three years ago.'

Alex is shocked. Whatever he expected, it was not this. He knew Martin was considerably older than Hester, and had been ill for much of his life, but the illnesses were never the kind that killed you. On the contrary, they were the sort that made you take better care of yourself, and so live much longer than anyone expected. So Martin dead takes some adjusting now for Alex.

'He was seventy-four, you know,' Hester says quietly. 'And his heart was giving him trouble over the last few years. The doctors said if he hadn't taken such care of himself, exercising and watching his diet, he'd have died years earlier.'

'I see,' Alex says, and is it bitterness Hester detects in his voice, or is the moaning of the sea creating imaginary disharmony? But then he continues, 'I'm sorry. He was a good colleague – I enjoyed the brief time I worked with him,' and Hester knows he is sincere, that the bitterness, if there was any, was fleeting.

'Martin was a good man,' she says emphatically. 'That's why I couldn't leave him, Alex. Not for you, not for anyone.'

'I know, Hester.'

'It was right, what I did. We made the right decision.'

Alex looks at her strangely. 'It was *your* decision, Hester, not mine,' he says gently. 'After all these years, you still think it was right?'

Hester looks at those gold-green eyes and the hard, deep lines around his sweet mouth and says firmly, 'Yes, I do. It was the only decision, Alex. The only one at all.'

Alex looks away, out to sea, and she notices again how long his hair has grown, but how grey, how white. When she last saw him he had only one or two flecks of grey amongst the dark, and those were underneath, above his neck, where only she saw them as they made love in the bright sunlight filtering through the pine trees in hidden copses and woodlands.

'And you?' she says quickly, because she doesn't want to think about these things right now. 'I know you and Angela never got back together, but have you married again? Or are you in a relationship?'

Alex remains staring out to sea for another moment or two before replying, almost nonchalantly, 'I never remarried – God, wouldn't do that again. But yes, I guess you could say I'm in a relationship.'

Hester finds this hard to handle. She no longer loves Alex, no longer wants that intensity of feeling she had with him; she wants peace, comfort, security. But the thought of him with another woman unsettles her. She looks out at the raging sea and suddenly feels slightly seasick.

Alex reads her thoughts, and smiles sadly. 'Did you really think, Hester, that I would – that I *should* – pine away for you all those years, a lonely eccentric hermit?'

Hester protests, since that's exactly what she did think. 'Why isn't she with you?' she says brightly. 'Surely you're not going on holiday on your own?'

Alex says, watching her carefully, 'I'm not on holiday, I'm going home. I live in France now.'

'Oh.' And Hester adds stupidly, 'With her?'

Alex watches her again, and she cannot fathom what he is thinking, which is odd for someone with such an expressive face. I no longer can read you, she thinks sadly, and then is angry with herself. She grieved over Alex for years, she reminds herself. Her grieving is *over*.

'No, actually,' Alex is saying. 'She's not living with me; she lives in the village. She'd like to move in, but . . .'

He shrugs in a very Gallic way, and Hester thinks – yes, he'll be fine in France, just fine.'

'I'm too old and crusty to live with anyone these days.'

'Me too.'

They smile, only half-meaning it. They are, after all, only in their fifties, but it is safer, perhaps, to think of themselves as old. When we were in our forties we acted like adolescents, Hester thinks wryly, and now we are maturing sombrely into an early old age. Or perhaps I should speak for myself: Alex may be living alone but unlike me he is involved, passionate. He is in a relationship, while I am alone, uncommitted, detached from all that excess of emotion that relationships usually entail.

Hester believes that she, not Alex, is the lucky one, but before she can get too smug she hears herself unwillingly asking, 'And what is she like, Alex? Your, um – your woman? More suitable than a lady poet, I hope, especially one so very tied as I was.' She smiles to show she is only teasing.

Alex doesn't smile; he is beginning to look somewhat strained, somewhat drawn. Perhaps he doesn't want to share this new love? Hester is ready to be affronted, but he says, albeit hesitantly, 'She's French. Lives with her two sons, they're ten and twelve. She's younger than me, thirteen or fourteen years younger, I guess. She spends most of her time in a converted barn full of barrels of herbs from Provence which she packages and markets. She smells like rosemary. We've been together, off and on, for three years.'

Three years. Alex found her at just about the time Martin died. While Hester sat at her husband's hospital bedside, holding his dying hand, Alex was in France, *their* France, smiling his sweet smile at a woman smelling of rosemary.

Somewhat stunned, she says, glibly, 'Well, I'm glad I didn't look you up when Martin died.'

But something is wrong, terribly wrong. Alex is staring out again at the sea which churns and gurgles like dirty bathwater thundering down old lead pipes, and now Hester sees there is a tiny bead of sweat along the side of his face which looks white as milk, and his hand on the table is clenched so tightly that all the veins stand to attention like soldiers.

Oh God, she thinks, he's ill, Alex is ill. The thought comes to her suddenly and with great certainty: *I'm going to lose him again*. She doesn't stop to analyze how she can lose someone she doesn't have any more, someone she hasn't seen in eight years. The boat tips from side to side and Hester's heart does too and she cries out, without thinking, 'Alex, have you been to England to see a specialist? You're ill, aren't you, I can tell. For God's sake, what's wrong?'

The look he gives her is so stricken that she panics, sure he is terminally ill. Taking his hand she says weakly, 'Tell me, Alex. For God's sake, tell me – I must know.'

He stares at her with glazed eyes. The boat is rocking dementedly like an overwrought mother rocking a cradle. 'Actually,' he says finally, taking his hand from hers and standing most unsteadily, 'I'm afraid I'm going to be sick.'

With that he walks hurriedly away from her, not looking back, just as he did the last time they parted, eight years ago. Only then he was trying to hold back tears, Hester thinks crossly, not going off to be seasick. She takes a deep breath, mortified, not for Alex but for herself, for her surplus of emotion. She is overwrought, she tells herself reasonably, not because of Alex but because of that wretched phone call from France two days ago, and this wretched unexpected visit that she is forced to make. She knew she would find France unnerving; after all, her last visit was traumatic and it is understandable that she feels slightly unhinged. If she just stays calm, she'll get over it.

Satisfied with her reasoning, Hester takes out her book again but cannot concentrate. The sea is still hissing and fermenting and suddenly she is hungry, famished, but the thought of walking across the rolling ferry to the cafeteria is not very appealing. Glancing around, she sees Alex's rucksack on the table; it is partially open, with her book of poetry falling out. Hester feels inordinately gratified; her first collection was published a year after Alex and she parted, and she sees by the smudges and marks that it has been well-read.

As she picks up the book, Hester inadvertently dislodges a plastic container. She starts to put it back but can see that it is full of sandwiches. She hesitates for only a moment, then opens it, marvelling that after all these years Alex still prefers mustard on his chicken sandwiches. They taste delicious, and she eats most of them, knowing he won't be fit to eat for some time.

There is still tea left in his flask: it is Earl Grey, and Hester helps herself to a bright blue plastic cupful. It tastes wonderful. Then she settles down to leaf through *Empty Bottles*, at which she hasn't looked for years.

Outside, the sea growls and grumbles and roars. Hester wonders where Alex is, and hopes he made it to the men's room. Her mind is as turbulent as the sea, but her stomach is calm and full. In spite of herself she feels extraordinarily well, and thinks how odd it is that after all these years she has found her sea legs at last.

Chapter Two

Alex returns a half-hour later looking like a man already drowned. Hester offers him the one chicken sandwich that is left.

'Aargh,' he moans, slumping at the table with his head in his hands. Hester offers instead her chunky cardigan as a pillow, suggesting that he lies down on the floor. He agrees and curls up under the window, right next to the table. As Hester covers him tenderly with his coat she thinks, I don't need this, this caring for someone else. I have done it for too many years – I have nothing left to give. She is pleased to feel like this. Alex, after all, has his French herb girl who smells like rosemary to comfort him in such moments and as for herself – well, she no longer needs anyone. She has her poetry and her garden, a dog she acquired when Martin died, and two very independent cats. Her two daughters supply her with filial respect and, she hopes, affection. She tells herself trenchantly that it would be churlish to long for anything more.

Alex sleeps for the remainder of the journey. Once he rolls over and gives Hester his special look, the rolling upward of the eyes with the slight smile, but she thinks, It is too late, Alex. That doesn't move me any longer. She notes that he looks slightly seedy: his once-strong jowls are wobbly and definitely stubbly, like an overweight hedgehog. His mouth is open and he is snoring, and his hair, once so sleek and shiny, is matted and tangled. Hester observes all this with conscious dispassion, deliberately detaching herself from this person whom she once loved so dementedly, this man for whom she nearly left her husband and home and daughters.

Nearly? Hester *did* leave – for three weeks. The irony was that no one knew she had done it, no one but Alex who was with her. Alex had just separated from his wife with a great deal of bitterness and acrimony; he had left her once previously, long before Hester even knew him, but had returned because of his two sons whom he loved inordinately. Simply, he could not live without his children, could not conceive of knowing them only at weekends, on the odd holiday. But in the end Alex was forced to admit he was wrong, and he never forgave himself for returning to a marriage that was loveless on both sides. Too late, he realized his beloved sons suffered more from the damage he and Angela inflicted on each other than they would have, had the family broken up. Years later they were to tell him: 'You and Mum should have split up ages ago, Dad. It was either constant quarrels and arguments, or stony silences and atmospheres.' But Alex, agonizing, couldn't leave them. It wasn't until both boys were at university, and he in his late forties by then, that he was able to make the final break.

'Be sure you're not doing it for me!' Hester cried on more than one occasion, when Alex was making his plans to leave Angela, move to France for a few months, and then return to England and, he hoped, a new life.

'You can't do it for me. I'm not free – I'll never leave Martin.' She warned him of this over and over again, terrified that Alex might make demands on her she would never be able to fulfil.

'God, Hester, how many more times do I have to tell you? I'm doing it for *me*! And for Angela too, though she can't see it. I fill her with such bitterness – she can't forgive me for not being the man she thought she married. Since the early years of our marriage she's wanted to change me. I've never been ambitious enough for her, she hated my being in education . . . oh, the list goes on and on. I can't bear talking about it any more.'

'Then why doesn't she let you go?' Hester wailed. 'Why did she fight to get you to go back all those years ago! Why is she clinging to you now, like a bloody leech, for God's sake!'

'Angie never lets anything go, you know that. Divorce to her would be a failure, like not returning a library book or falling behind with the mortgage repayments. Anyway, she still thinks I'll change. She's convinced I'm the way I am merely to annoy her, and that eventually, if she perseveres, I'll become the man she should have married. I hope that when I've been away from England for a few months, she'll realize that it's definitely over.'

'I don't want you to go away, I can't bear it.'

'Oh, Hester! I don't want to go either but I must, at least for a time. Come with me! Come with me to France.'

'I can't,' Hester despaired. 'I can't.'

But in the end she did. Not forever, as Alex wanted, but for three weeks, staying in a cottage in Brittany that belonged to a friend of his.

Alex described it to Hester on the ferry, the same boat they were on today, only then the sun shone and the sea was as sparkly and iridescent as new rain after a long drought.

'I'm glad it's calm,' Hester told him. 'I don't like boats much, they make me nervous as well as seasick. I don't think I could cope with a storm.'

'Really? I love the sea, the stormier the better.'

She had looked at him fondly, wondering if she could write a poem about the way his gold-green eyes reflected the ocean, but almost immediately discarding the idea. She wanted to live life, she thought passionately, not write about it. It was only later, when she believed she would never see him again, that she wrote her poems about Alex, and the first one, *Empty Bottles* – the title also of that collection – was about the house in France.

'Wait until you see it,' Alex had said. 'It's on the coast, not that far from Roscoff, outside a tiny village called Kerrocher. It sits at the end of an estuary, all on its own, and there's a balcony that looks down over the water. We could fish from it if we wanted to.'

They had laughed, delighted with each other, delighted in being on this ferry bound for France, delighted most of all with the heady knowledge that in the three weeks to come they could do anything they wanted . . . that for the first time ever, they would be together for more than just a few hours in any one day.

Then Alex had cried, 'Look, dolphins!' and there in the sea off the side of the boat were two of them, leaping up from the placid water into the sunlight and then disappearing like conjurers.

'Oh Alex,' Hester said, moved. 'I've never seen dolphins before.'

The cottage was perfect. Hydrangeas, newly flowering, burst out of control all around the stone walls, and the water at full tide came right up to their balcony, just as Alex had promised. On each side of the narrow waterway were lush green woodlands from which kingfishers suddenly flew out over the water, and in the distance, out to sea, came flickers of light from fishing boats and the lighthouse. Inside it was plain, undecorated, but felt lush and luxurious simply because they were together. As Hester described it later: *'The house was simple, a plain bottle/illuminated by its contents: love, we called it,/iridescent colours richly filling every contour.'*

For that was what it was like; the house was indeed an empty bottle which was soon transformed, becoming rich and magnificent and splendid as they filled it up with their love and with their lovemaking.

It was the first time they had ever made love in a bed, and this small pleasure gave them much erotic joy, being soft and sensual after their usual rendezvous among broken branches and tree roots. Hester had just had her fiftieth birthday – so she was long past the age when one is expected to do such cavorting, but love and sex and the vibrant good health that often accompanies these blessings were bestowed upon her that holiday. Already looking younger than her age, she seemed to shed years more as her skin became lightly tanned in the constant French sun, and her body relaxed and gained strength with the long walks in the woodlands by day, the lovemaking at night. She glowed, she radiated like a miniature nuclear reactor: Alex adored her.

'God, you're beautiful,' he told her, kissing the tips of her nipples, the flat of her stomach, as she lay spread on the strange luxurious bed, revelling in the softness. From the open window they could hear the tide coming in, the lapping of water on rocks, and later she remembered Alex's cry mingling with the song of a nightingale floating over the smell of sea and salt and sex.

And the Gauloises . . . Alex smoked them copiously in France and occasionally Hester would have one also, sitting on the tiny balcony surrounded by woodland and hydrangeas, looking out over the sea. Silently they watched the blue smoke from their cigarettes waft away down the estuary, content and peaceful after their lovemaking, locked in a moment that haunts Hester still, sneaks up on her unexpectedly, invading the sanctuary of her cloistered heart with the faint aroma of a French cigarette, the remembered image of hazy smoke drifting over the sea and disappearing into the sunset.

No one knew Hester was in France with Alex. Her husband and daughters thought she was in Normandy, visiting an old schoolfriend called Sarah. It was the first time she had gone anywhere without Martin, and she felt more guilt over leaving him behind, with his arthritis and angina and the strict diet he had devised for himself, than she did over the fact that she was going to be with her lover. Where she went, and with whom, didn't matter nearly so much as the fact that she had dared to go. Martin liked her at his side, always – a faithful guide dog, placid and biddable.

But this time Hester was determined. 'I am exhausted, Martin. I need this break,' she said to him when he protested.

'How do you think I feel?' he countered. 'My hip is so painful I can no longer take long walks, and yet the doctor says I must exercise because of my heart.'

'I know, and I'm sorry. But I've just finished teaching three hectic full-time terms for that tutor who had a breakdown, and now I can understand why he did! His timetable was completely exhausting, both physically and mentally. I must get away for a few weeks before I start my next dose of supply work.'

'And leave me to cope here alone. Thank you, Hester,' Martin replied sardonically.

'Oh, for God's sake! For the past few years I've pleaded with you to come away on holiday, but you've taken a sudden dislike to travel. If you won't come with me, I'll have to go alone.'

And indeed, for the first time Hester could feel relief, could secretly rejoice even, over Martin's sudden decision, made several years ago when he retired, never to take another foreign holiday. Travelling, he declared, caused havoc with his sleep and with his diet; he was healthier and happier at home, and home they would stay from now on. Hester, having Alex, went along with this, but now, for the first time, she objected. Martin had no choice but to let her have her way, albeit ungraciously. So, crossing her fingers and taking a deep breath, Hester packed her bag, took a bus to the ferry port, and met Alex who was waiting for her at the terminal.

They made the most of it, knowing that these few weeks were very possibly all the time they would have together, other than their usual few snatched hours. When they weren't hidden in the cottage like nesting birds they walked in the woods, swam in the sea, and sometimes went into Kerrocher, where they found a restaurant perched haphazardly on a lone cliff overlooking the waves.

'Oh look,' Hester said, spotting it in the distance as she and Alex walked along the cliff's edge early one evening. 'What a funny little place! Shall we go and investigate?'

Le Café de la Mer was empty, and remained that way during most of the evenings that Hester and Alex spent there. The owner – a large ebullient man – had just started up, he told them, and he hoped business would improve when the summer really got under way. Sensing that they were lovers, he gave them the most romantic table in the restaurant – a corner one by the huge window. Candles and fresh flowers were in abundance, and a *soupe de poissons* of a quality Hester had never tasted before; but best of all, there was the time to talk, and to look out at the lights of the boats at sea as they lingered over their evening meal.

They went to Le Café de la Mer often during those three weeks, getting to know the proprietor who spoke very good

English and always chatted to them amicably both when they arrived, and when they made ready to leave. But in between he was wonderfully discreet, disappearing into the kitchen and leaving them well alone as they sat for hours pretending that they had a future together.

It was banal, Hester thought later, all that self-delusion, wondering aloud what it would be like living together, when both of them knew it was not an option. They did a lot that was banal that holiday, and more that was foolhardy as well – like going deeper into each other, loving more, giving more. Peeling off layers of emotion like onions, so that they saw what was underneath, knew the core of each other and craved it, not for just these few weeks, but for always.

'Don't go,' Alex said suddenly as they stood at Roscoff waiting for Hester to board the ferry home. He had driven her to the port and Hester's younger daughter, Abigail, who had just passed her driving test, was to meet her on the other side, in Plymouth.

'I don't want to go,' Hester replied, waiting for the loudspeaker to call her on to the boat. Alex was staying behind for the next two or three months. He had taken a year's unpaid leave from his job and was remaining at the house to do some work on it for the owner – some badly-needed decorating and repairs. When it was finished, he would return to England and decide what to do next.

'Leave him,' Alex said, for the first and only time. 'Leave Martin, stay with me.'

'There's Abigail—'

'She's almost eighteen, off to her music college in a few weeks. You don't love Martin—'

'I do, that's the problem!'

'Not like you love me. You love him as you would an old friend you don't even *like* very much – one who has become a habit.'

'I know,' Hester said sadly. 'That's why I can't leave him. You can't do that to a friend.'

They clung to each other like limpets to rocks, then Hester had to go. They didn't intend this to be the end; they thought the parting was temporary, not final. If Hester had known, would she have left that day? She wondered agonizingly for years about that . . . and never came to any conclusion.

And now it is eight years later and Alex and Hester are back in Roscoff. The boat has docked and the passengers have picked themselves up and are straightening out their clothes, rubbing their faces, feeling relieved. *40 Today* has lost a shoe under the table and is nagging her husband to find it for her. The loudspeaker is telling them they have arrived and Captain Lamont and his crew are hoping the passengers will travel with them again. Alex scowls as Hester pours him the few remaining dregs of tea from his flask.

'I'm sorry about that,' he says, drinking it gingerly. 'I never get sick on boats.'

'Things change,' Hester says cryptically. 'Which reminds me – do you still smoke Gauloises?'

Alex looks quite ill at the thought. 'God, no. Gave up cigarettes years ago.'

'There,' Hester says triumphantly. 'I told you things change.'

'Bloody nuisance getting seasick like this. I wasted the whole trip.'

Hester smiles placidly at him. 'I didn't. I had a lovely time drinking your tea and eating all your chicken sandwiches.'

'Hester, don't be so maddening, you know what I mean. We haven't had a chance to talk, and now we're here in Roscoff. Where are you going? How long are you staying?'

'I'm going to see Imogen – she's married and living in France now.'

'Good God, I can't imagine her being married. I think about your daughters often, especially Abigail. I knew her so much better, of course, as she was still living at home. Is she married also?'

Before Hester can answer, the loudspeaker pings again and the voice tells them in French that they can now go to their cars.

'No, she's not married,' Hester says rather curtly, gathering her belongings. As she picks up her capacious red quilted bag she knocks over *40 Today*'s coffee. The birthday lady looks scathingly at Hester, though Hester knows full well the coffee is stone cold: Jimmy of the blue shell suit brought a tray of it over for his dispirited party a full half hour ago. Nonetheless she apologizes and Alex, who has only a rucksack, grabs her other bag, her precious book bag, and follows her through the bar towards the car exits. The boat's corridors are full of people; their pristine tracksuits look grimy now, their faces much the same. There is a distinct smell of vomit everywhere.

'Is Abigail in France as well?' Alex shouts above the whine of children and the swearing of French adolescents as they wait for the queue to the cars to subside.

'Yes,' Hester replies, manoeuvering her quilted bag away from an English child trying to stuff a half-eaten croissant in it.

'How nice for you,' Alex says, 'the whole family together.'

He sounds so wistful that it makes Hester cross, so she says, as they jostle and push their way down the stairs to the belly of the boat, 'Bullshit, Alex. Imogen rang me from France two nights ago to say her sister Abigail has run off with her husband Gordon. I'm going there now to try and sort things out.'

'Good God!'

'Yes. I was hoping never to set eyes on France again, just as I was hoping never to set eyes on you again.' This is harsh but Hester is beginning to weaken; emotions assail her from all directions and she is no longer used to it. She knew France would have a debilitating effect on her and is determined to overcome it.

'Anyway,' she continues, hoisting her quilted bag on her shoulder and knocking off the glasses of the passenger behind who swears at her in German, 'here is my car. Goodbye, Alex.'

She unlocks her car, an old MG that Alex stares at in some amazement (she drove a Volvo estate when they were lovers), throws her bag in, and starts the engine as already they are letting her row of cars out over the ramp and into France. She does not look back, just as Alex did not look back that last time in Roscoff, and the memory of it scratches Hester's heart like a bramble and she knows for certain, and despairs of it, that this parting too will mark her, though exactly how she is not quite sure.

But then the passenger door opens and Alex is sitting beside her, and before Hester can react the two are driving into France together as they did all those years ago.

'You're crazy! Get into your own car,' Hester hisses at him.

'I can't. It's in France, so I'm a foot-passenger. Anyway, you forgot your sack of poems.'

She looks at him incredulously; he is holding the old scarred leather book bag that she takes with her everywhere. It contains all her random jottings for new poems, her notebooks and pens, her favourite books and collections of poetry – her whole essence as a writer is in that floppy black bag. The fact that she forgot it says epics about her meeting with Alex.

Oh hell, she thinks wretchedly. Three days ago I was serenely gardening, my life and my emotions as clean and ordered as folded laundry, and now I am sitting in the belly of a boat with a man I thought I'd never see again. I am going to visit my daughters, both of whom seem to be ruining their lives, in a country I once loved but now cannot bear, because it stirs up passions that I hoped were dormant, like cold seeds in an even colder winter. Damn, she swears silently. Damn, damn damn. She knows that if she is not careful, the springtime sun of France will trigger an explosive sprouting of things that should always remain buried in the dark, things that should never see the light of day again.

But there is no sun in France. It is raining, and the wind is howling. It is quite dark, dark and late; the storm slowed the crossing considerably.

'Oh, God,' Hester cries in despair. 'Are things never as they were? Does even France have to change? I'd have so liked to remember it as it was.'

Alex starts to answer her but they are going through Customs. When this finishes Hester pulls into the terminal building, and parks the car. 'I need a coffee before I carry on,' she says to him. 'It's a three-hour drive to Imogen's house and I've never been there before. I need to look at the map again. Where are you going?'

'I have to go to the terminal, too. I'm meeting someone.'

Hester looks at him sharply. The rain whizzes around them as she locks the car and they walk towards the building. 'The herb lady?' she says.

'Actually . . . yes,' Alex replies rather lamely. 'She's brought my car.'

'How devoted. And where do you live; Alex? I hope the young woman did not have to travel far; it is not a nice evening for travellers.'

Alex looks at Hester strangely as they go through the steamy glass doors into the ferry terminal. 'As a matter of fact,' he says slowly, 'it's quite close, less than a half-hour drive.'

She stops and looks at him. He shrugs that Gallic shrug which so suits his thin frame, his slight wiry body, and says casually, 'I couldn't leave it, you see. The house. Not after you wrote to me, told me you would not see me again when I returned to England. I couldn't face England without you somehow.'

'Alex . . . I had to.'

'Oh, I suppose you were right, though I still don't know why you did it. I had hoped we could at least go on the way we had been for the last few years, finding a few hours a week for each other whenever we could. Obviously I was wrong.'

Hester says, in some distress, 'I had hoped we could too, go on in our bumbling way without hurting anyone. But – we couldn't,' she finishes lamely, knowing it would take too long, and it is far too late, to tell him now what she was never able to write him.

'Well, whatever.' Alex too seems unable to go on. Finally he says, 'At any rate, I had no desire to go back to England, not after your letter.'

'I heard you and Angie sold the house, but I didn't know you stayed in France. I quit my job, you see. I had no way of finding out about you, and I didn't really try. It was all too . . .'

Hester flounders again, and they are silent, looking away from each other and around the huge crowded room where passengers rush by with bags and knapsacks, ferry officials placate customers in French and English for the storm delays, and children lie collapsed in little heaps of sleeping bags, oblivious to everything.

'So I bought the house in France,' Alex says at last. 'After I'd been there a few months, my friend decided he wanted to sell. I had the money, for Angie and I had just sold our place in England. So that was it and there you are: my story brought up to date.'

So there they are. Shamelessly Hester's eyes fill with tears but she tries to bluff her way through them. I'm a poet, she thinks fiercely: I'm allowed to be sentimental on occasion. She acknowledges what could have been, then takes out a handkerchief and blows her nose.

At that moment, a girl who looks sixteen with hair like a rodent and teeth like a hamster appears and covers Alex in kisses. When she stops for a breath Hester can see that she is in her early forties and has a pert, pointy face under all that scrambled weevil-coloured hair.

'Goodbye,' Hester says brightly, rushing off towards the Ladies. 'Must hurry.'

'Hester, wait!' Alex shouts after her.

'I can't, I really can't,' she shouts back.

'Does Imogen have a phone?' he asks, running after her. A French crew member looks at him admiringly. Rosemary, or whatever her name is, clings to his arm like a mating gerbil.

'No,' Hester lies. She wants to get away, before she is introduced to this herbal child who smells like rosemary and looks barely older than her daughter. Hester does not love Alex any more, but, being human, she doesn't want him to love anyone else. Especially not in France.

'I'm glad you haven't let her move in,' she cries to Alex

impetuously, hoping the herb woman doesn't understand English. Then she blows Alex what she hopes is an appealing, tender and – most important – final kiss, before rushing into the Ladies.

Hester darts into the only empty cubicle, sits on the toilet seat, and bursts into tears. She hasn't cried for three years, since Martin died; she didn't even cry when her daughter Imogen phoned to say her sister Abigail had run off with her husband Gordon. She fumed, of course, and cursed that the even tenor of her life was to be spoiled, that her English country garden would have to be neglected for a few weeks, that she would have to return to France when she wanted to keep the reality of that country at arm's length, preferring to remember the fantasy – a doomed love affair and a profusion of hydrangeas.

But now something has broken in her, the wall she began to build after she left Alex, the wall that grew higher when she thought she would lose her daughters, the wall she completed when Martin died and she vowed to be through with attachments forever. It's breaking now like a cracked reservoir, letting in the torrential flood of feelings she has for so long held back, and she is as powerless to stop it as sand is to the tide.

And so here Hester sits, on a loo seat in Roscoff, crying for all she is worth: for her daughters, whose lives seem to be a total mess right now, and for her husband, who is dead and has left her alone to sort out his two children. Then she cries for Alex, whose hair has gone white, and when she finishes mourning Alex's dark hair she cries for France, which was sunny once and the air thick with the hot smell of the sea and honeysuckle, and nightingales sang in the night instead of the sodden wind which tonight shouts and rumbles and groans and farts like an old man having a nightmare.

Finally, Hester cries for herself, for the person she once was and never will be again, the one who made love on stones and roots and felt only ecstasy, the one who loved Alex who is no longer there but only some stranger with jaws like a hedgehog who kisses girls smelling of rosemary and whose hair has turned white like the foam on the sea.

And she cries because that woman who doesn't exist any more lost Alex in France a long time ago; then she is crying because the woman she is now has also lost Alex a second time, just a few minutes ago. Then she is so confused that she begins crying all over again because it is dark and late and stormy and she has a long, long drive ahead of her and she doesn't even know the way.

Hester cries for an inordinately long, indulgent time. An hour passes before she finally emerges from the Ladies, cleaned up, brushed and powdered, with a fresh new plait hanging down her back. She is feeling fragile but slightly better: she knows this because she is hungry again.

Before leaving the Ladies, Hester looks at herself carefully and critically in the brightly-lit mirror, something she has not done for some time. She decides that she has physically, at any rate, weathered the years far better than Alex. Her hair, attacked by salt and wind, has frizzed around her new plait and tumbles about on her forehead and around her cheeks – the 'wispy bits', Alex had called them, and Hester agrees they are not unattractive. The wrinkles around her fine dark eyes are all too apparent, but at least her jaw is firm, and though when she smiles her face cracks like an egg, her lips are still full and her teeth white.

Feeling curiously satisfied, Hester takes several deep breaths, as she does before a poetry reading, boldly opens the cloakroom door, and walks out. She is ready, albeit shakily, to face France for the second time in eight years.

Chapter Three

It is three hours later when Hester finally arrives at her daughter Imogen's home. Imogen, first impatiently, then with growing concern, has been pacing the floor of her well-groomed house. She is bursting with indignation, hurt pride, and a kind of furious grief which she is anxious to off-load upon her mother. She loves Hester, and so of course this gives her the right to make her suffer also, as Imogen herself is suffering. After all, it is Hester's other daughter who ran off with Imogen's husband: Hester must bear some of the responsibility.

And so when her mother finally arrives, Imogen is so relieved that she shows it by battering Hester with words before she is even properly in the sitting room. 'Mum, I've been so worried! Why didn't you ring? I've been frantically phoning the ferry office trying to find you. They said the boat was late because of a storm; you are naughty not to phone me. I never thought you'd attempt the drive tonight! Why ever didn't you stay the night in Roscoff?'

'I, well, I wanted—'

'God, Mum, you look exhausted. You really must take care of yourself. You're not as young as you were, you know. You really do look shattered, you poor old dear.'

Hester instantly feels irritated. She loves her older daughter, but detests the way Imogen, since Martin died, has relegated her to a poor old dear. Hester's hair is still dark, her body still trim and firm, and she walks more miles in a week than Imogen does in six months, but her daughter still sees her as a poor old dear. Hester suspects this is because she hasn't a man in her life, and this irritates her all the more.

She is reminded now that Imogen hasn't a man in *her* life, but Hester refuses to cope with this until the morning. Luckily Imogen too is tired, and has rather gone off the idea of raging and howling about her sister until her mother is more able to withstand it all. In the midst of her own misery she can see that Hester is not quite herself; her eyes look definitely puffy and her nose is red. Imogen thinks sadly that her mother can't take it like she used to, and decides to put her to bed after a cup of tea and a quick tour of the house.

It's magnificent, this house. It seems to Hester to be a mini-château full of interesting corners and crevices and windows and doorways. Although it seems huge, it's all wonderfully warm, as there are attractive woodburning stoves of intricate design in most of the fireplaces. The lovely, patterned wool rugs covering the sleek and polished wooden floors add to this effect, as do the thick velvet curtains in warm, antique yellows and golds and crimsons. The furniture is a mixture of old, heavy Breton pieces, delicate English antiques, and the odd bit of Victoriana, and surprisingly, everything works: it is both comfortable and easy on the eye. Aesthetically satisfied, Hester takes off her boots for the first time in almost twenty-four hours and paddles around in the depths of a thick, lush Turkish carpet, deciding that physical comfort is not a bad thing after a storm at sea and a chance meeting with your ex-lover.

After some desultory conversation, Imogen takes her mother to her bedroom, a large room with high ceilings and French windows shuttered against the night. Here there are the same polished floors, and an immense circular rug as white and thick and soft as an angora goat. Hester can't wait to plunge her bare feet into it. Facing the shuttered windows is an elegant brass bed, piled high with billowing pillows and a fluffy duvet cloud of sunrise-pink. On the wall next to the bed is a painting of market day in a French village which cheers Hester immensely with its *joie de vivre*, its opulence of colour and light.

Hester, delighted with it all, suddenly finds she wants to giggle: it is so far removed from her own bedroom in England with the old shabby carpet, the sparse furniture, the travel posters haphazardly splattered around the walls, the single divan bed with the Indian bedspread casually thrown over it. How neat and tidy everything is, not like her room at home with its piles of notebooks and paper and pens on every surface, or all those clothes draped on every chair because she could never decide what to wear when giving a poetry reading. My house is tangled, she muses, but my garden is immaculate, pristine. It is my garden and my life that I keep well-ordered and after all, that is what is important to me.

Imogen's house is immaculate. Tired though she is, Hester has taken in the order, the discipline of the house which looks as unruffled as a row of tulips. The furniture, the well-chosen ornaments, the vases of flowers . . . all look as if they have been carefully planted and nurtured here for years. Hester marvels at her daughter, knowing she works long hours and yet still manages to produce this.

And still looks bloody marvellous, Hester acknowledges. Stunning and completely unruffled, despite all the trauma of the past week. Her thick dark hair is neatly cut just under her ears and swept fetchingly to the side, fastened with a tiny ebony clip. Her lovely oval face is still, at this time of night, craftily made up, and she is wearing a long white silk nightgown, all lace and little straps, with a matching dressing gown. She looks enchanting, but also slightly forbidding. Hester wonders if that is why Gordon left her.

But she absolutely refuses to dwell on that now, and sits on the soft down duvet with a sigh of pure delight at the luxury of it all. Luxury, or rather the lack of it, has never been a problem for Hester, which is just as well for a poet, but she is sensuous enough to enjoy it when it is so blatantly thrust upon her. She sighs again, which Imogen mistakes for exhaustion. She kisses her mother solicitously before tiptoeing out and wishing the poor old dear a good night's sleep. Hester is relieved to be on her own, and after a wash and a change into her long brushed cotton nightgown, curls up like a furry animal and prepares to sleep for hours.

But oddly, tired as she is, she can't sleep. The wind has dropped and the rain ceased, and it all seems strangely quiet, ominously so. After a half hour of staring into the darkness, Hester finally gets out of bed, opens the window and sees, in the light of the stars and fresh new moon, a willow tree, a clump of peonies, and some bushes covered with a yellow flower that Hester can't quite discern. There is a smell of France in the air – a mixture of new blossom, honeysuckle and early roses, all mingled with the sea just over the hill, and the fresh scent of night after a rainfall. It is all so painfully beautiful, so evocative, that Hester wishes with all her heart she had not come, that she were back in England, in her tidy, ordered garden which she has painstakingly raked and plotted and hoed into submission just as she raked her heart back in line after the disastrous affair with Alex. She misses them both, her garden and her composed well-plotted heart, for they seem as out of reach to her here in this dangerous, alien place as the stars coldly distant in the dark night sky.

It is a long time before Hester finally falls asleep, and when she does she dreams fitfully of being in a troubled land, riotous with uncontrolled colours and scents and foliage and passions. She feels as tumbled and blown by the dream as a butterfly caught without shelter in a sudden summer storm, and as fragile. When morning comes and she awakes, she is definitely relieved – for whatever she has to face in the day ahead will certainly be less uncomfortable than the emotions that assailed her during the night.

And so Hester awakes to the sun trying so hard to get in through the shutters that she instantly leaps up to open them. At once she is in France, really in France. The house is just outside a village and her window faces the little road leading to the church which dominates the square, and the three or four tiny shops dotted around it. An old man on a bicycle is pedalling home with bread; he sees Hester, waves, and carries on slowly up the hill. Beyond the cluster of stone houses opposite, Hester can see the sea, calm and serene after giving her such a hard time yesterday. She opens the French windows and steps out on to a tiny balcony with wrought-iron railings, full of clay pots of red geraniums. The balcony overlooks part of the garden, a rather chaotic mass of peonies, roses of every colour, yellow buddleia, and an exquisite willow which sparkles like a chandelier as the sunlight catches the morning dew.

There is a discreet knock on the door and Imogen walks in with a tray of early morning tea.

'*Bonjour! Ça va, Maman?*' she says, and she and Hester talk a little in French which years ago Hester knew quite well, having taken the girls to France on so many holidays before Martin became adverse to travel. Imogen's French, Hester notices, is now as efficient and under control as the rest of her life, or rather as her life was before this recent crisis. Hester sighs, remembering why she is here.

'Lapsang,' Imogen says, pouring the tea from a white china pot festooned with poppies. 'I remembered you like it.' She smiles, looking amazingly unlike a woman whose husband has just left her. Though it is still quite early she is fully dressed in a rosy skirt with buttons all up the front and a pink silk shirt tucked in, with a smart leather belt buckled around her slim waist. The sun coming in the window lights her up like a glowing ember about to burst into flame. Hester notices with some admiration that her hair is combed, her make-up impeccable.

Tactfully Imogen does not mention her marriage or her sister, and leaves her mother to shower in an adjoining room which must have once been a small dressing room but which has now been converted into a perfect white bathroom. The hot water sings and sizzles. Hester washes her hair and dries it with the little blow dryer she found tucked in one of the drawers. Imogen thinks of everything: there is even a collection of poetry by the popular French poet, Jacques Prévert, on the bedside table.

Hester searches her hair carefully for signs of grey, something she has not done for years. There are a few grey hairs, yes, but not many. Hester silently thanks her mother, who did not turn grey until her eighties, for this genetic bonus.

Suddenly she puts down her comb and shakes her head with disgust, wondering why she is suddenly so obsessed with her hair. Crossly she plaits it and when, as usually happens, the shorter, wispier bits that do not fit tumble around her face, she remembers Alex on the boat last night, commenting on them. She smiles at her reflection in the sun-struck mirror and wonders how Alex is today. For some inexplicable reason, she derives great satisfaction out of imagining him in the French house – *their* house – though she knows it is not theirs any longer, never will be 'theirs' again. But Alex is in that house, and Hester can picture him in it. (She tries not to picture the herbal hamster there also, and determinedly puts Alex's Frenchwoman out of her mind.) For so many years, thinking Alex had left France, she could not visualize his whereabouts, could not place him, and although she was trying to forget him, the fact that she didn't know where he was irrationally made her feel that he could be anywhere: that she would see him in an open window in a city, or walking along a well-trod footpath in the countryside. This thought was not comforting, for she knew that if she saw him, she would have to walk away from him again, and she did not know if she could do it a second time.

But she did yesterday, she thinks, remembering how she ran into the Ladies. As she dresses in a pair of cotton khaki trousers, with a baggy olive-green woolly jumper (cast not a clout) and a long flimsy scarf the colour of a flock of parrots, tied loosely around her neck, she allows herself a spasm of anger against Alex. He could have waited, after all these years. Yes, she was in the loo for an hour, but what is an hour after eight years? True, she refused to tell him Imogen's phone number, but couldn't he, for old time's sake, have persisted?

This is futile; Hester is in a turmoil. Fighting down an impulse to write about it, she quotes to herself what Wordsworth said about emotions – that they should be recollected in tranquillity. Feeling far from tranquil herself at that moment, Hester decides that food is more important than poetry and marches downstairs to breakfast.

'You poor dear, are you rested now?' Imogen cries from the kitchen, where a blackbird sings in the open window and outside the sun gathers strength for the day.

The kitchen is tastefully modernized and smells

gratifyingly of coffee, but Imogen hustles her mother through into a courtyard where cobbled slabs of granite stone seem to fight with grass and wild daisies, and old apple trees cluster and hover and there is a profusion of flowers and colour everywhere. It's utterly enchanting, and Hester sits down with pleasure at the outdoor table laden with freshly-made coffee, huge white china cups, croissants, a mixture of French breads, Brittany butter, apricot jam, and piping hot milk for the coffee.

'What a splendid garden,' Hester says, itching to get to it, to prune a bit, tidy up a little.

'We're putting a courtyard in, a proper one. Neither of us are gardeners,' Imogen says abstractedly. Then she remembers. 'Or we were,' she says heavily. She puts down the coffee pot in a tragic gesture of despair and stares gloomily at a blackbird in the largest apple tree. She looks magnificent.

With regret Hester realizes the time has come To Talk About It. She takes a bracing sip of the excellent coffee, casts a clout (her jumper: it's hot in this wonderful garden), and faces her daughter.

'Tell me about it,' she begins gently.

But Imogen is not in the mood to be gentle. 'The bitch,' she says. 'The cow, the bloody—'

'Imogen, calm down.'

'I know she's your daughter – Christ, she's my sister! I can't believe it, my own sister – are you *sure* we're sisters? Maybe she's adopted.'

'Of course she's not adopted, Imogen. You came to see her yourself in hospital.'

'I know, how can I forget it? I was ten, and so looking forward to having a sister of my own, someone I could help look after, someone I could pour out all my love to.'

This is so outlandish that Hester has to interrupt. 'Imogen, what a lot of crap. You were mad with jealousy when Abigail was born. Surely you remember how you begged and pleaded with your father and me to send her back?'

Imogen sips her coffee and glares at her mother over the

china cup. Her eyes are black, broody, and quite cunningly made up. Her skin is slightly olive, flawless. Hester finds herself wondering if she can borrow her daughter's moisturizing cream.

'Oh, I might have had a fleeting second or two of sibling rivalry, but it soon passed,' Imogen continues after a moment. 'It's a wonder I didn't have more, you and Dad were so besotted with the little shit when she arrived.'

'Imogen! How unfair, we doted on you. Of course we were happy to have Abigail, we had been trying for years to have a brother or sister for you and it was such a surprise when it happened. But we went out of our way to make sure you wouldn't feel left out.'

Imogen takes another sulky sip of her coffee and looks darkly at her mother again. It's a look Hester remembers quite well, one her daughter has used for years – a mixture of wounded innocence and a smug certainty that she is right. It gets to Hester every time.

Feeling slightly out of control, Hester finds she is suddenly famished. All she's had for almost twenty-four hours were Alex's chicken sandwiches with mustard, give or take an apple or two she bought at the ferry terminal and the Brie and biscuits Imogen gave her with her tea last night. Hester, who is used to eating plainly and substantially, helps herself to a large portion of baguette and smears on the butter and apricot jam while her daughter quietly simmers. Hester has to admit that Imogen's eyes look magnificent, all lined with some kind of a black kohl thing, and her lashes longer and thicker than ever. They smoulder beautifully, and Hester, despite herself, is impressed.

And so they sit like this for some time, Hester munching lightly and Imogen brooding darkly. They played this game often when Imogen was growing up, Hester remembers – Imogen not saying a word, waiting for Hester to justify herself, explain herself – but she's not in the mood for it now. The game always began when Hester told Imogen something she didn't want to know: hard truths have never come easy for this fractious daughter. Though to be fair, Hester thinks that is probably true for most of us. Illusion makes a far greener pasture to graze in than the hard crust of reality, and anyone who tries to move us from the lush grass to the salient rocks often gets short shrift.

But now Hester does not want to play the game; she is too busy eating to speak and so she ignores Imogen's mood for the moment and lets herself feel the pleasure of bread still warm from the *boulangerie*, of full-fat, unsalted local butter softly melting in her mouth, of the taste of fresh apricots in the exquisite thick jam.

Imogen can't keep it up; she has too much to say to remain brooding, so she cries, 'Oh Mum, you forget things, it's understandable at your age. But I remember it all so well, the things I did for Abigail. I was always looking after her, pushing her around the garden in her pram—'

'Rubbish,' Hester says, reaching across the flowered oilskin tablecloth for a croissant. 'You tipped her over once, right into the flowerbeds. It's a wonder she wasn't concussed.'

Imogen ignores this. She sits back in her garden chair, the sun glowing on her face, and says dramatically to the apple tree, 'How could she do this to me? My own little sister! I used to play with her all day when she was growing up.'

'You begged me to put a lock on your door so you could get away from her.'

'I used to talk to her for hours . . .'

'You told her once that she was adopted. Upset her for weeks.'

'Yes, well, that was a joke, but she never could take jokes – no sense of humour. God, when I think of the way I used to put up with her when I was older, letting her follow me and my friends around everywhere.' She breaks off with a sigh.

Hester echoes that sigh, remembering Imogen's tantrums – and Abigail's sulks – when Abby wanted to tag along with her older sister and Imogen refused even to contemplate it. 'Imogen,' Hester says somewhat snappishly, 'forget the past. What about now? Where is Abby, where is Gordon? What exactly is happening?'

'Don't you know? Hasn't Abigail been in touch with you?'

'She sent a letter. It arrived a few days after your phone call.'

'What cheek. What did she say?'

'Only what you had already told me. She was with Gordon, they were going away for a few days together to sort things out—'

'Ha!'

'And she hoped that when you calmed down you would understand and forgive them both.'

This sends Imogen right over the top. She rants and raves: hell hath no fury. If Hester hadn't suckled this formidable woman as an infant at her breast, she'd have felt no little trepidation now as the younger woman vents her anger. Imogen is a strong, assertive woman, used to having her own way when she feels she is in the right, but one of her failings is that when she is crossed, her subsequent rages are hard to control. To give her her due, she has in the past been highly successful, thanks in part to the fact that she *is* usually in the right when it comes to furthering her career. In England she ran a successful modelling agency after becoming bored with being a model herself; here, in France, she masterminds the antique business she and Gordon began when they moved here over a year or so ago. All this, and her house is immaculate. Hester wilts, thinking of this energy and efficiency.

'Calm down, Imo,' Hester says now. 'I know the whole thing is a mess, and I can't think what Abigail is up to, but it won't do you any good shrieking and swearing like that. You're becoming dishevelled and your make-up is smearing. Do pull yourself together, for God's sake.'

Ordinarily this would have been enough to calm her, but to Hester's surprise, Imogen now bursts into tears. Like Hester herself in the Ladies yesterday, all these tears are out of character. In the past, Imogen's emotional outbursts have been anger, fury even – never grief, never tears. Hester, reacting instantaneously, takes her daughter in her arms and cradles her, soothes her like a baby. 'My poor darling,' Hester murmurs. 'My poor sweetheart.'

Imogen cries as if her heart is breaking. Hester, her composure still shaky from yesterday's encounter on the boat, does too, because her heart is breaking also. She loves her daughter, and her pain is her mother's pain; her heartbreak, Hester's own. Sod Abigail, she thinks as she tries to comfort Imogen, then she remembers, I love Abby too. It is all such a mess that she cries even harder.

Imogen finally stops and scrabbles around in the pockets of her skirt for a handkerchief, and the blackbird sings and sings in the apple tree while Hester's daughter hiccups and sighs and blows her nose. She looks pathetic and unsure, with her mascara smudged, hair all messy and her silky blouse pulled out of her rosy skirt. Hester finds herself wishing that Gordon could see her now for there is, paradoxically, something very appealing about the way she looks, the way she snivels. Perhaps it is because for once she is herself, and not on show, not putting on the façade she seems to need to cope with the exhausting standards she sets for herself.

For a few moments mother and daughter sit quietly in the sun, listening to the blackbird singing so gloriously that Hester's congested heart turns clear and untroubled for a second or two. But then a sniff and a sigh from Imogen bring her back to reality.

'Tell me all about it,' she says gently, thinking what a shame such a sad tale is about to unfold with the bird warbling his head off in the sunshine.

And so Imogen tells her. For the next hour she talks and Hester listens, inserting the occasional exclamation, the odd question. At times she wants to get hold of Abigail, her younger daughter, and shake her soundly; at other times, she could weep with anguish for her, for apparently the child thinks she is in love with Gordon. It is no excuse, of course, for what she and he have done, but Hester can understand the temptation. Oh God, how she understands, for even while Imogen talks, and cries, and rages, Hester's thoughts stray (Imogen does tend to repeat herself) to Alex, to their own love affair when she too was tempted to leave her husband and run off, as Abigail has done, with another man.

But the man wasn't married to her sister, she tells herself sternly, hardening her heart against her younger daughter.

The whole thing began, apparently, six months ago when Abigail moved in with Imogen and Gordon in France. For the past four years Abigail had been a music teacher at a comprehensive school in England, but she had never been happy in her job. She enjoyed one-to-one teaching, with students who had both the ability and the desire to be taught; what she detested, and as a consequence did badly, was trying to instil a love of music into thirty-odd pupils who so obviously wanted to be elsewhere. A mismatched love affair – begun by Abigail as a reaction to a series of rather ethereal romances in her music academy days – with one of the other teachers, didn't help the situation. He was the sports coach, given to dragging Abigail away on long rugby weekends. It ended on both sides in incredible boredom, and with great mutual relief.

After this Abigail gave in her notice, deciding to head for France where she had always felt at home, having spent some considerable time there. Abigail had done French A-Level, could speak the language well and had quite a few contacts in the country. She had the rather vague idea that she could give private piano lessons in France, with some English lessons thrown in, perhaps. It was all rather nebulous, but then so many of Abby's plans were: this one seemed as good as any.

Naturally, she gravitated first to Imogen and Gordon's house in Brittany. Although the two sisters had never been very close – there was the ten-year age gap to begin with – they were both rather pleased at this reunion, having seen each other only sporadically over the past few years. On the surface, it seemed like a good arrangement. They had shared a childhood marred by fierce rivalry: this would give them a chance to start afresh, get to know each other again. On the practical side, Imogen and Gordon were delighted to give Abigail room and board and a small salary, in exchange for much-needed help in the antique showroom and shop attached to the house. Abigail too was pleased: she was quite happy to work for her sister until such time as she had enough pupils to set out independently.

'I was really glad to see her,' Imogen says now, and Hester can tell that she is sincere. For years the sisters had lived apart – Abigail doing her music training in the south-west and Imogen living and working and marrying in London. The reunion must have been, at least to start with, a happy one.

Hester knew that Abigail was in France, and she heartily approved. It was time her younger daughter ventured out of the West Country, and particularly out of Devon, where she had lived most of her life. Before Abigail went over to Brittany she had actually moved in with Hester for a time, in the little cottage she had bought after Martin died. Abigail had suddenly decided that she hated her flat in Exeter, hated her job and her whole lifestyle, and needed time to sort herself out. Being a mother, of course Hester took her in, though within days her tiny house was in a shambles thanks to all of Abby's belongings: there was just not the room for more than one person. Hester was also quite busy during this period, writing prolifically as well as running a workshop in Cornwall and giving a series of poetry readings with another poet. And then there was her garden, of course. It was what kept her calm, and if she couldn't get to it as often as she needed she fell apart, became unstuck, unsettled. It sometimes struck her as odd that this strange need of hers, this gardening urge, had only surfaced after she had left Alex.

Abigail had been in Hester's house for about a month when she suddenly announced her decision to go to France. Hester encouraged her. She had learned to love her solitude like a well-worn garment, and so she quite happily waved goodbye to her younger daughter and turned back to her own space with the alacrity of a dog to a long-buried bone.

Imogen had no idea that Gordon and Abigail were lovers. 'I was so busy with the business – Gordon is useless at it, you know, even though he's supposed to be the expert – that they could have been bonking on the carpet every night for all I knew. I was either working or crashed out in bed, exhausted.'

And so when Imogen found out, it was as great a shock to her as it was to Hester when she received that hysterical phone call in the middle of the night.

'However did you find out, then?' she says now to Imogen, for the younger woman is brooding again and has lost track of her story. 'Did Gordon actually tell you?'

'Oh no, God no, he's too much of a coward, the bastard, to come out and just tell me.'

'Abigail, then?'

'Hah, her? Oh no, she was as secretive and deceptive as Gordon, the little shit. You know, I think they both thought they could go on forever like that, having their sordid fling while I slaved away and made piles of money for everyone.'

'Imogen, calm down. So how on earth *did* you find out?'

'The way the whole village did, Mum. I found out in the same sordid, despicable, and utterly blatant and tacky way the whole village found out.' Imogen closes her eyes and shudders, obviously unable to go on.

'Well?' Hester says, after a pause.

Imogen sighs, opens her beautiful eyes, and looks tragically at her mother. 'I suppose I'd better tell you all about it. From the very beginning.'

Hester sighs too, and unconsciously straightens her shoulders. 'Yes, Imo, I think you'd better.'

Imogen nods her head, sits down at the garden table opposite Hester, and begins to speak. It is a most extraordinary story.

Chapter Four

A visit from the village priest marked the beginning of Imogen's story. It was a pleasant Sunday, midday, and she was alone in the house when he appeared like a great dark bird of prey, his long black skirt flapping like wings around his ankles, his nose hooked and pointed like a beak. On his head, like a thick tuft of feathers, sat one of those squashy ebony felt hats that the clergy in France sometimes wear. His eyes, close-set and naturally bloodshot, seemed to merge when his passion was aroused, and Imogen said he looked like a Cyclops on that day with one burning red eye accusing her from the middle of his forehead.

'Madame, je voudrais parler avec vous,' he began in his most formal tones, though not bothering to take off his beanbag of a hat.

'Ah, Monsieur le Curé, bonjour,' Imogen said, not at all surprised to see him. Père Jacques Bonté had taken to visiting her on the odd occasion, ever since she had made the chance remark in the *boulangerie* one morning that she thought the Church in Brittany was much more interesting than in the rest of France, because of its fascinating profusion of saints. The priest, snapping to his heels, had mistakenly sensed a convert, and had hounded Imogen ever since.

And so the good Father was not unknown at the Boswick household, where he drank numerous cups of Imogen's strong coffee and preached to her on the merits of Catholicism, or, more importantly, depicted vividly how she would rot in hell if she didn't embrace the true faith. The poor man wandered sometimes, breaking into his native Breton language when he got carried away about the torments of hell. Imogen didn't understand a word of it, but being a well-brought up Englishwoman she listened politely, nodded her head at what she thought were appropriate moments, and silently wished he would leave so she could get on with her work.

So, on this warm placid Sunday, Imogen, though slightly put out because she was busy with the accounts, resigned herself to another wasted half-hour and offered the Father coffee in the garden.

Unusually, he refused. He followed Imogen into the garden but remained standing, pacing around the uneven stone courtyard and muttering to himself in a state of extreme agitation. He looked like a big black buzzard. Poor Imogen was at a loss; the man was definitely distraught, almost hysterically excited. She rather wished that either Abigail or Gordon were at home, but they had left separately right after breakfast, Abigail saying she needed a walk and Gordon presumably seeing a man who wanted to sell an *armoire*. The priest was declaiming darkly to Imogen, but unfortunately she couldn't understand a word he was saying because he spoke mostly in Breton. When he did lapse into French he still made absolutely no sense at all.

'Monsieur le Curé,' Imogen began, trying to interrupt the flow. *'Je ne comprends pas—'*

Father Bonté took no notice; he was so twitchy with outraged passion that he was having trouble breathing. Imogen was beginning to feel annoyed, and more than slightly cross that neither her sister nor her husband were around to help her do something with the priest whom, she suspected, was becoming completely unhinged. His strange garbling was increasing in volume, his long arms, cloaked in black, flew through the air like predatory birds, and he resisted all Imogen's efforts to calm him.

Finally realizing that she hadn't understood a word of his monologue, Father Bonté came closer and in his frustration grabbed Imogen by the arm and held her tightly, continuing his harangue but punctuating it with loud whispers in her ear. His claw-like fingers dug into her bare skin; his breath smelled wormy. Imogen was beginning to get worried.

'S'il vous plaît, Monsieur le Curé,' she began, trying to get away from him, but his grip on her arm tightened, and the

whispers in her ear became even more hoarse and passionate.

By now the normally intrepid Imogen felt the first stirrings of fear. Had the good *Père* lost all control and was he, God forbid, making a pass at her? He was certainly holding her close, and his breath was hot and rancid on her bare neck. With horror she looked down at her skimpy sunsuit with its extremely short shorts and top that was almost indecently low-cut. She hadn't been expecting company, of course, and the weather was exceedingly hot . . . Had her unsuitable attire totally unbalanced the celibate priest? She had heard about the temptations rampantly beguiling the priesthood, but God knows she hadn't intended—

And then, to Imogen's dismay, Father Bonté changed his tactics. Still holding tightly to her arm, he began to kiss the air around Imogen's face seductively, at the same time grinding his pelvis in a most suggestive manner.

'*Non, non, non!*' Imogen shrieked, appalled and helpless. Though she was not a small woman, she was slight in weight and the priest, despite his advancing years, was still a big man, tall and surprisingly strong.

'*Oui, oui, oui!*' the priest hissed, grinding away harder.

'*Non. Arrêtez! Au secours! Vous êtes un homme de Dieu!*' Imogen said wildly.

'*Mais si!*' he agreed, holding on to her bare arms with both hands now and trembling with the ecstatic knowledge that at last Imogen was beginning to understand him.

Sure that she was about to be raped, Imogen screamed loudly and relentlessly as she struggled to free herself. The priest, demented with excitement, fury and frustration, slapped her hard across the face. At that moment, the French windows leading into the house burst open and out rushed a magnificent Frenchman with dark dishevelled hair and a black leather jacket. '*Monsieur le Curé!*' he exclaimed. 'Imogen!'

'Oh, Bruno, thank God you've come!' Imogen said weakly, collapsing into a chair.

There was a moment's silence during which everyone

froze, as in the game of Statues that children play. Then Imogen opened her eyes and smiled tremulously at the man who had just saved her from rape – a sacrilegious one at that. The young man looked at her, at her frightened, vulnerable face, her trembling smile, her innocent troubled eyes, and perhaps it all started then, at that moment, for it was doubtful if any man had ever seen Imogen tremulous and vulnerable before.

The Frenchman, Bruno Lambert, who was the village doctor and a friend of the Boswicks', was rather nonplussed for a moment, seeing Imogen pale and breathless, and the village priest red-faced and dishevelled. *'Bonjour, mon père,'* he said politely to Father Bonté, then, in English to Imogen, 'Excuse me, Imogen, I was passing the house on my way to visit a patient and I thought I heard a shout. I wondered if you were in some trouble but I see I have made an error. It is only Father Bonté here with you.'

'Oh, Bruno, I've never been so happy to see anyone in all my life,' Imogen said faintly, standing up but looking exceedingly fragile.

'My dear friend,' Bruno said forcefully, remembering he was a doctor and responsible for this woman, 'you must sit down. Your face is white and you are trembling. Have you had a shock?'

Imogen meekly sat down again. Bruno was so authoritative, so commanding, that she was actually relieved to relinquish control.

He sat her under the old gnarled apple tree where one or two new green leaves fell delicately on to her bare shoulders and on to her creamy pale sunsuit, where they rested on her bosom like little boats safe in harbour. She felt calm, lulled; she mistakenly thought the crisis was over. Bruno laid his finely-chiselled ear on her bosom to hear her heartbeat and when he was satisfied she was not in any immediate danger, he turned again to the priest. 'I think we must all sit down', he said gravely, 'and discuss this. What has happened to upset the lady?'

'It was the priest,' Imogen said. 'He tried to—'

But a cascade of words interrupted her. Father Bonté had

taken Bruno aside and was shouting away at him, pecking at his shoulder with his long thin fingers, pointing first at Imogen then at the sky as if at God Himself.

'*Mon Dieu!* No wonder she is in shock!' Bruno said, when the priest had stopped. The young man went over to Imogen, took her hand and said with great passion and sympathy, 'My poor Imogen, my dear friend, how difficult for you.'

'Oh Bruno, it was dreadful, dreadful. That horrid man—'

'How stupid the English are – I beg your pardon, my dear – but sometimes it is true, especially in matters of love.'

'The English?'

'In France, if a man has a mistress (and it is not such a big thing as the English make out), he is discreet, he does not let his wife know – and of course he is not so tasteless as to choose a sister.'

'Mistress? Sister? What are you talking about, Bruno?'

'Forgive me, you are still in shock.'

'No, I'm not. For God's sake what are you on about? Who has a mistress? And what do you mean by someone's "sister"?'

'It is not unusual to be confused when you have had bad news and what Père Bonté has told you of course has given you much agitation.'

'Of course it's given me agitation. The poor demented man tried to rape me.'

'*What?*'

'I couldn't understand a word of what he was saying – all that garbled Breton mixed with archaic French!'

'You have not understood him?'

'I understood his intentions, all right, if not his words. He tried to rape me.'

Bruno shook his head. 'This is not possible, Imogen.'

Imogen, becoming cross, said, 'He was clutching my arm, whispering things in my ear . . . then he was making kissing noises and thrusting out his pelvis.' She shivered distastefully.

'And you thought he was trying to be indecent to you?' Bruno was incredulous.

'Of course he was being indecent,' Imogen said rather sulkily. 'Maybe you don't call those lewd gestures indecent in this country, but in England—'

Bruno shook his head. 'There is a terrible misunderstanding. Father Bonté was trying to tell you something, something very important indeed, Imogen.'

'Oh, naturally,' Imogen said sarcastically. 'That's why he practically tried to grind his groin into me.'

'Excuse me?'

'Obscene gestures. Bruno, The priest was making obscene gestures.'

'Because you didn't understand him, Imogen. He was miming, trying to make you understand.'

'Oh, for God's sake!'

'*Monsieur le Curé* prides himself on his acting abilities. Every year he plays Joseph in the Christmas play at the village church.'

Imogen swore impatiently. 'For God's sake, Bruno,' she repeated. 'He slapped me, too. That horrid man slapped me.'

'He thought you were hysterical, that is why. He thought at last you had understood what he was trying to convey to you, and the shock made you hysterical. He slapped you to calm you down.'

Imogen shook her head. 'I don't believe this. What on earth was he trying to convey, then?'

Bruno looked at her, then at the priest who said something rapidly and passionately to him again before throwing up his arms in disgust and frightening the wits out of the blackbird in the apple tree.

'Imogen,' Bruno said, taking her hand in the most professional manner, 'did you really not understand anything of what the priest was trying to tell you?'

'Not a word, Bruno. He didn't speak much French; he was so excited he kept lapsing into Breton. I honestly don't have a clue what he was on about. I really thought he was attacking me.'

Bruno sighed. 'Then it is up to me to tell you,' he said manfully. 'If I could keep it from you, I would, but by now the whole village knows.'

'Knows what, Bruno? Could you please tell me?'

Bruno nodded. 'It happened this morning. Today is the feast day of the Blessed Sainte Barbe. Sainte Barbe is a saint much beloved of the Brittany people. She is patron saint of many things, of those who lose their homes by fire, of sailors who are victims of great storms, of—'

'Is this relevant, Bruno?' Bruno, startled, admitted it was not. 'Then please go on to what is.'

'There was a Pardon, today – a solemn procession to the Blessed Shrine of Sainte Barbe. It happens once a year, on her feast day. Do you know the shrine, Imogen?'

'Yes, I saw it once, in the middle of the woods. Rather hard to find, if I remember. There's not much there but dense woodland and an overgrown path leading up to the shrine, which is rather dilapidated. I don't suppose many people go there.'

'They don't, hardly at all. Except today, on her feast day. Today, the whole village assembled in front of the church and began the solemn procession to Sainte Barbe's shrine, a half-mile away through the woods.'

Bruno stopped, not knowing quite how to go on. When Imogen kept silent, he continued slowly: 'So they set off, the priest and the altar boys, in their finest vestments, carrying solemnly a small replica of Sainte Barbe. All the devoted of the village were dressed in their very best clothes, everyone carrying flowers of every colour, beautiful fresh flowers to lay at the Blessed Shrine. They walked slowly, happily, for it was a magnificent morning, the sun shining, the woods filled with the glory of spring, the leaves blossoming out in the palest of pale green colour . . .'

'Bruno,' Imogen interrupted, not unkindly. 'Are these details necessary?'

Disconcerted, the doctor shook his head. 'It is hard to tell you this. I wish I didn't have to, but if I don't, someone else will.' He shifted in the garden chair, looked away from Imogen and said in a rush: 'As they rounded the corner of the wooden path to the shrine, there, at the feet of Saint Barbe, lay your sister and your husband . . .' Here Bruno faltered.

'Oh no,' Imogen said weakly. 'They weren't. . . ?'

'Yes, I am afraid they were, under a wild pink flowering rhododendron. Discovered in the act, *inflagrante delicto*, in front of *Monsieur le Curé* and all his flock.'

'Good God.'

'I am so sorry, Imogen. Would you like me to smash his head in?'

It took Imogen some time to assimilate this. Then she said, almost casually. 'No, thank you, Bruno – though it is kind of you to offer.'

Her second reaction was one of laughter. Bruno, thinking it shock and hysteria, opened his little black bag and rummaged around in search of some sedatives.

'No, no, I'm not hysterical,' Imogen said, laughing till the tears made little sparkling streams on the undulating curve of her cheeks. 'It's just that Gordon and Abigail don't even like each other,' she went on between giggles.

Bruno and the priest, who had at last calmed down, were silent, feeling immensely sorry for her. Bruno translated for the priest.

'No, they've never liked each other,' she went on musingly. 'Gordon thinks Abby is a bit wet. All that lank, bright-ginger hair, that freckly baby face, that music-teacher air she has – sort of prissy and ethereal at the same time. It drives him nuts.'

This was too much for Bruno to translate, so he remained quiet.

'As for Abby – when I married Gordon she asked me why I was tying myself down to a philistine who thought Baroque was a new brand of cigar.'

This again was beyond Bruno.

'So you see,' Imogen finished. 'It can't be true.'

This Bruno translated, and the priest burst into speech so vociferously that two yellowhammers perching in the large apple tree rapidly left it for the smaller ones at the bottom of the garden.

'What's he saying?' Imogen demanded.

'He is saying that it is certainly true, for he saw them. So did the altar boys, the visiting curé from our neighbouring town, the elders of the church, the parishioners—'

'Yes, yes, Bruno, that's enough, I believe him.' Imogen was silent for a moment, then she said sadly, 'Poor dumb Gordon. Only he would choose the one day of the year when someone actually visited that shrine. And then it was the whole bloody village.'

She closed her eyes and shuddered, and looked so pale and vulnerable that Bruno was moved to take her hand again.

'What did they do?' she asked with her eyes still closed. 'What on earth did they do, when they realized the whole village had stumbled upon them?'

Bruno put the question to Father Bonté. The priest muttered something angrily and Bruno, scarcely able to look at Imogen, said in a strangled whisper, 'They climbed the rhododendron tree.'

Imogen stared. 'They what?'

'The rhododendron. It is very old, very solid, very large and thick with leaves and flowers. They looked up, saw the priest and the villagers behind him, and hastened up the tree *tout de suite*.'

'Dear God.' Imogen, looking dazed, shook her head. 'What did the Father do?'

Once again there was another spirited exchange in French between priest and doctor.

'His first duty was to the Blessed Sainte Barbe. He proceeded as usual with the Pardon.'

'With Gordon and Abigail in the rhododendron tree?'

'They were well-hidden, the Father says. The tree is heavy with foliage. Thanks to *Monsieur le Curé*'s great dignity and presence of mind, the ceremony went on as scheduled.'

There was a silence from Imogen, who had once more closed her eyes. Bruno hoped she wasn't becoming hysterical again, for her chest was heaving in a most irregular manner. He held tighter to her hand, thinking dire thoughts about the man who had so dishonoured her. Suddenly Father Bonté, who had been standing under the apple tree muttering quietly to himself, began croaking and ranting and flapping his great black sleeves like a wounded crow.

'What's he on about now?' Imogen said faintly, not opening her eyes.

'Do not let him distress you,' Bruno said solicitously. 'He is in a great fury with your sister and your husband, because he feels they have committed a terrible sacrilege, desecrating the Blessed Shrine of Sainte Barbe.'

At this, Imogen revived. She sat up sharply, looked the priest in the eye and said, irreverently, 'Bugger Sainte Barbe.'

Luckily, neither of the Frenchmen understood her.

Imogen pauses at this part of her story. The garden is steeped in sunlight, as it was that day – only a week ago, only last Sunday – when her life was so dramatically altered.

'So what happened then? Did you face Gordon and Abigail with it? Did they come back to the house or leave straight away?' Hester prompts, as it seems Imogen will not go on. She is looking vulnerable again and Hester is not used to it. She thinks irrelevantly how it becomes her, but it frightens her mother. The formidable businesswoman in her sleek sexy suits, her glossy lips, reeking of power and efficiency, has always lulled Hester into thinking she does not have to worry about her daughter, that her own sealed-off heart need not stir itself too diligently for Imogen, for this strong young woman who has no need of the useless outpourings of maternal emotion. This has suited Hester in the past, for she finds love wrecks her, breaks her up into foamy salvage: she can't handle it. Now love breaks through out of the deep like a whale, and she finds she does not know what to do with her daughter's pain.

She tries by tentatively touching Imogen's hand. Imogen never liked to be touched as an adolescent and Hester has grown out of the habit of doing so, fearing rejection. But her daughter smiles and looks at her kindly. Something akin to understanding passes between them, something to do with love, and Hester is moved and shaken. Perhaps after all her garden hasn't been enough all these years.

The moment passes and Imogen goes on with her story. 'What did I do?' she thoughtfully repeats Hester's question. 'When the door shut on the two Frenchmen I tore the house apart. I came out of my shock, if that's what I was in, and ran around shouting and swearing in such a state of fury you wouldn't believe it. Then I took all Abigail's things and shoved them in bags and cases and boxes and put them outside the front door; then I did the same with Gordon's.'

'How energetic,' Hester says, allowing herself a small smile.

Imogen smiles also. 'Oh Mum, I was in such a fury. You know my temper, anyway—'

'Yes, I know.'

'So when they finally returned to the house about two hours later – they had been cowering in some café somewhere, too bloody frightened to come back – I was cold and rigid with determination, with loathing for them both.'

'I can imagine,' Hester says rather weakly. Imogen in a fury is a force no sane person would confront, and for a moment her mother's heart goes out just the tiniest bit to the poor lovers, quavering over *café au lait* in a seedy café knowing they must face Imogen's vengeance. 'So what happened then?' she asks with some trepidation.

'I threw them out. I showed them their bags and ordered them both out of the house.'

'Oh my. Didn't they protest?'

'Gordon tried. Abigail just cowered behind his back, whinging on about everybody talking things over, that they would explain everything. I ignored her, and told Gordon that if he didn't get out at once I would call the priest, the doctor, and anyone else I could find in the village and get them to throw him out.'

'Did he take notice of that?'

'Bloody right he did. The whole village was in a fury about it – not about the adultery, but where it took place. Sainte Barbe is much loved around here, and they've been talking about nothing else all week, the corruption of her ancient shrine, and on her feast day no less.'

'So Abigail and Gordon then left?'

'In a hurry, especially when I hinted that Father Bonté might be back any minute with a party of the church elders to confront them with the desecration of church property.'

'Dear God.'

'I know. Sordid, isn't it?'

Actually the word Hester was thinking of was 'farcical', but she let it pass. 'They've not been back?'

'No, they wouldn't dare!' Imogen said indignantly. 'I had a letter from each of them separately, a cryptic note from Abby saying she was sorry but I wouldn't understand, she loved Gordon – God what a pompous cow she is! – and has loved him since she first arrived in France, when their love affair began. Love affair, hah! More like—'

'What did Gordon have to say?' Hester interrupted hastily.

'Oh, he whined on about how he loved us both and he never meant me to find out and when they come back – they're somewhere in the south, apparently – can we three sit down and talk about it like rational human beings? The bastard. To think I loved him once.'

Hester looks at her sharply. 'Don't you love him now?'

Imogen looks as if she has just been caught out. 'Yes, of course I love him,' she says impatiently.

'Then why did you say—'

'Because I hate him, too. Look what he's done, and with my own sister. I'll never forgive him, ever. Or her.'

Hester sighs, and listens to the blackbird. The sun is high now and in the distance she can hear a barking dog, then some seagulls. She had forgotten how close they are to the sea, and she finds she wants to go to it, rush into it, wallow around in its sticky salt and frothy sediment until she no longer exists, until all these emotions that have, over the past two days, crowded in on her have ceased to exist.

But there is even more to fill Hester's mind, her heart, her bemused senses during this extraordinary weekend, for Imogen is looking strangely at the French windows leading from the kitchen to the courtyard.

'*Désirez-vous quelque chose?*' she says in her polite French, frowning at the person who has suddenly appeared at the kitchen door.

'I'm sorry to intrude,' the man says in English. 'I did knock on the front door, but obviously you couldn't hear. The door was open, and I heard voices, so I took the liberty of coming through.'

'I'm afraid I don't know you,' Imogen says accusingly.

'It's all right, Imo,' Hester says weakly. 'I do.'

For it is, of course, Alex.

Chapter Five

He looks wonderful, Hester has to admit, standing there with that apologetic and slightly wistful air, as if he isn't quite sure whether he should be there or not. He has shaved and showered and looks clean and fresh, like the apple trees; his jowls seem to have firmed overnight, his longish white hair is thick and fluffy. Hester longs to touch it, to see if it still feels the same as it did when it was dark and crispy.

Imogen, looking curiously at Hester and then Alex, invites him into the courtyard. Hester makes some feeble introductions, saying Alex is a colleague of hers from years ago when she was at the college, and explains about their accidental meeting yesterday on the ferry. Actually Imogen has met him, many years ago when he and Hester's husband, Martin, worked together, but of course she doesn't remember. It was her sister Abigail who knew him better; she did her A levels at the sixth-form college when Alex and Hester both taught there. But that, of course, was later.

Imogen disappears at once into the house, saying she will make some fresh coffee. Hester understands that her daughter feels uncomfortable with her tear-streaked face, rumpled hair and smudged make-up, and wishes she could tell Imogen how well this dishevelled state suits her: how natural she looks, and how lovely.

'So that's Imogen,' Alex says when they are alone. 'I hardly remember her. She looks like you, but not as accessible.'

Hester is so disarmed she is speechless. *Accessible?* She has spent the last eight years building a stone and bramble hedgerow around her emotions precisely to remain *in*-accessible!

'Don't look so fierce,' Alex says with a smile, stretching himself out on the recliner next to the table. Behind him a yellow buddleia beams and flowers, and beyond that the old stone house glistens and glows in the sunlight. Hester waits for the blackbird but he seems to be still now.

She says, 'However did you find me? I gave you no phone number.'

'I know. You were always such a stubborn thing. I see there *is* a phone in the house.'

'I'm sorry, I suppose that was churlish of me. But, well . . . I couldn't see any reason for us to be in touch again.'

Now Alex looks fierce. 'Good God, Hester, how formidable you have become,' he cries, and Hester thinks: What? Me, formidable? Like Imogen? Well, perhaps that will make me less accessible.

'You didn't answer my question,' she says tartly. 'How did you find me? You don't know Imogen's married name. So you couldn't have looked her up.'

Alex grins, enjoying this. 'It was your precious book bag, actually. You not only had your name and address in England blazoned on it a couple of times, but your address in France. I memorized it right away.'

Hester has to smile. 'I am rather obsessive about that black bag. It contains everything precious to me – my notes, my writing, my poetry books . . .'

'Oh Hester,' Alex interrupts. 'Do you really think I'd let you go a second time as easily as that? Becoming ill on the boat as I did, I never had a chance to ask you what you have been doing, how you are getting on – good God, I'd have waited outside that loo door for hours if necessary, if I hadn't had your address.'

'You couldn't,' Hester says with some asperity. 'You had Rosemary with you.'

'Who?'

'Rosemary, that Frenchwoman. The herbal hamster.'

'Hamster?'

'Sorry, forget it, private joke.'

'Her name is Ermi.'

'Fine, great. Ermi. Got it.'

'Hester, will you stop that?'

'Stop what, Alex?'

'Being so monosyllabic. And flippant.'

'Oh, was I? Sorry.'

There is a pause, then Hester relents and says, 'Alex, I'm finding this all very difficult. I knew I would, that's why I thought it best we didn't see each other.'

'I find this difficult too, Hester. But that's why I thought it best we *did* see each other.'

'I don't understand.'

Alex sighs and shifts himself in the chair, so that the sun isn't hitting him in the eyes. 'Don't you see?' he says. 'If we didn't still have unfinished business with each other, it wouldn't be at all difficult. We'd exchange banalities, wonder what we ever saw in the other, and go our separate ways without another thought.'

'And how do you know I don't feel that way?'

'Oh, Hester. Remember that I know you.' He sits up, leans over the table where she is shredding a croissant into ragged bits of crumbs, and puts his hand over hers.

She is not unmoved. Another stone in the wall shifts, topples. 'Oh Alex,' she says softly, and with some anguish.

Imogen appears at the kitchen door. 'I'm making some more coffee,' she says politely. 'Please, both of you, help yourself to bread and butter and jam, and the croissants.' She looks slightly disapprovingly at Alex, who has not let go of Hester's hand.

'Mum,' she says in a most offended manner. 'You hardly had a thing to eat, you must be starving. Whatever is the matter with you?'

Refraining from saying that she couldn't very well tuck in when Imogen was having a crisis all over the breakfast table, Hester thanks her for her thoughtfulness and breaks off great chunks of bread for herself and for Alex. Imogen nods approvingly and goes back inside. Hester is rather relieved that her daughter didn't refer to her as the poor old dear again.

And suddenly, Hester is starving. Emotion always does that to her, and she has had a gutful this morning. Alex is hungry also and he accepts a large hunk of the crispy-crusted baguette which is fresh and perfect and curiously comforting. Hester feels quite light-headed, as if she has thrown off weights and chains, and wonders why. She decides it's probably because she has abandoned her breakfast muesli and wholemeal toast for a second helping of the sunny joys of white French bread, pure Brittany butter, and golden sweet apricot jam.

Not to mention the croissants . . . Imogen brings out a pot of aromatic coffee, fresh cups, even clean napkins, but refuses to sit with them, saying she must get on with her accounts. Hester wonders how the antique showroom will thrive without Gordon, but doesn't feel like asking now. Certainly the business does not seem to be one of Imogen's worries.

After they have drunk the coffee they pull the deck-chairs under the shade of the apple tree and recline side by side, for all the world like a contented married couple on their holidays. Alex is wearing very old, very faded, jeans – can it be, Hester wonders, the same pair that he bought new, eight years ago, to take to France? – and a long-sleeved pale-blue cotton shirt. He had a jumper but he shed that as the sun gathered momentum; now he rolls up his shirt-sleeves. She notices that he is still slim, doesn't seem to have put on any weight, though he has many more wrinkles (as no doubt she has) out here in the morning sunlight than he did in the storm-darkened ferry. They are mostly in intricate clusters around his eyes; they are like road maps, and Hester finds herself wishing it had been possible to travel them with him during those lost years . . .

Ah, regrets. *Non, je ne regrette rien.* With a little sigh Hester slips off her espadrilles and watches her toes uncurl like flowers towards the sun.

'Ahh,' she murmurs. 'Nice.'

'Hmmm,' he says. 'Yes.'

They both close their eyes for a few moments, savouring the first sun of spring on their faces.

And then, at the same moment, they open their eyes, sit bolt upright, and look at each other, speaking simultaneously.

'I can't believe this—'

'How very strange to be here—'

They laugh, easily. All the tension of yesterday, of the first moments of Alex's arrival, has gone. They are as comfortable and relaxed together as two lazy old cats, and Hester finds herself thinking wistfully that maybe that's not what she wanted after all.

Alex lets her speak first. 'I can't believe we're here, wallowing in the sun like two grizzled hippos in a mudbath, not after the anguish of our last meeting all those years ago.'

'I know. Do you want to talk about it, Hester? What happened?'

She looks around at the little courtyard and garden. Wild violets poke out amongst the tiny ornamental hedges that seem to zigzag all over the place with no rhyme or reason, pansies edge the old stone of the makeshift courtyard, and the apple trees are once again filled with birds. The smell of the sea mingles with the scent of some blossoming pear trees.

'No,' she says finally. 'I don't want to talk about it now.'

'Fine,' he answers. 'We have all the time in the world.'

This makes Hester inordinately happy, though she suspects she would find this feeling dangerous if she tried to analyze it. So she doesn't, and Alex goes on: 'Tell me about you – about Martin, if you like. How he died.'

'It wasn't unexpected, though that didn't seem to make it any easier. He had a heart attack and was in hospital for several weeks. He was improving slightly, but then he suddenly had another one and died instantly.'

'I only knew Martin professionally – before I met you, of course, but I liked him. Most people did, actually.'

'I know.'

They are both silent for a few moments, each with their different memories of Martin. Alex remembers him not as Hester's husband but as his boss, for Martin was the headmaster of the large comprehensive school where Alex taught science. Professionally, the two men liked and respected each other's work. Alex could never reconcile the calm, efficient headmaster with the husband of Hester, the father of Imogen and Abigail; perhaps it was just as well. Alex's admiration for Martin's proficiency did not stop him from loving Hester, although this did not happen until Alex left the comprehensive.

'And when he died,' Alex says after a short time, 'what did you do?'

'Sold the house. You know, try as I did, I never liked that house. You only went there a few times, but do you remember how dark and damp and cold it was? So huge, so inadequate in everything but size. There was no light, no heat – it was always uncosy and unwelcoming, no matter what I tried to do with it.'

'It had belonged to Martin's parents, hadn't it?'

'Yes. Martin was born in the room which later became our bedroom. It had been the old rectory for the village years ago. You know his father was a vicar?'

'I remember. I also remember how Martin loved that house, how he used to tell everyone it had been in the family for years. The first time I went there was for a wine and cheese get-together for Martin's department heads. My head couldn't go and I was deputy, so he sent me along.'

'That's right, I remember.'

'You didn't remember me, though, not at that first meeting.' Alex looks doleful, as if this slight has only just occurred.

How odd, Hester thinks. We've had this same conversation before, years and years ago, as lovers do. 'When did you first begin to feel this way? When did you first notice me? Do you remember when first we met?'

She smiles. 'There were so many people, it was a large comprehensive. What with all the deputy heads there as well, it was quite a large gathering.'

'The governors too, they were invited.'

'I hated those parties. They used to be excruciatingly boring. I always wished I were somewhere else.'

Alex smiles. 'You didn't show it that night. You walked around with the cheeseboard looking like a schoolmarm yourself, with your hair very properly and primly pulled back on top of your head.'

'Odd that you remember me so well, since I looked so plain and austere.'

'Who said anything about plain? I watched fascinated as the evening wore on, how your hair began gradually to slip away from its clips and fastenings, how first the wispy bits that later I so loved, then the other longer darker strands, broke away and slithered down your neck.'

Hester laughs. Alex has told her all this many times before, but it somehow seems new and fresh, sitting in this French garden, listening to the blackbird which has started up again.

'And then,' he goes on, 'you said you were a poet. That clinched it: I was besotted with you.'

'I'm still amazed at my temerity.'

'You and Martin were talking to a cluster of the guests and someone asked – I'll never forget it: "And what do you do, Hester? Do you work outside the home or do you find your two daughters and husband enough to keep you fulfilled and happy?" '

'Bumptious man, he was one of the new deputy heads.'

'Everyone looked eagerly at you to hear your answer, but before you could speak Martin said, proudly of course, "My wife teaches part-time A level English at the sixth-form college in Exeter." '

Hester smiles, because she knows what is coming next. Alex, his expressive face twitching with remembered merriment, continues: 'That impressed them, and just as some of the more ambitious ones began trying to charm you, not only because you were the Head's wife but also because the sixth-form college was a prestigious place to work, you said, quite loudly and plainly, "Actually, I'm a poet." '

Hester and Alex look at each other and grin. 'God, what cheek,' Hester says. 'My first poem had only that day been accepted for publication. *Children Like Leaves*, it was called. I was heady with success: I felt a true poet at last.'

' *"Children like leaves/drift away in autumn. Trees tired now/from summer in the sun/loosen their hold, and children like leaves/drift slowly into the next season . . ."* '

Hester is moved. 'Oh Alex,' she says. 'You remember that first verse?'

'I remember all three verses, Hester. I was one of your first fans, remember?'

'I remember.' They both wallow in nostalgia for a moment or two, until it becomes too painful. Then Hester says, 'I don't know who was more surprised that evening, when I announced I was a poet. Me, or Martin, or all those heads of departments and governors.'

'It stopped them dead,' Alex says gleefully. 'They didn't know whether to say how wonderful it was or oh dear, what a pity how sad! Poets are rather suspect with the English, I'm afraid. Even Martin looked quite disapproving.'

Hester shakes her head. 'He never took me seriously as a poet. I think poetry made him very nervous. When I gave him the odd shopping-list I could see him holding it out gingerly between his fingertips and looking at it suspiciously until he was satisfied it wasn't a poem.'

'I loved your poetry.'

'I know. But then, later, so much of it was about you.'

There is another pause, as both Alex and Hester wrestle with memories that they thought long subdued. Then Hester says, so quietly that Alex can only barely hear, 'Alex, why are we doing this? All this reminiscing?'

He's not surprised at the question. 'It's because we never were able to talk about it with anyone else. That's one of the sad things about relationships that must be kept secret – you can't share them. I never told anyone about us, did you?'

'No, no one. I wrote it all in my poems.'

'I know. Your first published collection. I saw it in the bookshop a year or so later, when I was in England for a few days. I nearly got in touch with you then and there.'

'I'm glad you didn't. I couldn't have coped.'

'I was a fool.'

He is frowning, troubled; Hester is also starting to feel agitated. Their placid memories are starting to hit rough waters, and Hester realizes she cannot safely cruise through them yet – maybe not ever.

When she tells him this, to her relief Alex doesn't push her. Instead, he talks about his sons, who are both married now and living in London.

'Do you see them often?' Hester asks. 'You were always so close to them when they were growing up.'

Alex nods. 'We're still close. They and their families spent Christmas with me in France last year, and every time I go to England I stay with one or another of them.'

'And Angela? How is she?'

'Re-married and living in Scotland.'

Hester is surprised, and says so. 'She liked the idea of being married,' Alex explains. 'That's why she tried to hold on to our marriage, even when it had turned into something hollow, something completely empty. When I stayed in France, Angela at last realized it was finally over, and found someone else not long afterwards.'

Hester, though she is aware this might be disturbing, cannot help but ask, 'Why did you not go back to England, Alex, as you had planned?'

'Oh Hester, you must know why! After those letters from you, those dreadful letters, saying I must never try to see you or contact you again, I simply couldn't face England. I sent in my resignation to the college, gave up teaching and became a carpenter in France.'

He says this succinctly and without emotion, but Hester is not fooled: she knows what a drastic step this must have been. But she is not surprised at his change of profession: she knows he has not always been a teacher. Alex actually worked for years as a builder when he left school at sixteen, first for other people, then gradually branching out on his own. Shy, and with a slight stammer, he had been slow at school, ponderous, and the combination had been enough to condemn him to life in the bottom stream at his large Midlands primary school. At the age of eleven he was labelled, categorized, and programmed for failure: never once was he expected to do anything even vaguely academic.

He was saved by what he calls instinct, a feeling he had, a gut feeling, that his teachers were wrong. Because he was quiet, and thought carefully before he spoke, no one listened to what he had to say; no one tried to bridge the wide chasms in his learning with special help, or with encouragement. His parents, both scientists, were so delighted with Alex's older brother, a child prodigy destined for brilliance and prominence (though in fact he ended up a minor government official), that they were only too happy to accept the fact that Alex just wasn't very bright. Because the brother, only a year older, had come top of the class every year at his school, they felt it only just and right that Alex should be at the bottom. After all, they weren't greedy; they did not want to tempt the gods. One child, thank you, of such brilliance and promise was quite enough for them.

It wasn't until Alex was twenty-five that he set out to prove his parents and teachers wrong. Instinctively, he had always known that just because he was slow to verbalize, and a late developer in his writing skills, it did not indicate a lack of basic intelligence. It was confidence he lacked, and as he learned to build houses, and carve intricate patterns in wood, so he at last gained a belief in himself that neither his home nor his school had been able to instill.

Alex began with evening classes, which gained him the exams he needed; then he rather hestitantly, and with sheer terror to begin with, attempted his A levels. By the time he had passed these he was brimming with confidence and went on to do a biology degree. From the start he wanted to teach – probably, he sometimes thought, out of a quixotic desire to right the wrongs he had witnessed there in the bottom stream.

But he had been in the building trade for nine years, and had always, even as a teacher, found relaxation in handling wood, making toys for his young sons, or frames for pictures, or even simple shelves in the kitchen or living room.

And now he tells Hester: 'I didn't miss the teaching, you know. I enjoyed being a teacher, but in some ways it was almost a relief to be out of it. It was rather therapeutic, working with my hands again.'

Hester does not pursue this, but says instead, 'Was it hard to find work here in France?'

'No, no problem at all, especially as I took on any jobs

that came up, like making kitchen units, or bookshelves, or converting a barn.'

'You were always a good craftsman,' Hester says. 'I still have the little tree you carved for me. I take it everywhere.' And then she wishes she hadn't said it.

Alex is moved, like Hester was when he quoted her poem to her. Finally he says, to cover his confusion, 'Well, I hope I still am a decent craftsman. As a matter of fact, I've been able to make a fairly good living lately, doing just that. Being a craftsman, that is. But I think I'd rather show you, instead of explaining.'

Again Hester feels inexplicably happy. She is not sure that this is a good thing, for she knows it has to do with Alex being back in her life, and long ago she was forced to teach herself not to rely on anyone for her emotional contentment.

'I was lucky, of course, when you left me,' Alex says, and the irony is not lost on Hester. 'Angie and I sold the house when prices were high and I was able to buy the property in France at only a fraction of my share. So I live frugally but contentedly, and now take on only the jobs I find satisfying. It's not a bad life.'

'And you have your Rosemary,' Hester says rather waspishly, and wishes she had bitten her tongue immediately the words are said.

'What?'

'Your little bit of lavender blue. You know, tarragon, basil, chervil – Ermi, that's it! Sorry, couldn't remember her name.'

Alex narrows his wrinkly eyes at her – oh, they do look so interesting, she thinks, all those road maps! – and he says, 'Hester, I do believe you're jealous.'

'Don't be silly.'

'You are!'

'I'm not. How can I be jealous, when I've never met the herbal hamster. Oh yes, briefly at the ferry terminal, but I don't remember her at all,' she says spuriously.

'Actually, Hester, I don't mind. That you're jealous.'

She knows he is teasing her, but because he happens to be right it makes her cross. So she says, 'Look, Alex, what happened between us was years ago. It was an accident we ever met again, and though it is very pleasant seeing you here, relaxing with you in the sunlight like one would with an old friend, I doubt if we'll ever see each other again, what with me living in England and you in France, and besides, you have your little oregano and I have my garden.'

At this crisp little speech Alex shakes his head and says gently, 'How transparent you are. You always were: it made you very endearing.'

Hester smiles, a bit sadly, and says nothing. She and Alex look at each other, helpless under the weight of all those lost years, and the happiness she was feeling only a few moments ago vanishes, leaving her suddenly bereft, empty. Alex too looks troubled, and starts to move towards Hester, but then hesitates, uncertain.

'Ah, Hester,' he says. 'How I wish . . .'

But she is never to find out what it is he wishes, for suddenly loud shouts hammer the peace of the garden and it is transformed, with people running into the courtyard, all speaking angrily and gesticulating wildly and shouting in both French and English. Alex, bewildered, falls back into his deck-chair while Hester sits hypnotized by the capacious display of emotion bursting and exploding like fireworks.

'Get out of my house! Get out, you little slut!'

'Don't you start bullying me again!'

'Conniving little tramp, I have nothing to say to you.'

'God, you're so unreasonable. Can't you even listen?'

'Now calm down, you two—'

'And you, you monster, get out!'

'*Mon Dieu, mon Dieu, mon Dieu, vous êtes le diable lui-même, un vrai démon!*'

'Calm down, please. Will everyone be quiet! We must all be calm. FOR FUCK'S SAKE WILL EVERYONE BE CALM.'

'Watch your language, Gordon you creep. Thank God the priest doesn't understand English.'

'Imogen, do not agitate yourself, please.'

'God, Bruno, how can you say that, with him standing there, and her? I could murder them both, I . . . oh, Mum, I forgot you were out here! *Do something*.'

'Mum, is that Mum? Oh *Mum!*'

There is a stunned silence; everyone freezes as if someone has stopped the video, and turns to look at Hester. Before she can gather her wits about her, a small female shape hurtles into her arms crying hysterically. Then before she can say another word, a slightly larger female shape is doing the same, and then everyone is talking at once and the emotional fireworks start to explode again so Hester finds her voice and says loudly, in French and in English; 'WILL EVERYONE PLEASE STOP SHOUTING.'

When they do, she turns to the two cringing, weeping, shaking figures huddled in her arms and says grimly, 'Well, Abigail? And you, Imogen. What the hell are we going to do now?'

Chapter Six

There is a merciful silence for a few moments, disturbed only by the hiccuping sobs of Hester's two irascible daughters. Then a male voice says unctuously, 'Thank goodness you're here, Mother. Now perhaps we can all sit down and discuss this situation reasonably.'

Hester looks at the owner of this voice with distaste. It comes from a pleasant enough human frame, a fairly fit body wearing dark baggy trousers, a white collarless shirt, and a trendy waistcoat patterned with what looks like an artist's abstract of a rain forest. He has a well-shaped head, curly sandy hair and a straight sandy moustache. He looks well-oiled, as if ready for anything; his smile, Hester has noticed, is particularly greasy. As she regards him he smiles ingratiatingly at her again and she suddenly takes umbrage. He has married one of her daughters and run off with the other: Hester doesn't know if she can forgive him for either.

So she says, with dignity, 'Sod off, Gordon. If you please.'

He does, or at least he shuffles ignominiously away towards the bottom of the garden, there to frighten away all the little furry things in the borders, Hester supposes. She allows herself a moment of small satisfaction; it is the first time she has said what she thinks to her son-in-law.

She then tells her daughters, in slightly gentler terms, to stop their sniffling so that she can sort out her thoughts. There are still two strange men in the garden talking loudly and excitedly in French, and Hester tells them also, in their own language, to please hush. They apologize profusely for the intrusion, and introduce themselves.

But of course Hester knows them: Imogen's descriptions were so vivid she would have known the priest, Père Bonté, and the young French doctor, Bruno Lambert, without any introduction. Père Bonté's eyes are so close together that when he is agitated they do rather seem to merge together, giving him the appearance, as Imogen had noted, of a demented Cyclops. His habit, black and dusty, flaps around him like the broken wings of a rook, and as he hovers over Hester to kiss her hand, which is made difficult by the fact that her arms are still wrapped around her daughters, a musty smell, like churches, emanates like incense from his clothes. It is strangely comforting, like the smell of honey.

Bruno Lambert is something else. He looks like a rock star, a classy one, or the latest French cinema idol. He has a natural sexy slouch and his pelvis, encased in tight jeans, tips forward both innocently and provocatively. He wears a plain black T-shirt and extremely dark sunglasses. His hair, longish, shines clean and straight and black like a raven's in the glistening sun. A light spring suntan glosses his smooth skin and his smile manages to be both seductive and appealing. On closer inspection Hester notices that one of his fine strong white teeth is slightly crooked, but this imperfection only enhances his charm: were he perfect, perhaps he would be boring. Like this, he is absolutely irresistible.

Bruno goes to Hester and speaks to her in English. 'I am so sorry, Madame, that I and *Monsieur le Curé* have come here like this. The Father and I, we have only just arrived, separately, here at your daughter's house. I to call in and see if her health is okay (I am a doctor, you see), and the Father to see that her spiritual life is in order. As we meet at the door and are knocking, a car comes and the husband, Gordon, arrives with . . . with Imogen's sister.'

He stops and looks pointedly at the back of Abigail's head, which is still nestling like a salamander under Hester's arm. 'With Imogen's sister,' he says again loudly, with rampant disapproval.

At this point Père Bonté starts booming something in his thundery voice and Hester can see why Imogen could not understand him. His French, heavily accented, is interspersed frequently with Breton words and phrases, and with obscure exclamations which sound remarkably like the croaking of great, large birds.

Bruno, translating as best he can, says, 'The Father, he is disapproving of this delicate situation here. When he saw those two, the husband and the sister, stepping out of the car, he began to abuse them. Not physically you understand, but with the words. The French words, of course.'

'Of course,' Hester says weakly, for Bruno has stopped and is looking at her expectantly. 'Please do go on.'

'I say to Père Bonté, "We must go, we must not intrude. Come away with me and I will buy you a drink in the café in the village."'

Another pause. 'How very kind of you,' Hester manages to mutter.

A shrug, a slight wriggle of the hips. A wisp of an intense frown. '*Alors*, it was nothing. *De rien, madame*.'

'Oh.'

'But this priest, do you think he will go? *Non, non*. This priest follows Imogen's husband and Imogen's sister right into the house, shouting at them all this time. And it is tragic, we all come here into this beautiful garden, shouting in the French and in the English, disturbing your most precious peace and tranquillity. I make the profuse apologies, Madame. To you and to Monsieur' – he nods to Alex – 'who were both so enjoying this beautiful Brittany morning before our arrival.'

He wrings Hester's hand, the one on Imogen's backbone, and Hester notices how it lingers on her daughter's silky spine for a moment or two. Then he goes to Alex, shakes his hand firmly, man to man. Hester splutters out some introductions, feeling rather silly performing this formality with her two daughters more or less collapsed on her shoulders, and wonders distractedly what to do next. Père Bonté seems to be praying out loud in a grating monologue under the apple tree, Bruno has slouched up against the garden table oozing sex appeal all over the place, and, worst of all, Gordon is creeping back up the garden like a tenacious slug.

It is Alex, dear Alex, who saves the immediate situation, much to Hester's relief. He has not moved from his chair during the whole procedure; he has not spoken except to acknowledge Bruno's introduction. But now he stands up, smiles reassuringly at Hester, and then says in French to Bruno, 'I think it is time we men left the women alone; I am sure they have many things to discuss.' He puts his hand firmly on Bruno's shoulder to emphasize the point.

Bruno understands at once and nods his beautiful head. He speaks to the priest, but before the Father can answer Alex says to Père Bonté, 'I believe I saw a café in the square when I arrived, perhaps we should go there for an apéritif while the women talk. I do not know your village, but it looks charming.'

The priest is gratified and agrees at once. By this time Gordon has slunk his way back to the courtyard and is looking most disgruntled. He is just about to sit down at the garden table and pour himself a cup of the coffee Imogen had brought out for Alex and Hester, cold though it is by now, when Alex says, 'Ah, you must be Gordon. I'm Alex Chrichton, an old friend of Hester's. I was just saying to these two gentlemen here that we should go to the village and have a drink – give Hester and her daughters a chance to talk. Will you join us?'

Gordon says sourly, 'Sorry, I'm dead tired. We've driven a long way. I'm not moving from here.' He starts again to pour the coffee but Alex stops him.

'I think you should reconsider, you know,' he says conspiratorially. 'I'm sure the women need some time on their own. You'd better come with us, there's a good chap.'

It isn't exactly a threat – Alex is the picture of innocence –but after a slight hesitation, Gordon acquiesces. With a scurrilous look at Hester, and at Abigail and Imogen who are still refusing to face the world, he turns and walks through the kitchen door, with Bruno and Père Bonté behind him.

Alex turns to Hester and says, 'I'll head for home after I've had a drink with the others. It's a long drive, almost three hours, and I must get back, I have some work to do. And your daughters need you, obviously.'

'Oh,' she replies stupidly. She hadn't expected to lose Alex again quite so soon.

'I've taken your daughter's phone number; you forgot to give it to me,' he says mischievously. 'This was just a preliminary visit, so that we didn't lose touch again after that chance meeting yesterday. I hope you will come up to see my little house in Kerrocher soon. I think you would like it. It's right on the estuary facing the sea, and there are masses of hydrangeas running riot all over the place. It's very cosy.'

This is so brazen that Hester has to smile. Alex leans down and kisses her lips briefly, and she could swear that after all these years the shape and the feel and the texture of them are as familiar to her as her own hands, her own body.

'Goodbye, Alex,' she says faintly.

'Non, non, Hester. Au revoir, n'est-ce pas?'

'D'accord, Alex. C'est vrai – au revoir.'

Then he says, politely and without a hint of irony, to the back of Hester's daughters' heads (their faces are still hiding in their mother's shoulders), 'Goodbye, Imogen. Goodbye, Abigail. So nice to have seen you both.'

He goes, and at last the two women struggle up out from their mother's bosom and face each other like feisty little bantam hens, one ginger and one dark, ready to peck each other to the death. But before they can begin Hester says threateningly, 'I don't want to hear one word, *one word*, until you are both calm and in control of yourselves. Is that understood? Or I shall get right into my car and head for Roscoff and home.'

There is a sullen silence. 'Good,' Hester says. 'We are agreed. Now, daughters, can we try to talk sensibly about this bloody mess?'

The next quarter of an hour makes no sense to Hester at all. Imogen at first is silent while Abigail tries to explain her version of what happened, but she is so incoherent that Hester cannot understand a word she is saying. Then Imogen, unable to keep quiet, starts interjecting phrases like, 'How can you listen to her, Mum, how can you?' and 'Will you get out of my house, Abigail? I can't stand the sight of you.'

Finally Hester realizes that any hope she has of discussing this rationally with both her daughters is totally illusory, so she says firmly, 'This is getting us nowhere. Abigail, will you please stop talking and keep quiet for a moment. Imogen, you and I have talked all morning; I think it is time for me to have a private chat with Abby. Anyway, you are only upsetting yourself hanging around here.'

'Bloody hell, Mum, it's my house! She should be the one to go.'

'I appreciate that,' Hester says reasonably, 'but it would be very difficult for me to talk to her if she went. As a matter of fact, I am terribly hungry. It has been an exceedingly long morning and lunch would be most welcome. Besides, you are looking sadly woebegone. You'll feel better if you wash your face.'

Imogen gives in. She has been dishevelled off and on all morning, which is extraordinarily out of character, and Hester suspects she is beginning to feel disarmed. 'All right,' she says with spirit. 'I'll go, so that my deceitful sister can wheedle and whine to you to her heart's content, trying to justify all she's done. I'd rather not hear her whinging anyway, it makes me feel sick.'

She walks with dignity to the house, then pauses at the French windows and says dramatically, 'I'll make lunch for you, Mother, but you can tell your other daughter I expect her out of my house by then.'

Hester sighs, sensing her lunch retreating. She turns to Abigail, who is pacing around the garden and courtyard like a little fox. 'Well, Abby,' she says with resignation. 'Whatever do you think you are doing?'

Abigail doesn't answer at once. She sniffs, blows her nose on a clean tissue she has found in her trouser pocket, and sits down at the table. Her ginger hair looks rich and polished in the sunlight; she has had it cut short, which suits her tiny face and frame. Abby has always hated her hair, about which she was teased endlessly at school, and has always envied Imogen's dark, rich colour. Is this why she ran off with her sister's husband, Hester wonders.

Could it all be reduced to hair-colour? She shakes her head and tries to concentrate.

Abigail finally meets her mother's eyes and has the decency to look slightly ashamed, though there is defiance there also. Hester hasn't seen her since she left for France six months ago, and scrutinizes her daughter carefully. Abigail has put on a bit of weight, which Hester thinks suits her as she was always too thin. Her skin is still pale, retaining the freckles that plagued her through her adolescent years, and Hester suspects she still resents them and her ginger hair. Nothing her mother or anyone could say ever convinced Abby that the combination of her fine hair the colour of a healthy fox, the endearing freckles, and her clear blue eyes, were just as appealing as Imogen's classic model's features, and a great deal more interesting. Abigail wanted beauty, and fretted a great deal that it seemed to have been all unfairly distributed to her older sister.

That Abigail was creative, and Imogen not (though she was always academically able), was not appeasing to this younger daughter. Abby could make music almost from birth; she sang like a thrush, a lark, a blackbird. Later, any instrument she picked up she could manage to wring melody from. As for the piano, her teachers said she was a natural, but she turned away from performance and chose instead to pursue a teaching career.

Martin and Hester often wondered why she chose not to train as a concert pianist. Her teachers, all of them highly qualified musicians themselves, insisted she could be successful on the concert circuit. But Abby had always been a diffident child, seeming not to want too much from life other than hours of playing her piano – to herself, not for an audience. Her only other interest was reading: mostly copious biographies and autobiographies, not just of musicians, but a random selection of theatre people, politicians, literary figures, explorers, adventurers and courtesans.

An escape from the tedium of her own life? Perhaps; some would say obviously so. But Abigail could have had a life just as glamorous, if that was what she wanted, as some of the people she read about. But she made a conscious decision to reject it.

It was a shock to her tutors, and to her parents, when she decided to turn to teaching, but where Hester accepted Abby's decision, Martin found it more difficult.

'Why?' he thundered at her. 'You're gifted, Abigail. How can you even think of giving it up? Teach when your concert career is finished, if you must. Don't waste time on it now.'

'How can you say that?' Abby replied. 'You're a teacher. I want to follow in your footsteps.' She said it demurely, rationally, as she did everything. Martin suspected irony but Hester wasn't so sure.

'Anyway,' Abigail went on cunningly, 'isn't one daughter as a performer enough? Surely you don't want both of us in the limelight.'

This irritated Martin beyond reason. 'You are not comparing the aesthetic life of a concert pianist with the meretricious life your sister Imogen leads as a fashion model, I hope?' he said stiffly.

Abigail shrugged. 'It's all to do with fame, isn't it?'

'My God, Abigail, surely you are intelligent enough to comprehend the difference between fame and notoriety. At least your sister is bright enough to admit that her own meteoric success was due to a pretty face and plain hard work, a far cry from creative talent.'

Abigail looked away from her father. 'I'm really not interested in talking about Imogen right now, if you don't mind. Whatever you say, I don't want to be a performer, in the public eye, as she is. It's brash and too ego-pushing for me. I thought you'd agree, I thought you'd be happy if I became a teacher – *like you*.'

Hester, hearing of this conversation later, wondered if Abigail was being disingenuous or merely naive. Whatever, it worked, for Martin, rather flattered that his younger daughter wished to follow in his footsteps, soon succumbed and supported Abby in her decision.

Later, Hester was thankful that he never lived to see how Abigail grew to loathe teaching in the classroom. Though her husband accepted Abby's reasons for giving up the idea of becoming a concert pianist, Hester was never quite sure. She often wondered if it had been a lack of confidence, or a fear of failure. Her sister Imogen had been so overwhelmingly successful in her modelling career that if Abigail had pursued a career as a concert pianist, and then for some reason failed, she would never have forgiven herself. The rivalry between the two sisters was still exceedingly, almost dangerously, strong, but by choosing to become a teacher, Abigail had removed herself from competition. At least, from *that* particular competition, Hester had thought ruefully at the time. There were other, darker jealousies, which she knew one day would have to be faced.

But now, sitting in this French garden with Abigail tearfully opposite her, Hester knows there are other things which must be confronted first. 'Well, Abigail,' she says to her daughter, regarding her with both love and exasperation. 'What do you have to say for yourself?'

Mother and daughter are alone. Abigail doesn't look at Hester but at an empty coffee cup as she says, trying to sound defiant but only sounding churlish, 'I love him.'

Hester groans, but has the sense to make it inaudible. This is just what Imogen said when Hester tried tactfully to ask her, six or seven years ago now, when she was at the height of her modelling business, with a number of the world's top models on her books and she herself doing the odd, prestigious job, why it was exactly she wanted to marry Gordon.

'I love him,' Imogen had answered, far more defiantly than Abigail's declaration.

Hester, perhaps unwisely, had tried to ask Imogen precisely why she loved Gordon, when her choice of eligible men was seemingly endless. 'Mum, you don't understand,' was Imogen's reply.

'Try me,' Hester insisted briskly. 'I really would like to know.'

'Well, there's something about him . . . something about

the way he is when he's with me. He makes me feel, all the time, at every moment, like there's no other person in the whole world as special and as precious as me, that there never was, and never will be.'

This Hester could understand; Gordon had that effect not just with Imogen, but with everyone he met, even the most casual acquaintance. It was a gift, a talent, like a flair for making soup or a genius for playing the recorder. Hester could see that if you were attracted to a man like Gordon, it would be difficult not to love him, not with all that charm beaming on you like a high-powered torch.

Hester tried to love Gordon also; he was her son-in-law, her daughter loved him. At their first meeting she found him pleasant enough. He was respectful without being obsequious, and praised Imogen highly.

'Your daughter is extremely talented,' he said to Hester. 'I sat in on one of her photo sessions recently. She managed to look warm and spontaneous, but at the same time was highly professional and efficient.'

'Have you known her long?' Hester asked, for Imogen had not been very forthcoming.

'Several months. Long enough to hear about her family, about you – Imogen's very fond of you, talks about you very affectionately.'

This surprised Hester, for she suspected that Imogen, in London, had barely enough time to think about herself, let alone her mother. But it gratified her, and she was happy enough to have Imogen bring Gordon down to Devon for frequent weekends. Gordon was then running a large and respected antique business in London, his father, who had built it up, having conveniently died and left it to him. Gordon was around thirty at the time, slightly older than Imogen. He had been married before and had two children somewhere in the north-east whom he never saw because, he hinted darkly, of his ex-wife who was so awful she was beyond the pale.

Imogen seemed fond enough of Gordon, in her usual brisk, efficient manner. Her passion, Hester knew, was reserved for her work, and her intensity surfaced primarily during her outbreaks of volatile temper which she had never been able to control.

'You handled that magnificently,' Hester once heard Gordon say to Imogen after her daughter had furiously reprimanded, on the telephone, one of her models who had arrived inexcusably late for an important photograph session.

'Oh Gordon, do you think so? I suppose I shouldn't have lost my temper.'

'You needed to. There was no other way to get through to her.'

'It's exhausting. We're supposed to be relaxing here in the country, for God's sake.'

'You relax. Here, I'll rub your feet the way you like, and then I'll get you a drink. Come on, put your feet up. You look gorgeous, you know. Losing your temper becomes you.'

Hester had to admit that he seemed perfect – eligible, presentable, successful, a confirmed heterosexual, of a suitable age, presumably doting on her daughter. However, a gradual foreboding began to shadow her relations with her prospective son-in-law. The feeling crept up after a few consecutive weekends in Gordon's presence; his willingness to please, his easy good manners, cloaked a shallowness that Hester found disturbing. He skirted around any subjects that were even slightly controversial, his ideas seemed to be a cloudy rehash of the popular themes circulating in the media and his interests in people seemed to pale when they responded with real feelings, real pain or sorrow or even joy. He would turn anything that threatened to become a serious conversation into something frivolous, light-hearted – and because he had wit and charm, he got away with it.

It wasn't long before Hester began, against her will, to dislike the man. As she got to know him he seemed to her to be too perfect, too superficially sincere. His eyes always looked directly into Hester's when he spoke, he hung on to her every word: it was too much, too spurious. That he did this to everyone Hester could have overlooked; that it seemed, at times, too practised, too studied, she couldn't. She supposed that if you were in love with the man, as Imogen said she was, such attention to every word, every gesture, would be exhilarating, but as she was not, it merely filled her with dismay. She wondered what would happen when love, as it usually did, became bogged down in domestic mire and togetherness. Hester feared Gordon was specious, but nonetheless she tried hard to overcome her prejudices against him; after all, they were no more than instinct and suspicion. Reluctantly, she gave him and Imogen her blessing, since Imo would have married him anyway, whatever she said.

It was a different story altogether with Martin. Gordon ingratiated himself with Imogen's father, not because it was necessary to charm him, but because it was a challenge. Imo had warned him how difficult Martin was within the bosom of the family, but Gordon prided himself on his ability to be liked by everyone, and he was certainly not going to let his wife's father be an exception.

'Well, Dad, what do you think?' Imogen said to Martin after they had announced their engagement. She said it challengingly and provocatively, as she said everything to her father, but there was some trepidation there also, which annoyed her.

Martin answered cautiously. 'Well, he's not the man I would have chosen for you,' he began slowly.

Imogen agreed. Perhaps this was one of the reasons she had decided to marry Gordon.

'But then,' Martin went on, 'you are not the daughter I had anticipated having.'

This was more like it. Preparing for battle, Imogen allowed herself a tiny smile. 'But you have another daughter, Dad,' she said sweetly. 'You have Abigail.'

'That is not the point, though you are quite right. You know how I feel about your modelling career, that you have thrown away your life and your intelligence—'

'Oh Christ, Dad, not again, please not again. God, what does it take to please you, anyway? Not only am I still one of the top models in this country, I also run the most prestigious agency in London. I'm a successful businesswoman, for God's sake! Can't you say once, just once, that I've done a good job? Even, maybe, that you're proud of me? I know that I'm not talented like my shitty little sister—'

'Imogen, I don't like you swearing! How many times have I told you—'

'Shit, shit, shit. Oh hell, I'm sorry, Dad, but Jesus Christ!'

Martin got up stiffly and started to leave the room. 'There's no point in talking to you, Imogen, when you get like this.'

'You make me like this!'

'But before I go I will say what I feel about Gordon, as you asked me to. I have had a number of talks with him during his weekends at our home and feel that he will make a good husband for you. Like you, he is a prosperous businessman. Like you, he is affluent and used to life's little luxuries.'

'Oh, for—'

'Don't interrupt me, Imogen. Whatever you say, you know I care deeply about you and have at all times only your interests at heart. I believe this Gordon loves you; he is a likeable young man, an ambitious young man, and certainly quite well-known in his field. I feel you are very fortunate indeed to have found him, and give you both my sincere approval.'

When Imogen, fuming, told all this to Gordon later, he was delighted. 'There, I told you I'd charm the old bugger, didn't I?'

'Oh, shut up.'

'Of course he's right, you know. You *are* bloody lucky to have found me.'

'Gordon, I said shut up.'

'Imo, what's the matter with you? Can't you ever joke about your father?'

Imogen thought about this for some time. Finally she said, 'No, Gordon, I can't.' Something in her voice made Gordon, finally, shut up.

*

And now, over six years later, Hester is listening to her other daughter telling her she loves this same detestable man. Hester finds it impossible to believe yet knows she must; she will have to accept this basic premise if she is to get anywhere with Abigail.

'Right, you love him,' she says to her daughter. 'Does he love you?'

'Of course he does!' she cries, rousing herself indignantly from the dregs of cold coffee she has been stirring up in the stale breakfast cups, and looking quite passionate.

Abigail doesn't often become emotionally aroused, so Hester is rather impressed by this, as she was by her daughter's outburst of tears when she and Gordon first walked in. Abigail has always, even as a child, been remarkably unruffled, which perhaps was just as well with Imogen throwing tantrums and creating scenes all over the place. Imogen, in her unkinder moments, accuses her sister of being so laid-back she might as well be dead, or alternatively, says she is a wimp. Abigail is neither; Hester has always suspected that in her own quiet way she is just as formidable as her sister.

'Well,' Hester says now, 'so Gordon loves you and you love Gordon. However, you seem to have forgotten something. Imogen, your sister, loves Gordon also, and we all of us, her included, assumed he loved her. In fact,' Hester speaks vociferously, for Abigail seems inclined to interrupt, 'this is more than an assumption, for he has always, up until your débâcle by the Blessed Shrine of Sainte Barbe, said so.'

Abigail shrugs. 'Of course he says he loves her. He has to – she's his wife.' She says it so scornfully, as only the unmarried can. But how can she know the peculiar ties – chains, perhaps – that bind two people together in those words *husband*, *wife*? Hester cannot tell her: no one can.

'All right, forget that for a moment. Suppose he doesn't love Imogen any longer, but you. Where does that leave Imogen? She's your sister, for God's sake, and she's suffering, Abby. Can't you see that?'

Abigail looks at her mother as if she were demented. 'Oh Mum, you know Imogen hasn't loved Gordon for years.'

This is news to Hester. She says, 'Ah, Gordon told you that, I suppose?'

Abigail looks sulky, and goes into one of her sullen silences that used to take the place of emotional outbursts when she was growing up.

'Abby,' Hester says, trying to be calm and reasonable. 'Of course you and Gordon want to believe that Imo no longer loves him; it's simpler and much less painful that way.'

'Oh Mum, you haven't lived with them, you don't know what's going on. Even back in England you could tell Imo was getting fed up with Gordon. All she did was work work work, never wanted to go out with him, never wanted to talk to him.'

'Come on, Abby. When his business failed she was most supportive, was quite happy to sell her own agency and uproot herself to start again with him in France.'

'That was only because she was bored herself with the modelling world, she's told us all that often enough. And she's always loved France, you know that.'

All this is true, Hester can't deny it. But that doesn't mean Imogen was bored with her marriage, or with Gordon, and she says so.

'Besides,' she continues, 'whatever the condition of Imogen's marriage, whatever went on between her and Gordon, it is still no justification for what you and Gordon have done. Imogen trusted you, welcomed you into her house . . .'

'Oh rot,' Abigail says with spirit. 'She let me in the house because it was handy, I helped prepare meals, served in the shop and diverted Gordon, for which she was quite thankful. Mum, you haven't visited her in France before, so you don't know what she's like. She's more a workaholic than ever; the business has taken off and is making piles of money, and she works at it day and night, long after Gordon has given up. He says she makes him feel like a useless appendage.'

Hester stops herself before she says, 'Yes, this is true: he is.' It is no secret that Gordon's antique business in London, which his father had so meticulously built up into a thriving little gold mine, deteriorated from the moment the son took it over. Gordon is not only inept, he is also incredibly lazy. No wonder Imogen has to work so hard, Hester thinks, the whole busines would go under if she didn't. The fact that Imogen also enjoys the work is immaterial.

Hester edits this quite a bit and tries to discuss it with Abigail, but she will not listen to a word against Gordon.

'Oh Mum,' she wails with such anguish that Hester's heart is suddenly moved for this wicked, wayward child of hers. 'You can never understand. The only man you ever loved was Dad, and he was yours right from the start. I've loved Gordon for years, and kept it all to myself.'

'What? You never even liked him – you said so often enough.'

'That was at first. Later, I pretended to go on disliking him, because I was falling in love with him.'

'Oh, Abby!'

'You don't know, you can't understand. He was so different from all the other men in my life, the ones at music school who were so wrapped up in their own talent they couldn't tell you what colour hair I had if I wasn't in the room.'

'And the sports coach? The men in your life haven't all been musicians, Abby.'

'He was an aberration, Mum. You know that.'

'Isn't Gordon?' Hester asks gently.

Abigail shakes her head. 'Even before . . . before we became lovers – ages ago when I was only Imo's sister, Gordon treated me like something special, something precious. He always noticed what I was wearing, or if I had changed my hair, and he always asked me about my studies. He looked at me, listened to me.'

Abigail stops. It seems as if she is not going to go on, so Hester says, 'When did you and he become lovers?'

'Not until I got to France – that's when he fell in love with me too. Oh, I knew he was my sister's husband, but she didn't appreciate him, didn't love him the way I did. Oh God, explanations are useless! I loved him, and I love him now, beyond sense and reason, and you'll never ever understand that and I'm sorry for you.'

She starts to cry again, slumping on the grass under the apple tree, her shiny ginger hair holding its own against the pansies and tulips and primula, and as if in exquisite sympathy, the blackbird begins once again its most glorious singing. And then the last stone crumbles in Hester's wall and nothing but love is left: for Alex whom she loved and lost and most likely will lose again; for Imogen who seems to have turned to jelly inside, leaving her hollow and vulnerable; and now for Abigail, whose life is breaking with emotion and who feels she will never love this way again.

Hester sits on the grass next to her daughter and holds her in her arms, as she did with Imogen earlier during this long morning which now has turned to afternoon. As she cries, Hester's own eyes fill but she knows they are selfish tears, the odd ones left over from her long-ago anguish over Alex.

And yet, as the blackbird keeps singing, Hester feels that it doesn't really matter who the tears are for, and that indeed they are for all of them, for Imo and Abby and herself, for love and loss and regret, for chances taken and chances missed, and in the end they all blend into each other; they are all one grief, one sorrow.

But there is something else that stands out in this moment, something as clear and as special as the blackbird's song. It is the fact that at this moment Hester feels closer to her daughters, and they to her, than they have for years, perhaps ever.

Hester succumbs to the moment. In the midst of this bloody appalling mess, at this moment she feels at peace.

Chapter Seven

'Bonjour, Madame! Ça va? Une baguette, s'il vous plaît.'
'Une baguette, oui; c'est tout?'
'Oui, merci.'

The plump, dimpled woman in the *boulangerie* hands Hester her purchases after exchanging a few pleasantries about the weather which has remained fine all of this week. When this amiable ritual is complete, Hester ambles out into the square which is, as in most Breton villages, built around the old stone church that squats like a mother hen in the middle of her nest. Imogen's village, Pont-Plouay, is not that small; there are two bakeries, a pharmacy, a small grocery store, a bicycle shop, a *tabac*, and a few other modest places of commerce, including a very busy shop which deals in equipment for both boats and fishing, for Pont-Plouay is located at a very salubrious spot just before the river widens and dissolves into the sea. In the summer the place has its share of holidaymakers but now, in May, it is just about right – bustling, but mostly with locals and those from the smaller villages scattered around. Even in the high season it is made bearable by the fact that most visitors from abroad bypass Pont-Plouay in favour of the more renowned Pont-Aven, which is not all that far away. The few who actually holiday in this village are usually from Paris or one of the other French cities. There is no beach in Pont-Plouay but there is a tiny harbour where people potter around in boats. It is all very laid-back and low-key.

Today is Friday, and being market day, the village is quite busy. Hester roams the square looking at crates of chickens squawking their heads off next to rows and rows of sturdy corsets and heavy no-nonsense bras. She browses through boxes of wooden clogs and acrylic jumpers; she purchases fresh goat cheese from a young jean-clad farmer's daughter.

As she wanders Hester thinks about how quickly she has

adapted to this French village, especially considering how she never wanted to come here in the first place. This last week, she has been sleeping much later than she normally does in England, ambling down to the village for fresh bread and vegetables, then blissfully letting herself loose in Imogen's garden while the younger woman tends to the business. Imogen has a little office in the back of the antique shop, which is built right on to the house. It used to be a stable, but Imogen and Gordon had it converted into two lovely airy rooms with a small but comfortable office in the back. Both rooms are filled with antiques: the showroom with large expensive pieces of furniture, the shop area with smaller items, mirrors, ornaments, lamps and so on, as well as some less expensive items of furniture.

At midday Hester and Imogen meet for lunch, in the shaded courtyard while the weather remains fine, and though Imogen rarely lingers but soon rushes back to her work, Hester takes her time, working her way greedily through fresh bread, an assortment of soft cheeses, salad, olives, sometimes a glass of deep red wine that reminds her of the richness of plums in summer, or of blackberries in autumn.

And then, of course, Hester dozes. She drifts over from the garden table to the chair under the large apple tree which is now laden with blossom, and the garden is so fragrant with scent she feels permanently intoxicated by it. With her she has two or three collections of poetry by people she has been anxious to read for ages, so she reads a poem or two, and then wafts away into a slumber as gentle as the breeze that sometimes blows from the sea. Often when Hester wakes she is covered with a soft coating of blossom.

Then she goes to the sea. From the small harbour there is a coastal path that rambles around indecisively for miles, sometimes losing its way and meandering a good half-mile away from the coast, but always managing to find its way back. Hester likes it when the path wanders off; you can look in people's gardens and see the poppies and peonies and pansies in bloom.

In the evenings, at night, Hester has been writing. The poetry flows and she writes and writes, instinctively knowing she has something good going but not stopping to analyze it. She just lets it flow like the river that runs alongside the town and into the sea.

Abigail and Gordon have gone away again, further south where they are living in a house belonging to an English friend of Gordon's. He didn't want to go, but Imogen was at her most formidable. When Gordon returned from the café an hour or so later on that dreadful day almost a week ago, he was in an unattractive mood, having been scathingly chastised by the priest, contemptuously ignored by Bruno, and having found no sympathy in Alex. So, in a foul temper and dispirited by his lack of allies, he was no match for his wife who had repaired her make-up and her dignity and ordered him and Abigail out of the house.

Abigail was quite happy about this and said she had no intention of staying, anyway. She would rather rot in hell than spend another minute in the loathsome place. Surprisingly, Imogen did not rise to the bait but refused to talk or even look at her sister, acting as if Abigail were a nasty but insignificant splodge of muck on the landscape. Gordon tried several arguments – that they all needed to talk reasonably about it, that the business needed him, that it was his house anyway as much as Imogen's.

Imogen replied in no uncertain terms that there was nothing at all to talk about after such scurrilous behaviour. The business had actually been doing better than ever in the past week since Gordon had left with 'that evil little wimp' and although the house might be half his in name, he had certainly relinquished every right to live in it with her.

Gordon was beaten, as well he knew. His downfall had begun at the local bar, where the other customers had avoided him like a man in the infectious stage of mumps. The fact that he had been found bonking with a woman not his wife might have been looked upon tolerably, even with sympathy, by the locals, but the woman being his wife's sister was just not on, and then of course there was the contempt shown to the Blessed Sainte Barbe. They were a moral lot, these townspeople, and Gordon would have to pay dearly for his sins.

And so they left, Abigail kissing her mother distractedly and saying she'd keep in touch, Gordon forgetting Hester's earlier affront and kissing her also, saying, 'One day, Mother, perhaps you will understand and forgive us.' Yuk! Hester thought. She wanted to hit him.

Since then, Imogen has refused to talk about it. She says she no longer has a sister or a husband, and isn't it lucky that she can now run the business without Gordon to hamper her. Hester has to admit she looks quite well, stunning even, but although she is once again glossy and perfect, Hester feels she rather liked her daughter uncertain and disordered. She was more approachable, somehow. Perfection is often a strain to live with, she thinks, and wonders if that was not perhaps how the fierce, unhealthy rivalry between the sisters started, all those many, many years ago.

It wasn't that Imogen was perfect as a child – far from it; nor, for that matter, was Abigail. But Martin, their father, seemed always to imply to each of his daughters that the other possessed something they themselves lacked. To each he compared the other, forcing impossible standards on both of them. And yet the irony was that he prided himself on being a model father. Certainly he doted on both girls, although in later life the way he expressed his feelings was both complex and destructive.

Before Abigail was born, Martin was devoted to Imogen, his first-born, and loved her fiercely, possessively. He played with her often, read to her, took her on outings to the zoo, the park, museums, adventure playgrounds. Imogen in turn adored her father: both were well pleased with each other.

'How good Martin is,' Hester's friends said. 'Such a wonderful father.'

And he was, of course. Hester agreed wholeheartedly, though even then she suppressed a slight uneasiness, a feeling that Martin's love would one day turn oppressive, that her high-spirited daughter would one day question the suffocating standards his love set for her.

But until Abigail was born, things went fairly smoothly. The birth of this winsome, cuddly sister with the disposition of an angel would have been a trial to someone of Imogen's temperament at any age, but at ten, with puberty approaching, she found it particularly hard to handle. Delighted that he was being made a father for the second time long after he had given up hope, Martin engulfed Abigail with the same enthusiasm, if not the same intensity, as he had his first-born, ready to mould her in the same way he felt he was moulding her sister.

But things were changing. By the time Abigail was two or three years old, Imogen was precociously well into adolescence, travelling far away from her father or perhaps (and Hester will never be certain) deliberately distancing herself from him to repay him for sullying their relationship with a sibling.

Whatever the reasons, Imogen was already rejecting the academic future her father was planning for her. Instead of hours spent over schoolbooks, she pored over fashion magazines, experimented with all the latest sophisticated styles, tried the newest make-ups on her face, and twisted her long dark hair into complicated and exotic creations.

'She's far too young for that,' Martin said to Hester in disgust. 'She's becoming vain, shallow.'

'Most girls go through this sort of phase,' Hester replied. 'It'll pass.'

One day Martin found Imogen in her bedroom, standing in front of her full-length mirror studiously, yet with a strange detachment, looking at her reflection. She was wearing a long black velvet dress she had picked up in a jumble sale somewhere; it had a low-cut neckline which emphasized her newly-acquired breasts and healthy glowing skin. Around her neck were several strings of crimson glass beads, glistening like drops of blood on the rich black of the dress. But what startled Martin was her face; fully made up, in bright and vivid colours that boldly pointed up her sultry dark eyes, her sensual mouth, this child of his, this daughter who was not yet thirteen, looked about twenty.

Martin, veins turned to ice, torn between rage and an inexplicable grief, felt like throwing himself on her and howling like an animal. Instead he said, in a frozen voice, 'Get it off. At once. Take that vile disgusting stuff off your face.' His own ascetic, pallid face was as impassive as one sculpted in marble.

Abigail, then only a toddler, had followed her beloved Dad up the stairs. Her first reaction at seeing her older sister was to cry out with delight. How strange and exciting and colourful Imogen looked, how pretty with the bright red lipstick echoing the crimson colour of the long beautiful beads.

'Oh, Imo, pretty lady,' the child cried. 'Please make me a pretty lady too, Imo, please?'

'Shut up.' Martin's voice lashed like a slap, and Abigail began to whimper. Ignoring her, he said again to Imogen, 'Go and wash your face, do you hear me?'

Shocked and flustered by her father's tone, Imogen said, 'Dad, I'm only playing.' She understood that her father, whom she adored, was in a cold-white rage but she could not comprehend why. 'I'm . . . pretending,' she stammered, not knowing quite what she had done wrong, but driven to explaining herself. 'It's a game. I'm not going out like this.'

Martin silently took Imogen by the arm and pulled her roughly away from the mirror, through the bedroom door, and into the bathroom opposite. Running both taps at full strength with one hand, still holding on to his daughter's arm with the other, he pushed her against the bathroom sink. Abigail, following, stood behind the open door and stared while her father began to scrub harshly at her sister's face with a pale-blue face flannel.

Tears gathered in Imogen's eyes and streamed copiously down her face, but she didn't say a word as Martin, silent also, rubbed the blood-red lipstick from her mouth, the blusher from her cheeks. When her face was scoured clean he turned off the taps, handed her a towel and said, his voice still icy and measured with suppressed fury and distaste, 'You are beginning to grow up, Imogen, and you are fortunate in that you are going to be beautiful. I will not have you spoil it.'

As he turned and walked away from her, he suddenly noticed Abigail. 'Shall we go to the park?' he said, taking her hand and smiling tightly at her. 'Mum's out shopping for a few hours, so would you like a ride on the swings?'

Relieved that her father was himself again, Abigail threw herself into his arms. 'At least *you* love me, Abby,' he said, his smile still tight but his arms lifting the toddler fondly on to his shoulders. 'You may not grow to be as beautiful as your sister, but if you turn out less vain and superficial I shall be more than happy.'

Without another word to Imogen, Martin carried Abigail down the stairs and out of the house. Imogen, her raw face buried in the soft blue towel, sat on the floor of the bathroom for a long time, listening to the drip of the leaky cold-water tap echoing mournfully in the large, empty house . . .

All these years later, Hester ponders these matters – incidents she witnessed herself, things her daughters told her later. She was never afraid to confront Martin over his handling of the girls, never afraid to state categorically when she disagreed with his management of a situation, but now she wonders if it was enough. Could she have done more? 'You've got to let her go, Martin,' she cried more than once, as he tried, with less and less success, to direct Imogen's life.

'She needs discipline, direction.'

'Of course, I agree. But not tyranny and threats.'

'You're being dramatic again, Hester. Perhaps that's the way you handle your sixth-formers, and that's fine: just leave me to handle our children. You're too emotionally involved to deal with them objectively.'

The old memories trouble her, and she tries to suppress them as they float in her consciousness like rotting seaweed, polluting the clear blue water of these balmy French days. Determinedly, she writes more poetry, takes longer walks.

And then Alex phones, and Hester knows, as soon as she hears his voice, that she has been waiting for this call since he appeared in Imogen's garden so unexpectedly that Sunday morning.

They talk animatedly for quite a while. 'I've thought so often about our meeting,' he says when they have exhausted all their other topics. 'It was so extraordinary.'

'I know. Me too.'

She waits for him to go on but he only says vaguely, 'How strange it all seems, to be back in each other's lives.'

'Yes. Yes, it is.'

'I've given you my telephone number, Hester. Have you written it down?'

'Yes.'

'We must not lose touch again. I have a big job on right now which I must finish, I've given my word. It shouldn't take long. Then will you come and visit me, spend some time with me here in Kerrocher?'

'Oh, Alex, I don't know. I just don't know.'

'Hester . . .'

'I'm not sure if it would be a good idea. I think I'd rather remember it the way it was when . . . when I was there before.'

What she does not say is that she has no desire to see his house – *their* house – littered with the scattered débris of the herbal hamster. Although the woman does not live there, Hester is sure her things will be discarded all over the place like cracked nut-shells: the odd cardigan, the mislaid hairbrush, the pungent scent of rosemary and lavender.

'We'll talk again soon,' Alex says. 'I'd like you to come up.'

But Hester will not commit herself, and they say goodbye hesitantly, almost fearfully, as if each is afraid the other will suddenly vanish before the past is laid to rest.

Hester tries, in these soft spring days, to put Alex out of her mind but he keeps reappearing in her poetry. She finally stops battling with herself and lets it go, writes about it, hoping it will run itself out. Now that the *ménàge à trois* seems to be on Hold for a time (though Hester is perfectly aware that nothing has been sorted out), she has time to sieve through her feelings for Alex. She realizes with regret that the emotions she has kept lidded for so long are simmering back into her life; things are moving, bubbling, stirring.

Hester is not happy with this. Things could get worse, so she decides it would be better not to see Alex. Having taken this decision she rushes for the phone when it rings; she broods jealously about that sweet-smelling rodent with the gerbil hair and large teeth and aroma of basil. She is, in short, acting again like an adolescent, just as she did when she was in her mid-forties and first fell in love with Alex. She decides crossly that this has to stop; it is undignified to go straight from adolescence into senility.

Her preoccupation, as she absentmindedly wanders around the village square choosing vegetables, is broken by a deep voice pounding her with French while clasping her on the shoulder. It is Père Bonté, flapping around the market stalls in his black skirts looking like a threatening storm on a sunny day. He talks at length about the weather, the market, and then, at even greater length, about Abigail and Gordon. He is obsessed with them, with their sin, and has personally taken on the task of avenging angel. Hester is not exactly pleased with either of them herself, but she does think the priest is rather over the top.

Taking her leave as quickly as she can, Hester heads for home, ignoring the good Father's hints that nothing would be sweeter than a dark, thick coffee in the pretty little garden with the enchanting and long-suffering Imogen, as well as her even more enchanting mother. Hester longs for the garden herself, but on her own.

However, when she has walked up the hill and reached the house she is met under the willow tree by Imogen and, following closely, Dr Bruno Lambert, whose tan has deepened during this week of sunshine and whose hair sweeps the rim of his dark glasses with sensual style. Hester wonders irreverently what his eyes are like. Perhaps they are little red piggy eyes! Perhaps he will stop looking like a rock star when he takes them off, and start looking more like a doctor.

'Mum, we've been waiting for you. We were just going down to the square to look for you!' Imogen cries. She looks cool and elegant in wide, flowing calf-length trousers made of some silky translucent material; they are navy-blue with tiny polka dots all over and they swish and sway as she walks, sounding like a gentle wind going through summer trees.

Bruno charmingly kisses Hester's hand; he has been to the house on several occasions, presumably to check on Imogen's health, though he surely must notice she is looking radiant, not at all like the abandoned wife. She does remember sometimes, especially when Père Bonté is around, to look tragic, although Hester has noticed that when anyone mentions her husband she looks more furious than distressed.

Bruno, still holding on to Hester's hand, says, 'I have the day off today, and because the sun shines I come here to see if Imogen and her charming mother would like to accompany me to Pont-Aven. The galleries will be open, the boats will be on the river, and you will take lunch with me at a very fine restaurant owned by a great friend of my family's.'

My God, the French are something else, Hester thinks admiringly. Things stir in her, as they have been doing ever since she boarded that wretched ferry boat. No wonder her emotions are totally out of control; how can they not be in this land of red wine and fulsome Frenchmen?

She looks at Imogen. Her daughter's hair is tied back with an elegant gold clip; her face looks chaste, demure, perhaps because she is wearing less make-up than usual. Her skin is luminous, glowing. Hester wonders if it is art or nature and decides it doesn't matter. Whatever it is, Imo looks much better than she did when Hester arrived not even a full week ago.

'I thought you were working,' Hester says to her with a smile.

'Well, I do have a customer in Pont-Aven, the same man who owns the restaurant where Bruno wants to take us. He's interested in some porcelain and I have some pieces to show him.'

'So we will combine *le travail avec le déjeuner*. A working lunch, very English,' Bruno says, smiling. His smile is amazing, like the flash of a lighthouse on a dark sea, magnetic and reassuring. That crooked tooth only adds piquancy, like thorns on a rose.

Hester is tempted; she has never been to Pont-Aven. But she tells herself it would be good for Imogen to get out alone with this splendid young man. After all, her daughter has had a most harrowing fortnight. So she says, regretfully, 'I have some work to do, unfortunately. My editor is expecting my next collection at the end of summer, so there's a lot to sort out.'

Bruno looks so wracked with disappointment that Hester wonders what's wrong with him. Why doesn't he want a day out alone with her daughter? But he says, 'Ah, but my parents are expecting you both! They are lunching with us in Pont-Aven.'

Imogen says, 'I took the liberty of accepting for both of us, Mum, and Bruno has just rung his parents at their gallery. You'll like them. I've only met them briefly before, but they are very interesting – your sort of people, I think.'

'They are both artists,' Bruno explains. 'They have a small gallery in Pont-Aven.'

This Hester cannot resist, so she accepts. Though both Imogen and Bruno assure her she looks fine, she insists on going upstairs and changing out of her jeans and shirt into a full cotton skirt the colour of olives, and a rusty-red, thin cotton jumper the colour of the pimento inside. Before going downstairs Hester grins at her reflection in the mirror, wondering if the Lamberts, artists that they are, will notice her resemblance to a stuffed olive.

Imogen and Bruno are waiting in Bruno's car, a nippy black Citroën. Imogen is already in the back so Hester is ensconced royally in the front with Bruno. The car smells of new leather and, less strongly, of Imogen's expensive perfume. As they drive off, Bruno puts in a tape; the stereo is perfect and waves of Verdi lap over them. So much for the rock star.

It takes them less than a half-hour to get to Pont-Aven, even going the scenic way past little villages tucked into green fields unrolling from the sea, and tiny harbours with boats nestling like white ducks under stone wings. They easily find a parking spot right along the river and walk languidly through the town to meet Bruno's parents.

The dozens of art galleries that have sprung up like mushrooms after rain in this town where Gauguin painted are all shut for the long lunch-hour, but Bruno assures Hester that she will have ample time to explore when they re-open for the afternoon. She is surprised that Imogen does not insist on rushing home after lunch, but the younger woman seems both unhurried and untroubled. Perhaps her daughter intends to spend the afternoon with her client, Hester decides, for she notices Imogen is carefully carrying the package with the porcelain.

They walk along the river towards the centre of town, admiring the houses snuggled alongside and on the wooden hillsides sloping away from the water. The town seems hushed and serene, the colours vibrant in the midday sun. Hester can see why so many painters chose to live here in the past, and still do.

Turning down by the stone bridge in the centre of the town, they come into a tiny side street, at the end of which is the Lambert gallery. There is a Closed sign on the door but it is open and Bruno invites the two women inside. While he disappears into the back, calling out to his parents, Imogen and Hester look around.

There are two large adjoining rooms in the gallery, each filled with paintings. In one the canvases are bold and vivid with colour and movement: they depict crowds of merry-makers at a carnival; a street in Paris crammed to capacity with pavement cafés, traffic and people; and a view of Pont-Aven, obviously in midsummer, with holidaymakers and art-lovers bursting out of the shops and galleries like beans from an overstuffed beanbag. Hester is delighted; she recognizes the work as being by the same artist who painted the picture she so loves in her bedroom at Imogen's house. And now, here, are a dozen in the same bold style, the colours alive and singing, using every shade of red and yellow, and blues as pure as morning skies. There is a kind of glorious joy radiating from each one.

Imogen points to the corner, where the name *Colette Lambert* is signed in a tiny neat script. 'Bruno's mother,' she whispers. 'I have one of her paintings.'

'I know, they're wonderful,' Hester whispers back. 'They resemble the kind of poems I would like to write – ecstatically joyful, in love with life, vibrant.'

Imogen doesn't answer; Hester doubts if she's ever read her poems, or Abigail either. It has never bothered her, this lack of interest in her poetry. In actual fact, it frees her, knowing none of her family reads her writing.

Hester and Imogen wander into the next room to look at the other paintings. Hester smiles and says, 'But these, I suspect, are what many of my poems are really like.'

The contrast is startling. These paintings are as misty and mysterious as the others were light and cheery and open. There are many of the sea, obviously of the Brittany coast, with vast stretches of shadowy sand and twilit sky, with perhaps a tiny boat moored dolefully at the end of the expanse. There are several of rain: empty houses along a river fuzzy with mist, and opaque silhouettes hunched under huge umbrellas the colour of sky just before nightfall. They are reflective, meditative, and not without a certain haunting power.

The signature on these paintings is large, scribbly. Hester can just barely make it out: *Luc Lambert*.

'Well, at least there is no competition here,' Hester says to Imogen. 'Their style and content are so vastly different. Both are quite good, don't you think?'

Imogen agrees, and they look around for a moment or two and then Bruno returns with an older man and woman. 'My parents,' he announces proudly.

Hester knows the couple are in their seventies. She learned from Imogen that Bruno was a complete surprise to them, arriving unexpectedly after they had been married almost twenty years and had given up all hope of children. But if these are the seventies, Hester thinks as the pair greet her warmly, then let the years roll on, for the Lamberts are delightful, full of health and sparkle and bounce and vitality.

'Bonjour à tous!' Luc Lambert cries, kissing Hester on both cheeks, twice on each side, then doing the same to Imogen. He is little and spry and still quite handsome with an over-abundance of white hair on both his head and on his eyebrows, and clear, deep-brown eyes which seem perpetually amused by everything.

Colette Lambert kisses Hester also, welcoming her in French and English. 'I am so very pleased to at last meet Imogen's mother,' she says. 'Bruno has spoken of you highly.'

'As he has of you both. He told me you were artists, but I was still unprepared for how marvellous your work is. So different in style, and yet all so memorable in such contrasting ways.'

Colette and Luc are genuinely gratified by this praise, as pleased as if they were amateurs in the art world, instead of highly regarded artists in their own country.

Colette is tall, much taller than her husband, and looks younger, though in fact Bruno has said they are, almost to the day, exactly the same age. Her hair is superbly dyed a pale ash colour, and piled crazily on top of her head seemingly at random, but it is her face that Hester finds intriguing – it is round and soft and delicately wrinkled like the bottom of a newborn baby. She has plump protruding lips that seem hard to control, so often do they wriggle out into a smile, and a magnificent Roman nose under large and myopic grey eyes that slightly cross when she gets excited.

As they all leave the gallery and walk down the street to the restaurant where a table has been booked for lunch, Hester smiles to herself at the Lamberts' clothes, for they are quite contrary to what she had expected of them, having seen their paintings. Colette, whose paintings are as rich and bright and quirky in their colours as Luc's are heavy and sombre and dark, wears all black and grey: a black fine silk suit with a long skirt almost to her ankles, and little black leather boots with a tiny heel and laces, and underneath the loose flowing jacket, a soft grey blouse. The only colour is in her jewellery: long dangling earrings the colour of tropical fish, beads the turquoise of the sea in summer, a bracelet of chunky ceramics painted like parrots.

And Luc? Luc of the haunting skies and lonely black seas, and solitary figures brooding in boats, is wearing a royal-blue jumper with a bright paisley scarf tied around his neck. His pale-blue cotton trousers are immaculate and his shoes are of the softest Italian leather, rich green like clover, which picks out the predominant colour in his extraordinary scarf which is long and flowing, rippling like the Aven around his shoulders and down his chest.

Ordinarily Hester would have felt rather dowdy amongst all this flair, resembling a stuffed green olive in her cotton skirt and jumper, but the Lamberts have that rather special knack of enhancing the well-being and confidence of everyone around them. Colette and Luc are like their son, Bruno, exuding warmth and sincerity. Hester, thoroughly enjoying herself, enters the restaurant in a mood of complete contentment and anticipation.

The Lamberts, who obviously use the restaurant frequently, usher their guests to a fine, heavy polished oak table (which, Imogen whispers to Hester, she brought over from England and sold to her client, the owner of the restaurant) and they all settle themselves, Hester in between Colette and Luc with Imogen and Bruno opposite.

As the owner approaches there is a flurry of greetings, four kisses for Colette whom he obviously knows well, a brief but warm kiss on each cheek for Imogen who hands him the parcel with the porcelain, firm handshakes for the men, and then Hester is introduced with a flourish.

'*Enchanté*,' the man says, shaking her hand across the heavy table. Hester acknowledges the introduction and comments on the beauty and elegance of his restaurant. There are only six or seven tables in all, of various sizes, all different, all old and glowingly polished. A small granite fireplace, obviously much used in the winter, is now filled with masses of flowers, primarily daisies but of every conceivable colour. The ceilings are low, darkly beamed, and on the cream-coloured walls are numerous paintings, two of which Hester recognizes as the Lamberts'. There is a massive old sideboard in the corner with a huge spray of dried flowers and two very old patterned china water jugs. There is a good *ambience* about the place, one not only of richness and comfort, but of mellowed age and tranquillity.

And so Hester says, sincerely, as she shakes the owner's large firm hand, how delightful she finds his restaurant. But something in her voice alerts him; he looks at her more closely. Hester is unnerved and starts to take her hand away, but he only grips it tighter as his mind steps backward into the past, trying to identify this woman. And then suddenly Hester has her own moment of recognition and it is her turn to stare. He is older, of course, and his restaurant on the sea was more modest than this, but there were dried flowers there also, and even before Hester recalls the man she remembers that the massive sideboard, obviously a family heirloom, had stood in the corner of that restaurant also, eight years ago: Le Café de la Mer, on the cliffs of Kerrocher, near Roscoff.

M. Dupont has also made the connection. 'Madame,' he says excitedly, 'do you not remember, years ago, we have met before? Often you ate at my modest restaurant on the sea – I even remember how you adored my *soupe de poissons*, is this not so?'

Hester is nonplussed; she wants to dissemble but is too shocked and slow-witted at this moment to do so. She mumbles confusedly, 'Yes, of course I remember. How are you, M. Dupont?'

'But this is such a coincidence! We must share a bottle of Champagne – how extraordinary. And you must tell me what has become of – I can't remember his name, never mind, it will come to me. He came many times to eat alone after you had returned to England.'

He rushes off to get the champagne and everyone at the

table turns to Hester questioningly. She is bombarded by Luc and Bruno: when was she in France before? How did she get to know M. Dupont? And from Imogen: was that when she had gone to visit a friend on her fiftieth birthday? But wasn't that her old friend Sarah – who was this mysterious man M. Dupont remembers? Imogen laughs when she says this, and for once Hester is glad her daughter thinks of her as the poor old dear.

But as their host returns with the Champagne, Hester feels the onset of panic. Surely he will mention Alex, remember his name, tell everyone that he and Hester were lovers . . . say how they held hands across the table and kissed while they watched the sea darken as the long days turned to night and still they sat there, eyes lovingly on each other for hour after hour.

Hester sits stricken, feeling her face go cold and clammy; her thoughts are buzzing incoherently in her head like angry bees. Having found her daughter she will lose her again: Imogen does not understand passion, will condemn what her mother did as soundly as she condemns her sister. It is only a matter of time until M. Dupont mentions that his restaurant was in Brittany, when Hester was supposed to be in Normandy where her friend lived. But will Imogen remember that Sarah lived in Normandy? Probably not, Hester thinks, but she can't be sure. She is cold with fear and foreboding.

Everyone is waiting for Hester to speak, but she cannot. Luckily M. Dupont has finished pouring the Champagne and starts to make a toast, so they all turn to him expectantly. Hester's heart lurches: she is terrified the man will toast her and Alex, for surely he will have remembered Alex's name by now.

M. Dupont raises his glass and calls for attention. Hester wishes she could faint, like one of those Victorian ladies in moments of crisis, but she is far too strong and hearty. So she closes her eyes and waits for it: embarrassment, exposure, ruin.

But just as the man is about to speak, Colette quickly but gracefully gets to her feet, holds up her glass in a flamboyant gesture, and cries in her mellifluous voice; 'Gérard, my dear old friend, could you grant the wish of someone you have known a long time and drink to the future on this most fortuitous day, not to the past which is behind us? For we have in our hands Champagne, and the promise of a splendid lunch, and the company of new friends whom I hope will one day become dear old friends like you are to us, Gérard.'

She does this with such grace and style that Gérard and Luc '*oh la! la!*' with delight and then everyone breaks into agreeable chatter while picking up their glasses and drinking to the future, and to new and old friends. In the general babble that follows, Hester grabs her drink gratefully, swallowing great mouthfuls of Bubbly. Everyone is merry and expansive, French and English flows as freely as the Champagne, and for the moment Hester is forgotten.

Except by Colette. Her rosy plump lips, still delicately perched on the rim of her glass like a fat bumblebee on a tulip, twitch into a smile; she looks at Hester as innocently as an ageing cherub in a cracked Renaissance painting. Then, carefully and conspiratorially, she winks.

Chapter Eight

The lunch is of course magnificent, and dazed as Hester is, she eats heartily. M. Dupont's fish soup is as succulent and nourishing as she remembers, but today it is just a starter. There is chicken to follow, with spicy rice, and mushrooms in butter and herbs and garlic, and cauliflower, and later a lemon sorbet and an assortment of cheeses. The wine is rich and hearty and there seem to be copious amounts of it.

As the restaurant fills and M. Dupont becomes quite busy, Hester starts to relax, hoping they will finish and leave before the man has time to pursue their old acquaintance, or start asking questions about Alex. Hester watches him surreptitiously, wondering whether to feign illness and leave, but she hasn't the heart to break up the party and anyway, she doesn't want to draw any more attention to herself.

As the meal dawdles to a close Hester becomes slightly frantic. Her affair with Alex is intensely personal; she told no one either at the time or later, not even her closest friends. Perhaps that was a mistake; speaking of him to someone might have made the pain of separation less intense: she will never know now. However that may be, the fact is that now Hester is suddenly aware that someone else knows about it, and she finds this very uncomfortable.

As they linger over coffee, Hester wonders just how often Alex went to Le Café de la Mer after she left France. M. Dupont said many times. They must have talked, for the restaurant was usually empty – did Alex tell him about her? What could he have said?

As the restaurant begins to empty Hester grows increasingly uneasy. Will the gregarious owner come up to their table again and resume his reminiscence over Le Café de la Mer? Will Imogen start to question her again about the identity of this mysterious man?

And then Colette stands up and with relief Hester assumes they are leaving, but she only excuses herself and makes her way towards the *Dames* at the other end of the restaurant. Hester watches her cross between the tables regally, making a point of stopping near M. Dupont who has just come out of the kitchen. They talk intensely for a few moments; they seem like very old friends and have a great rapport with each other. Hester, watching them, sees that the restaurant owner is still extroverted and expansive, as she remembers, and his laugh, deep and resonant, bellows often and heartily throughout the cheery restaurant. He seems to have got no older; perhaps his moustache was not, eight years ago, then entirely silver, and perhaps his chin had not quite lapsed into an embryonic second. He is even taller than she remembers, quite easily several inches over six feet, and large, extraordinarily large, but not fat, not at all – just big. He seems oversized for his restaurant, but manoeuvres himself around the tables to greet his customers with remarkable agility. Hester thinks he must be around sixty, and envies the healthy vitality bouncing off him, like a Brittany fisherman just home from a satisfying day's work.

With dismay Hester realizes that she was right: they are not to get away without more conversation. When Colette returns to the table M. Dupont joins them. He offers Cognac and more coffee, and asks Hester to call him by his first name, Gérard. Imogen, already on first-name terms, comments on the delicious meal, and the others add their compliments warmly.

Gérard looks pleased and gratified. '*Ah merci*, but it is my life, the cooking, the restaurant, so naturally it must be always perfect,' he says with his wonderful laugh.

'Gérard has never married. His women could not compete with his love of food,' Luc teases.

'*C'est vrai*, it is true.'

'But you have no regrets, *n'est-ce pas?*' Colette asks rhetorically.

'*Mais non!* The cuisine, she eases the soul. A woman – not always.'

Everyone laughs, and then Imogen says, 'So tell us how you met my mother all those years ago – what an extraordinary coincidence! Who was this mystery man with you, Mum – one of Sarah's friends?'

'Oh, well . . .'

'Ah, I know, it must have been Henry, Sarah's husband. I remember him from my childhood – didn't he come to visit us at the rectory?'

'Perhaps, yes . . . oh, it was so long ago!'

'It is much too long ago to remember,' Gérard says firmly, as Imogen is about to go on. 'All I can now recall is Madame here looking much as she does now, only perhaps less beautiful all those years ago.'

Everyone smiles and exclaims benevolently over the charming compliment and then Gérard changes the subject, turning instead to the porcelain ornaments Imogen had discreetly handed him as they entered the restaurant. With relief Hester realizes he will no longer pursue their earlier encounters eight years ago, and with a deep breath is able to turn her attention to what he is saying about the porcelain.

'They are so fine, so beautiful, these pieces. Of course I must have them.' He turns to Hester. 'I have such good fortune in finding your Imogen. I have filled my house upstairs with many of her treasures.'

They talk of antiques for a time. Gérard is knowledgeable, and of course Imogen knows her new profession impeccably. The rest of the party listen with fascination as they discuss Chinese jade and Japanese bronze. By the time they leave, no one seems to have remembered that Gérard and Hester once met many years ago.

Outside the restaurant Imogen, Bruno and Hester say goodbye to Colette and Luc, and are urged to visit them one day at their house on the other side of the river. By now Hester is ready to go back to Pont-Plouay; the day has been rather traumatic one way and another. Imogen, she is sure, will also be ready to return, to her accounts or her cataloguing, or the numerous phone calls she is always making to customers and suppliers in that austere office in the back of the showroom.

But to Hester's surprise it seems that Imogen and Bruno want to laze about in the sun by the river, looking at the swans and seagulls, admiring the boats moored up and down the harbour, bobbing around like multi-coloured ducks. 'Well,' Hester says, 'then I can wander around all the art galleries for an hour or two.'

'Yes, that's the idea,' Imogen says. 'Do take your time, there's a lot to see in Pont-Aven.'

This is so unlike Imogen, who has been in a rush since she was ten years old, that Hester looks at her suspiciously, but she is swanning around in the grass, half-sitting and half-reclining, and only smiles at her mother innocently. Hester wonders that she is not mad with worry about grass stains on her flimsy, opaque trousers, but she seems totally unconcerned about anything at the moment. It is hard to remember that only a couple of weeks ago her husband ran off with her sister, so remarkably does she seem to have recovered. Hester wonders if this is just a very good act, that she is perhaps walling in her emotions as she herself learned to do many years ago. But this also is unlike her older daughter: Imogen has never been one to dissemble where feelings are concerned.

Hester leaves them dawdling at the river's edge and spends the next hour and a half immersed in a world of paint and colour. She resolutely makes herself forget the strange meeting with Gérard Dupont and all the memories it has conjured up, and indulges herself with art, staying as long as she likes in front of the exhibits that appeal to her, being more cursory with those that don't, and buying some Gauguin posters of his Brittany work, before she finally rejoins Imogen and Bruno.

They look as if they have hardly moved. Bruno is holding a worn paperback of Baudelaire's poetry, and Hester could swear he was reading aloud from it to her daughter before she approached. Oh ho, Hester thinks, and then – Never! He is never ever Imogen's type, this sultry, intense French doctor who never seems to take off his sunglasses. The thought is so bizarre that she discards it at once, and the three wander slowly back to Bruno's car.

This time Hester jumps in the back seat before Imogen can insist that the poor old dear sits in front. She needs time to collect her thoughts, to think now about the freak coincidence of meeting Gérard Dupont so soon after encountering Alex. How often it happens this way, she thinks. People disappear from our lives for years, and then they crop up one after the other, in batches like snowdrops or mushrooms.

Though perhaps it isn't so strange. After all, for years Hester never set foot in France and then suddenly here she is, back in Brittany, and perhaps it is natural that she should be reacquainted with old places, old friends. What is odd is how contented she feels, being in France once again. Yes, she is worried about both Abigail and Imogen, and knows that that situation will eventually have to be resolved; and yes, she knows that Alex and she still have many things to talk about, some of which are troubling. But in spite of that Hester feels quite calm. She doesn't even miss her lifeline –her English garden, nor her dog or cats, yet when she first received that furious phone call from Imogen, summoning her to France, she was quite frantic and, yes, angry. She didn't want to go, didn't want to leave her snug, smug life for that precarious place abroad, seething with both old and new emotions. Yet here she is, serene, contented, not even thinking about going back, not yet. She finds it all very perplexing.

Another week, almost two, pass idyllically. On the surface, things seem to be at a lull; there is no word from Abigail and Gordon, no signs of distress from Imogen who still won't talk about them, and Hester has not seen Alex. He phoned again and as usual seemed preoccupied, pressed about a certain piece of work he had to complete, but not particularly keen to elaborate about it. 'When it's finished, in about a week or so, we must meet.'

'Yes. Ring me then.' She changed the subject quickly, so that he wouldn't ask her again to visit the house in Kerrocher. She would rather remember it as it was eight years ago, when it was just hers and Alex's, their escape, their haven. Sentimental – yes. Foolish – yes. Hester knows all this, but there you are – she blames it on France.

On the phone she told Alex about Gérard Dupont. 'Good God, Hester, how extraordinary. I would very much like to see him again – perhaps some time I will. And he remembered you after all these years?'

'Well, you and I did spend quite a bit of time there. And the restaurant was just starting up then, so there were very few customers.'

'That's right. Actually I can remember some evenings when we were the only ones there. No wonder he remembered.'

'He said you came in alone quite often, after I left.'

Alex hesitated for a few seconds before saying, ambiguously, 'It was hard to let you go, Hester.'

Hester had intended to ask Alex whether he had spoken about her to Gérard Dupont, but something in his voice kept her silent. She realized she was not yet ready to face the pain she had caused him when she left him the way she did, and she knew it was cowardly, but she told herself that the telephone was not the proper means for this type of communication. They each held on to their respective phones for some moments in silence, neither of them quite knowing what to say, and neither of them wanting to hang up. And so the trauma of all those years ago hung palpitating on the lines between them, as they finished their conversation in a desultory way and put down the phone, neither one of them satisfied.

Hester thought later she should have asked him about his woman, about the herbal hamster, but in retrospect she admitted she would have done so churlishly. Alex had every right to have another woman and actually she was quite pleased (she told herself), because now neither one of them, Hester or Alex, would have any illusions about getting together again.

Hester tidies up her thoughts, which have scattered messily since her conversation with Alex, and concentrates on Imogen's garden, happily rescuing pansies from strangulation by couch grass, and pampering the rhododendron, which seems rather neglected. The weather is once again superb after a couple of days of rain and Hester finds an old floppy sunhat which she wears while she works.

'Don't you miss your garden back home, Mum?' Imogen says to her one lunchtime as Hester seems reluctant to drag herself away from the peonies to join her at the courtyard table.

'Oddly, no.' Hester takes off her gardening gloves and stretches her arms towards the sun. 'It will be beautiful now, too. The roses should all be out, and the clematis.'

She goes inside and washes her hands and face, thinking of her garden in England. It will be at its most glorious now, and Hester is missing the whole display, yet it doesn't seem important somehow. A year ago she would have been frantic to be separated from it at this time.

'I have someone in the village who is looking after it,' Hester tells Imogen as they sit down to lunch. 'A spry pensioner who has no garden of his own. He was so delighted when I asked him that he wanted to pay *me* for doing it, instead of vice versa.'

Imogen offers her a huge tomato which Hester slices and stuffs into the baguette she has copiously buttered. 'And the animals?' Imogen asks.

'Simnel is on a friend's farm, quite deliriously happy, I should think.' Simnel is Hester's yellow labrador.

Imogen says, quoting, ' *"We called him Simnel, because of his Marzipan ears and coat the colour of egg yolks . . ."* '

'Goodness, Imogen – I didn't know you read any of my poetry!'

'Oh, I just picked up your latest collection. Hope you don't mind – I saw it in your room and couldn't resist. I love the poem about Simnel, the way you compare him to an Easter cake.'

'It's one of my lighter poems. I didn't really want it included in the collection but my editor thought it was different – "surreal", he called it – and insisted.' Hester opens her mouth wide to take a bite out of the baguette. Ripe Brie oozes out of the sides and Hester captures it with her tongue. Bliss, food is – she loves it.

'I like your reminiscence poems,' Imogen goes on casually, spooning out some mushroom salad on to her plate. 'The ones that recall things that happened in the past.'

'Oh?' Hester says suspiciously.

'There was one about me, about that time I defied Dad and went to the folk festival in Glastonbury. I came back hungry and caked with mud and chilled through, and in a state of terror about what Dad would say, and you fussed over me, gave me hot soup and coffee, as I talked about it.'

'I remember. In spite of all your stories about the diabolical weather, high winds, rain, tents blowing away and everything drenched and sodden – you had had a marvellous time. You were radiant, glowing with happiness.'

' ". . . *Commiserating over coffee I feed you/stoking you like a furnace/till the glow on your face blinds me,*" ' Imogen quotes.

'Oh, Imo—'

' "*Then I remember: that other country,/and dreams like rucksacks/hard across my shoulders . . .*" '

Hester feels her eyes dangerously full. 'Imogen,' she finally says carefully, 'why this sudden interest in my poetry?'

Imogen looks both startled and sheepish, as if Hester has caught her out in some minor misdemeanour. Then she decides to come clean. 'As a matter of fact, it was Bruno. He reads poetry.'

'I see.'

'He's very impressed, you know, that you're a published poet. He's read your stuff. I lent him that last collection, hope you don't mind. I found it on the shelf in your room and I meant to tell you. He's given it back and now I'm reading it.'

'Well, well.' Hester is not sure whether to be pleased or wary, and she makes a mental note to hide her first collection, the one full of poems about Alex, under her pillow.

'You know, Mum, I never knew you felt that way.'

'You mean the poem?'

Imogen nods. 'I remember that day, coming home from the festival. I was so full of myself. I was young, on the brink of success, the whole world waiting in front of me—'

'I remember.'

'And yet you were feeling, as you put in that poem, such a nostalgia for your own youth, such a sense of loss too.'

Hester is nonplussed; this child of hers, who has never read a line of her work, knows this poem inside out.

' "*I celebrate you*" you wrote,' Imogen continues. ' "*Harbinger of my past, traveller/from that world I touched on/twenty years ago.*" '

There is a silence. Hester is too moved to speak and Imogen is far away in her own thoughts. Finally she says, 'I wish we could have talked about it then, Mum. What you were feeling at the time.'

Hester smiles. 'It was *your* day, Imo. I guess I didn't want to spoil your moment. It was your turn.'

Imogen shakes her head. 'I wouldn't have listened anyway, even if you had tried to tell me. I was a pretty selfish person, I know. I only saw you in relation to me.'

'It's okay, Imo. It's hard to be unselfish at that age. Very few of us manage it.'

Imogen smiles. 'I feel I know you much better since I read your poems. Do you want to know my favourites?' She goes on to quote other poems, talking quite intelligently about them. Hester can't help but be pleased; and even if it is Bruno who has instigated all this, Imogen seems a more than willing pupil.

Just as Hester is enjoying the novelty of talking poetry with a member of her family, they are interrupted by a polite but superfluous knocking on the French windows leading out to the garden, for the doors are wide open and the newcomer is already standing in front of them.

'Ah, I rang the front bell, but no one heard me,' booms Gérard Dupont. 'So I took the liberty of coming through. I think also', he says to Imogen, 'you have some customers for your antiques. They are standing outside the showroom door looking very forlorn because it is shut for lunch.'

Imogen rushes off, after inviting Gérard to sit in the garden and offering a glass of the red wine she and Hester were drinking with their lunch. He accepts the wine, refuses food, and settles expansively in one of the recliners.

Hester says, rather uneasily, 'And why aren't you in your restaurant, preparing your superb cuisine for today's lunch?' She knows that though Gérard can and does employ help in his kitchen, he still insists on preparing most of the food himself.

'We are always shut on Tuesdays. It is our "day off" as you say.'

'Of course. I forgot that many of your businesses shut up shop on a Monday or Tuesday, like our Thursday early closing.'

They talk desultorily for a few minutes, then Gérard shifts slightly in his chair, leans towards Hester and says, 'Madame – Hester. There is something I must say to you before your daughter returns. May we talk in French?'

He is not laughing or smiling; his strong mouth under the massive silver moustache is well-hidden. This must be serious, Hester thinks. Suddenly he looks ominous, his white eyebrows, bushy and fine like a rabbit's tail, are pressed together in what she feels uneasily is a sinister frown. The eyes underneath are probing into things which should be left unprobed.

'It is, perhaps, a delicate subject. I am referring to our past acquaintance, years ago.' His eyes narrow – malevolently, it seems to Hester. She is suddenly wary.

Blackmail. The word lodges itself in her brain and, like a tick on a dog, will not be dislodged. The scurrilous sod, she is thinking. So that's why he never pursued the subject at lunch last week. He must have suddenly realized that she had something to hide when she didn't warm to his recognition. And Alex . . . he must have been lonely, missing her. When he knew their affair was irrevocably over, did he often, for comfort, solace, visit the restaurant? Distressed, and over a bottle of wine, who knows what he told Gérard Dupont?

Hester's instant reaction is to ask him to leave at once; she does not want to talk about her private past with this shifty Frenchman. But at least the years have made her less impetuous and she decides to hear him out. Also she is nervous, scared witless as a matter of fact. This would be the worst time ever for both Imogen and Abigail to find out about her affair with Alex. So she too narrows her eyes and says, in what she hopes is an intimidating manner, 'Yes, M. Dupont? And what about our very brief acquaintance of many years ago?'

Oh, how insensitive the man is, Hester thinks in despair, as he ignores her tone of voice and says smoothly, 'My dear Hester, is it not astounding, the connections we have? There is not only the past, but now also the present: your friendship with the Lamberts who have been my friends for many years, and my business association with your daughter.'

'I cannot think what you can have to say to me,' Hester says dismissively.

He looks pointedly at the French windows to see if Imogen has returned, then says conspiratorially, 'Hester, I say it again, this is a very sensitive topic we are discussing. It is hard for me to know how to continue.'

'Try.'

'I know about your past. In the restaurant, after I had met you, as I was seeing to my customers, I suddenly remembered your companion's name – Alex, yes? We talked on several occasions after dinner, long into the night over one or two bottles of Beaujolais.'

'Ah,' Hester says breezily, 'the Beaujolais. It will have coloured your memories of those nights. Confessions made under the influence of the Beaujolais should be instantly discarded.'

'*Non, non, non*, you misunderstand. It was not the drink that compelled us to talk so intimately to each other, but our mutual unhappiness. I, too, was suffering from a tragic love affair. This was why I made my subsequent decision, you see, to devote my life to *la cuisine* rather than *la femme*.'

'M. Dupont,' Hester says sternly, 'what exactly are you trying to say to me?'

'Gérard, please.' He tries to take her hand, but she draws away as from a viper, which throws him somewhat but he goes on sanguinely: 'I wanted to speak to you in private.'

Hester is distraught. Not only can she not bear talking about Alex like this, especially with Imogen likely to return at any moment, but by this time she is convinced that an attempt at blackmail is imminent: it will be something sordid and outlandish, like the price of porcelain knocked down to rock-bottom in exchange for his silence about her lover.

She says faintly, 'I'm sorry, but I don't like talking about Alex, and I don't know why you are here, and if it is why I think it is, perhaps you should go.'

This confuses him even more, but he gathers his wits and says hurriedly, 'I will try to explain, quickly and succinctly, even though it is very awkward for me as well as for you. I am afraid I am very slow to grasp things sometimes, things that other people see clearly.'

He waits for a comment from Hester, but she remains stonily silent which Gérard misinterprets. 'Perhaps you do not understood my French?' he says. 'Let me try to explain in English.'

She does not bother to say she understands his French exceedingly well, thank you very much, but continues staring at him, setting her face like granite.

Gérard goes on, 'In my restaurant at Pont-Aven I am so excited to see you I do not think you could be married to someone else, not Alex. I only remember you and he together and so in love. For your Alex, he never told me much after you left, only that he loved you. It was enough; I knew there was tragedy there soon after you left, knew it in the face of this man Alex.'

He looks at Hester. She is impassive: he will never know how her heart is racing.

'So when I see you at Pont-Aven, all these years later, I am so happy, I think maybe you are with Alex, and I hope to ask you all these things when lunch is finished and I am not so busy.'

'I see,' Hester says faintly.

Gérard Dupont shifts in his chair, takes another sip of the dark red wine. It is obvious that he is becoming slightly agitated, remembering the moment. 'It is my dear sweet friend, my darling Colette, who reminds me, just before I come to you to sit at your table and talk of Alex. She says to me, "Gérard old friend, do you not see how the English lady blushes when you speak to her of Le Café de la Mer near Roscoff? She is a widow of only three years. It is very likely the man she was with at your restaurant was not her husband. Can you not be discreet, old friend?" '

He pauses, shaking his head in annoyance with himself. 'And then, my dear Hester, I remembered, of course. I remembered how Alex had said, one night, so simply and so tragically, that it was not likely you two would ever meet again. He said nothing more, but I remember well his distress; I remember too the sadness of it all.'

They are both quiet. Hester too is remembering the sadness of it all.

Gérard puts his hand on her arm kindly and this time she does not pull away. 'So I came here to tell you – do not worry. Your secret is safe with me, for not even Colette will know. She may suspect, she is a Frenchwoman and not unknowledgeable in the ways of *l'amour*, but I know also she is totally discreet.'

His eyes soften as he says this and as he looks out over the garden, so obviously lost in reverie, Hester sits quietly, letting him have his moment, though she wonders what it is he is thinking.

When he turns back to her he says simply, 'A wonderful woman, Colette.'

And now it is Hester's turn to touch his hand, to say gratefully, 'Thank you, Gérard. I appreciate your tact, and the trouble you have taken to tell me all this.'

'I wondered whether to be silent, but then I thought that would be worse for you. Colette and Luc think you are enchanting, and plan to invite you for dinner at their house soon. And I, who as an old friend am always around, I am to be invited also. I have as well my connection with your daughter, I see her often on business. I felt, if I did not speak, that you would always feel uneasy in my presence, wondering what I knew, what I might say . . .'

'Yes,' Hester admits. 'I would have wondered, would have felt uncomfortable. You were right to come to me, to talk about it.'

At last he smiles, for the first time since he began this topic. 'No more about the past, then. Let us talk about the future, shall we? Can you come to dinner at my little house next Tuesday night? I will cook you the most magnificent meal you have ever tasted.'

'Why . . . yes, thank you! I hesitate only because I must eventually make plans, decide how long I am going to stay in France.'

'Ah, but your daughter tells Bruno, who tells his mother Colette, who tells me, that she is so very happy to have you here with her, and that she hopes you will stay for quite a while.'

This makes Hester inordinately pleased. She hasn't felt necessary in Imogen's life since she embarked on her modelling career, when she was not yet seventeen.

'I feel she's coping so well on her own since Gordon left,' Hester confesses, 'that she doesn't need me.'

'Ah, Gordon, the husband.' Gérard spits out something incomprehensible in his own language, but the contemptuous expression on his face says it all.

'The man is a snake,' he hisses. 'From the first I hated to do business with him, as he was always trying to make the fast deal, you understand? Now Imogen, she is honest and efficient. Always I tried to work with her.'

'Gordon is supposed to be the antiques expert,' Hester says. 'He had a business in London but it lost money, so he had to get out.'

'I tell you something, *chère madame* – the man is useless at his job. Every one of Imogen's customers would agree. If it were only your son-in-law running the business, he would be bankrupt in France also.'

As Hester mulls this over, Gérard observes, 'Ah, I see your daughter coming into the kitchen. Her customers must be gone.'

'I'm making coffee, would you two like some?' Imogen calls out through the window.

'*Oui, merci*. And now, Hester, is it definite? You will dine with me next week?'

'Yes, it sounds lovely. Will the Lamberts be there? I look forward to seeing them again.'

'*Ah non, ma chère Hester*, you misunderstand. You will see them again certainly, but not on that night. It is to be *une soirée à deux*, you understand?'

Hester does. Her first reaction is to refuse. She hasn't been alone with a man since Martin died three years ago, and then of course there is Alex . . .

But then she thinks of the hamster, Alex's little Rosemary, and hardens her heart. Unprotected by her garden, her cats, her labrador, and the wall which has crumbled inside her, she thinks – and why not?

She turns to Gérard and says warmly, 'That sounds even better. I look forward to it.'

They look at each other and smile. Enough of memories, Hester thinks with exhilaration: let the past remain the past. She will, as of now, start looking towards the future.

Chapter Nine

Before Hester's dinner with Gérard, she sees Alex again. He telephones her at the weekend and says, 'Do you know Concarneau? It's an old medieval town on the sea, touristy now, I'm afraid, but not quite spoiled, not if you go at the right time.'

'No, I've never been there.'

'I have to be there Monday, on business actually, but it shouldn't take long. Concarneau is not that far from you, so will you come with me? I know a good restaurant just outside. I'll take you to lunch.'

Because it is a long drive from Concarneau back to Kerrocher, Hester invites him to spend Monday night at Imogen's house.

'That would be great,' Alex says. 'I could take you and Imogen both out to dinner. I'd like to get to know your daughter.'

Imogen, when Hester tells her, seems pleased, but adds, 'Could we ask Bruno as well? He said he liked Alex, and admired the way he handled Gordon on that dreadful day when he and Abigail arrived here and there was that appalling scene.'

Hester looks at her sharply. It is the first time Imogen has mentioned her errant husband and sister since they were imperiously ordered to leave her house, several weeks ago now. Despite Hester's attempts to talk to Imogen, her daughter has refused to discuss it.

Relieved that she has finally opened the subject, Hester says, 'Imogen, something will have to be done, you know. Abigail and Gordon will need to come back eventually, and you will have to talk to them. There is not only the house, but the business—'

Imogen interrupts impatiently. 'I have seen both an accountant and a solicitor. I am in a position to buy Gordon out of the business, and as for the house, he left both it and me. I don't want any of his money – though God knows he wouldn't have a penny if it weren't for me – but I like this house and eventually I shall buy his share of it also.'

'You're simplifying everything a bit, aren't you, Imo? I mean, what if he refuses?'

'I hardly see how he can. He'd be ostracized if he stayed here. Anyway, I will offer him far more than a fair share just to get him out of my life. I've discussed it all with my *notaire*, and if Gordon still balks at giving up the business I have plenty of witnesses to the long hours I've worked while Gordon was out swanning around with Abigail. Even before she came he was never here, not when I needed him. He hasn't given a damn about the business in France any more than he did in London.'

Hester has to admit this is true. By now she has come to know many of the village people, and lately has been hearing uncomplimentary things about her son-in-law.

'Your daughter, she works hard,' the woman at the *boulangerie* told Hester. 'Not like her husband, this I can tell you. Often customers would come, and to their *chagrin* the shop would be closed. Your daughter had perhaps gone on one of her necessary buying expeditions, leaving her husband in charge – and he would shut the shop, disappear. A scandalous way to do business.'

'Ah, Madame, I must say your daughter is looking very well,' said M. Darris at the *charcuterie*. 'It was difficult for her, before. The antique shop, a house, a garden – a husband always down at the harbour, preparing to go out in his little boat – it was too much for her. I did not know the husband well, for he rarely shopped, but when he did come in with a list from his wife he always complained about my prices. *Trop cher*: I think those were all the words he knew in French!'

Madame Cadet at the local café was more blunt. 'The incident at the Shrine will turn out to be a blessing in disguise,' she told Hester confidentially one day over a black coffee. 'That man, your son-in-law, was here every evening, sitting in this corner where you are sitting, reading the English newspapers and never bothering to speak to the other customers, though as you know we in the village are not unfriendly. Perhaps if he had troubled himself to learn French . . .'

'Hasn't he learned the language?' Hester asked, surprised.

'Hardly a word. The only time he attempted to speak French was when he was trying to impress one of our young, pretty village girls.'

'What – Gordon?'

'*Mais oui!* Everyone knows M. Boswick liked our young Frenchwomen, but they only laughed at him, at his hopeless French, and pretended not to know what he was after when he tried to flatter them and charm them. He had hoped to have more luck with my daughter – you know, Bernadette, who helps me in the café when she is home from university. Bernadette speaks perfect English, which he thought would be an advantage. And so it was, to Bernadette – she told him to stop being so stupid and act his age!'

Hester, sipping her coffee, didn't dare ask if this incident had happened before Abigail arrived in France or after. Either way, it did not bode well for her younger daughter.

'Imo,' she says now, carefully, to her older daughter, 'what about Abigail?'

Imogen shuts herself up like a forbidding fortress on an inaccessible hillock. 'I no longer have a sister,' she says coldly, reminding Hester of when she was twelve and had announced the same thing to all her friends. Abby had just turned two, a rounded, appealing child with a mass of ginger hair and huge blue eyes, who toddled about good-naturedly looking adorable. It was more than Imo could take. She announced one day to all her friends: 'That baby is adopted, you know. I have no sister. My parents took her in out of the kindness of their hearts because no one else wanted her.' Imogen's friends all told their parents, many of whom had children in Martin's school, and it was months before Hester was able to sort things out, with some considerable embarrassment.

Hester bites her tongue so as not to remind Imogen about this now. Then she changes tactics. 'What about Gordon and you? How do you really feel? You've not said a word recently, and to be honest I'm beginning to feel rather superfluous. I mean, you called me over here in quite a state. I went frantic trying to get a ferry cancellation on a Bank Holiday weekend – and now you tell me you have everything all sorted out . . . Perhaps I should leave now and go back to England. There's not much need for me here.'

Hester and Imogen are talking in the antique shop, which shines and gleams with old wood and fine china and lovely things lovingly cared for. Imogen has left her tidy desk in the back office to talk to Hester, and is sitting on a Victorian settee finely upholstered in damson velvet, while Hester prowls around, looking at things, admiring. But now Imogen gets up and walks over to her mother, and suprisingly, puts her arm around Hester and gives her a little awkward hug. Hester thinks rather confusedly that living in France has been good for her daughter; she has always been wary of physical contact and seldom, in the past, initiated it herself.

'Mum, you're not thinking of going home, not yet!' Imogen says. 'I'll miss you, surely you can stay longer.'

This for some reason makes Hester's eyes blur, but then she seems to have shed a copious amount of tears one way or the other since arriving in this unsettling country.

'Imogen,' she says, pulling herself together, 'I've loved staying here, but surely you want to be alone now? I do understand.'

Suddenly Imogen looks uncertain, vulnerable. She says, 'It's the last thing I want, Mum, right now. To be alone.'

Hester, nodding wisely, says, 'I understand, love. You're putting on such a brave show of things, but of course you miss Gordon, you're grieving terribly for him. I just wish you wouldn't bottle it in like you do, it will just make it harder for you in the long run.'

Imogen, who has been pacing the floor during this conversation, stops and stares at Hester so peculiarly that Hester feels quite odd.

'Imogen, are you all right?'

'Oh Mum, oh God!' Imogen gives a little shriek and then, to Hester's horror, starts to laugh loudly, almost out of control.

So here it comes, Hester thinks wildly, the breakdown, the crack-up. She blames herself, as mother always do, for not seeing the signs. Imogen has not given herself time to grieve properly, has not let herself weep and wail over Gordon. Instead, she has been burying all that emotion in her work, in going out practically every evening with the young doctor, putting on a very credible show of cheery normality when in reality she was falling apart.

Just as Hester is wondering how she is going to handle this, Imogen suddenly stops laughing and begins crying. As Hester goes to her she looks up, smiles radiantly through her tears, and says, 'Oh Mum, I'm so unhappy,' looking so amazingly joyous that Hester is speechless with bewilderment.

Then she starts talking, first hesitantly, then gathering speed. 'Mum, I don't love Gordon, I'm not grieving for Gordon. I haven't loved him in years. You probably haven't noticed it, but to be quite honest he's not a very lovable person.'

'As a matter of fact, Imogen, I have—'

'Oh, of course I didn't think that at first. I suppose I loved him; I certainly loved the attention he gave me. I imagine he loved me, too, though I think it was mostly my lifestyle that attracted him – you know, all that modelling stuff. Gordon always found it very glamorous. He played up to me at first – maybe it was a game, maybe he meant it, but whatever I did, he seemed to think it was wonderful.'

'That's heady stuff.'

'I know. And he was – is, I suppose – attractive. Women seem to like him . . .'

'In England, perhaps,' Hester mumurs, but luckily Imogen doesn't hear her.

'At first, we got on all right. We were in London, our life together was pretty full, there were parties and first nights at the theatre, there were night-clubs and charity galas, we both had dozens and dozens of friends . . . ' Imogen trails off.

'So what happened?' Hester asks gently. 'What went wrong?'

'It's so hard to pinpoint, it really is. I suppose we started to change. I began getting bored with the social life but Gordon didn't. I stayed at home more while he kept going out, but on his own. Before long we discovered we hadn't much to say to each other, and soon after this I realized I didn't really love him at all. What I had thought was love was nothing more than a superficial attraction.'

Imogen stops, but Hester says nothing. She can think of nothing to say.

Imogen takes a deep breath. 'I also realized around this time that I had never really loved anyone, not properly, and maybe it wasn't Gordon's fault that I couldn't love him, it was just me.'

'I'm not so sure—'

'That's why we never had children, you know. I'm not exactly anti-kids, I just wasn't wild to have Gordon's children. He never cared one way or the other, as he already had two children from his first marriage whom he never saw, so it didn't much matter anyway.'

'Imogen—'

'God, it makes me so angry!' Imogen cries, and sets her mouth tightly the way she did when she was a child, when someone or something ignited in her a slow flame of rage that would often turn into an inferno. 'When he and that cow of a sister of mine were so embarrassingly, so indelicately, caught fornicating on poor Sainte Barbe, and I rang you up, of course I was upset. Here I had been protecting that bastard Gordon from the fact that I didn't love him any more, and probably never had – and there he was getting it off with my sister, the slimy bastard. I mean, if they had only told me when it all started, I'd have given them my blessing, for God's sake!'

Her voice rises, her eyes darken in anger, her hands curl up into tense little fists at her sides but then, suddenly, she loses steam, shrugs her shoulders and shakes her head as if she were finally at a loss for words. Hester, rather stunned, tries to gather her thoughts and finally says, 'But Imogen, if that's the way things are, why are you so unhappy? I know the circumstances are unfortunate, but you have got rid of a husband you didn't much like, and that is surely a bonus? Is it Abigail you are unhappy about? I don't blame you, and I know she has been a wicked, wicked girl, but you must understand she too is mixed up about Gordon, and about you, and—'

'Oh Mum, sometimes you are so dense! Sorry, didn't mean that. What I do mean is, of course I'm not unhappy about Abigail, I just hate her of course and always will, the ginger-nut freckly-faced foxy little bitch, or I suppose I should say vixen—'

'Imogen!'

'Well, she is, Mum, face it, even if she *is* your darling daughter. God, no, it's not *her* making me unhappy, I've washed my hands of her. It's – oh Mum, it's Bruno!'

She says this with such anguish, and looks so radiantly blissful, that Hester feels out of her depth. 'Bruno?' she echoes stupidly.

'I love him!' Imogen wails.

'Oh.' There is a short silence as Hester struggles to assimilate this information. A few moments later she says, as calmly as she can, 'Imogen, what seems to be the problem? You say you love Bruno. Now if you still had a husband, that perhaps would be difficult, but since Gordon has conveniently left, and since Bruno appears unattached, and totally devoted to you, I can't quite see the difficulty. I'm sorry to be so obtuse.'

Imogen goes to her mother and hugs her – the second time within an hour, Hester thinks wonderingly. Then she says quietly, 'I'm scared shitless, Mum.'

'What? Why?'

'I've never felt this way before, you see. So . . . so wild and sort of out of control. And yet so tender and defenceless too. When Bruno is supposed to meet me and he's five minutes late I am frightened out of my wits, wondering if he's been hit by a bus or something—'

'Hardly likely in Pont-Plouay, my love.'

'And when he says he loves me, it's even worse. I go all odd and want to cry. I think of him all the time, and for God's sake, Mum, I'm thirty-bloody-five and have been married for six or is it seven years and before I married I had lovers since I was—'

'Never mind the details, Imogen.'

'And I have never been in love, if that's what this miserable condition is.'

'Sounds like it.'

Imogen is pacing around like a cat in a room with a hamster cage. 'You won't believe this next bit, Mum.'

'Do you think you should tell me?' Hester asks rather nervously.

'Until Bruno, I never had an orgasm.'

'Ah, oh. Oh.'

'Would you believe it? All those years of marriage and I don't know how many lovers—'

'All right, Imo.'

'And I'm thirty-bloody-five. And last night with Bruno, the first time we made love—'

'Last night?'

Imogen stops pacing and looks sheepish. 'Yes, we went out, remember? To the cinema at Pont-Aven. And then back to his house in the village. Bruno says he's been . . . you know, aware of me, attracted to me, since we moved here, but of course he thought Gordon and I were happily married, and I hardly noticed him. I was so wrapped up in the work and anyway I thought I was frigid so what was the point of noticing men . . .'

'Frigid?'

'Well, of course, no orgasms, and most of the time I found sex boring—'

'What?'

'But last night with Bruno . . . oh Mum, why didn't anyone ever tell me it could be like that?'

'Oh Imogen, my darling!'

'But it is terrifying too. You feel so vulnerable. All of a sudden someone has this power over you, to hurt you or to make you happy. Oh Mum, I just can't explain it. It's something you can't understand until you've experienced it.'

And thus Imogen dismisses Hester's thirty-odd-year marriage to Martin, for of course she knows nothing of Alex. Hester can only say inadequately, 'I *have* been in love before, Imo. I do know something of what you're saying. And of course, it's wonderful! It's all terribly new and strange, that's why it's so frightening. But I like Bruno, I think he's lovely.'

At this Imogen becomes radiant again. Like all lovers everywhere, she is happy and indeed eager to talk about her beloved for hours. So mother and daughter spend the next half hour discussing how marvellous Bruno is, until finally the business phone interrupts and Hester leaves the showroom, reeling from this new development in her daughter's rather eventful life.

Going into the garden she puts on her sun hat and gloves, and starts distractedly to dig out weeds. She is stunned by Imogen's revelations, though when she thinks about it she has to admit she always thought Imogen's young men were more in love with her than she appeared to be with them. But Gordon? Abigail had accused her sister of not loving Gordon and Hester had admonished her, but Abby was right perhaps. Imo supposedly loved him at first, but not that much, not enough, not as she loves Bruno now . . . oh, how confusing it all is, Hester thinks as she digs deeper to pull out a root. And Abby – does Abby really love Gordon, or is this affair based on childhood rivalry running dangerously riot?

She remembers the weekend when Imogen told them she was going to marry Gordon. By then, the young man's meretricious charm had begun to grate on Hester, and she found herself watching him detachedly, finding him unbearably affected in even the little things: the way he glanced at mirrors and fluffed out his thick, pale curly hair; the way he wore his dark silk shirts as if he were entitled to nothing less, nothing more ordinary; the way he began each sentence as if he had something marvellous to say and wasn't everybody lucky to be able to hear it . . . By then, Hester had begun to wonder whether her daughter was really in love or was merely trying to irritate her father, for Gordon, though extremely eligible in some circles, was everything Martin disliked: divorced, rich, privately (and badly) educated, and too charming for his own good.

Abigail thought so too. After Imogen had talked to her father about Gordon, she went to look for her sister.

'Well, Abby,' Imogen said, finding her sister in the study playing her piano, 'and what do you think of Gordon? Our father approves, you will be happy to know.'

Abigail was cross at this. Their father always, in the end, gave in to Imogen, she thought, even when initially his older daughter shocked and appalled him. Ignoring her sister she kept playing the piano. The music was Beethoven's *Moonlight Sonata*, one of the first proper pieces she had ever learned, and she played it now to annoy Imogen, who had always hated it.

Imogen draped herself over the tatty old sofa, looking as if she was about to be photographed for *Elle* magazine. 'Abigail, could you please stop playing the piano while I talk to you?'

Abigail played on, louder.

'I know you are listening to me, Abby,' Imo shouted. 'Now stop being so stupid and tell me what you think of Gordon. We can talk: he's out now with Mum, helping her carry the shopping.'

'Creep.'

'That's better. Who's a creep – Gordon? Remember, sister dear, you are talking about the man I am marrying. Oh God, can't you play anything else but that bloody *Moonlight Sonata*?'

Abigail suddenly stopped playing and turned to her sister. 'I'm surprised Dad approves,' she said primly. 'Gordon hasn't very much substance, has he?'

'Oh God, you talk like a schoolmarm already, and you haven't even finished college.'

'I actually thought Dad valued intelligence more,' Abigail said, turning back to the Beethoven.

'You are a nasty, sarcastic little shit, Abby,' Imogen said, exploding. 'I'll have you know that Dad thought I was quite fortunate to be marrying someone like Gordon.' She was shouting now as the *Moonlight Sonata* began to crescendo.

'i know you're listening to me, abigail. And I know that it'll be a long time before anyone as handsome and charming and worldly as Gordon even takes a look at you, you horrid little fox.'

And so saying she ran out of the room, leaving Abigail thumping out the *Moonlight Sonata* at such a volume that it sounded like a stormy wind in a pitch-black night with not the slightest chance of even a glimmer of moonlight.

'Actually, that doesn't surprise me in the least,' Alex says as he drives Hester in his white Renault van to Concarneau. Hester has been telling him about Imogen and her new love affair with the doctor. 'Bruno was so indignant at the way Imogen was treated by Gordon, I thought it showed rather more than professional interest. Are you really pleased about it?'

Hester hesitates. 'Yes and no. I do like Bruno, and after Imogen told me all this, he came to see me and have a chat. What a dear lad. I think he wanted me to know his intentions were honourable. He seems totally besotted by Imogen but they're so different. For all his Frenchness and the fact that he looks like a rock star, Bruno is a provincial doctor in a small village not far from his parents' home.'

'That sounds ideal for Imogen. You said she was happy to leave London, move to the Brittany countryside.'

'Perhaps it's what she needs, who knows? She's only a few years older than him but seems a thousand years older in experience.'

'Has Bruno never married?'

'No, but he was engaged for years, lived off and on with the woman, a painter apparently, in Pont-Aven until she ran off to Paris to be famous or something.'

Alex is driving the car up a hill and into the entrance of a rather grand house overlooking the sea near Concarneau. 'I think it sounds perfect, Hester,' he says warmly. 'From what you say, Imogen settled quite happily in France even before she became involved with Bruno. Be thankful you are rid of Gordon.'

'Oh Alex, that's the trouble, I'm not. He's with Abigail, remember? It seems to be my albatross, having that unpleasant man as a son-in-law.'

Before Alex can reply, the door to the house opens and a well-dressed, rather sophisticated young woman runs out to the car, talking verbosely in French. 'Ah, Alex darling, you've arrived, you've brought it. How exciting, and such good timing, Jean-Luc is away at a friend's house for the day. You must help me hide it for his birthday which, as you know, is tomorrow. Ah, you have a friend with you! *Bonjour, Madame*. You will both stay for lunch, of course!'

Alex introduces Hester, refuses lunch, then goes to the back of the van where he begins to unload a large object that has been carefully wrapped in blankets.

'Ah, Alex, it is beautiful – beautiful, superb, wonderful,' the woman rhapsodizes.

Hester stares. Indeed it *is* beautiful, and she tells Alex so. It is an exquisite wooden rocking-horse – large, a perfect replica of a Victorian rocking-horse, painted a beautiful glossy black with a red saddle and reins and stirrups. The face of the horse is splendid; the eyes are large and brooding, framed with long black lashes made of real horsehair, the nostrils flare proudly, and the mouth is strong and life-like.

'Did you make it?' Hester asks. 'It's magnificent.'

'I started a few years ago, made one for my first grandson. Word got around, people began writing to me, ringing me up, ordering rocking-horses of all sizes. I loved doing it, and gradually I've taken on less and less building work and have devoted most of my time to this.'

'So you should. It's beautifully crafted, a real work of art.'

'I was hoping you'd like it. That's why I was in England when I met you on the ferry, you know. I had been delivering one in Devon.' He mentions the name of a famous stage actor who has recently retired. 'He wanted one for his grand-daughter. I like to deliver them myself, you see. I can wrap them properly, see each horse safely to its destination.'

'But you were a foot-passenger! You didn't even have a car.'

'My old Ford van packed up after I had delivered the horse and was on my way to see my son and his family in London. It was beyond repair so I just left it. I bought this second-hand van when I got back.'

When the rocking-horse is safely installed in a spare bedroom, and the business transaction completed, with Alex putting away a handsome cheque in his wallet, the two at last escape from the gracious but effusive woman and find the restaurant which Alex has chosen for their lunch.

'What does this remind you of?' he says as they sit down at the table. They are at a window and the view is of the harbour and the sea beyond.

'Le Café de la Mer, of course,' Hester says fondly.

They eat first the *soupe de poissons*, which is thick and rich and spicy, though not, they admit to each other, quite as good as Gérard's; and then they have mussels in garlic butter. Hester dives into this sea of food with alacrity, as does Alex, and they are silent for a while. Then, as they sip their wine, the ubiquitous Muscadet – a favourite in Brittany, Hester describes Gérard's visit, and how he has assured her of his discretion.

'Gérard was right,' Alex nods. 'I did go there after you left. At first I went because it made me happy, reminded me of the good times we had had. Later, when I realized that you and I were really finished, I guess I kept going back because we had been happy there. Very self-indulgent,' he finishes wryly.

Hester is silent and Alex continues, 'Gérard had moved to Roscoff to get away from a woman he had loved and lost, that's all I know, just as all he ever knew about me was the same thing. Except that he had met you, of course. He knew just how much I was losing.'

Alex says this last lightly, for Hester's sake, but he can see it distresses her, so he does not pursue it. Instead, he says, 'I liked Gérard. We suffered companionably together. I'm not surprised he has moved his restaurant – he was never really happy in Roscoff.'

'I like him too,' Hester says, glad to be talking about Gérard rather than herself and Alex. One day the talk will have to come, and soon, if there is to be understanding between them, but not yet, not yet.

'As a matter of fact,' she goes on, 'he's invited me to a meal at his house – he's cooking it especially for me.'

'Oh?' says Alex, sounding surprised.

This annoys Hester. Why should he be surprised, him with his herbal hamster? Does he think, because he has a bimbo – well, an ageing bimbo – that Hester is no longer attractive to men?

But before she can decide to take umbrage, Alex asks her how long she plans to stay in France.

'I'm not sure,' she says, looking out at the sea which is as rich and green as a woodland in summer, 'but I'm not going home just yet. Imogen wants me here, and I have told her if I'm going to stay she must let me help in the antique shop. She was quite delighted with that, since without Abigail or Gordon she was wondering how she would cope during the summer months when the place is at its busiest.'

Hester stops and eats another mussel, digging the meat out of the shell with another empty shell and dipping the succulent bit in the melted butter and garlic sauce. After she has savoured the taste to its fullest, she goes on, 'Eventually I shall have to see Abigail and talk to her. Sooner or later she and Gordon will have to come back and sort things out. But so far there hasn't been a word from them.'

'Where are they?'

'Still in the south somewhere, renting a house from a friend of Gordon's. I do worry about her, constantly. It never stops, does it, Alex? How many times in the past did you have to listen to me, as I worried and fretted over my daughters?'

She spears another mussel out of its shell. 'Hmm, delicious. I do love food. I'm lucky I don't get fat.'

Alex pours more wine. 'I never minded listening to you, Hester. Not then, not now.' He sips the wine. 'I'm glad you'll be in France for a while, and not rushing back to England.'

'There's nothing to make me rush back, only my garden.'

Alex shakes his head. 'I just can't imagine you a gardener, you never used to be.'

Hester stops eating and looks out over the water. How does she tell Alex that gardening, along with her poetry, was what kept her sane after she had to let him go, how it became her barrier against a world that kept trying to crowd her with emotion. She craved dispassion, detachment, and gardening helped to cultivate her erratic feelings, plough them into some kind of order. Pruning her roses, or mowing her lawn, she learned to stop yearning for Alex, learned to control the desperate voices howling inside her head telling her wickedly that she had made a mistake, betrayed her own emotions in letting him go and condemning herself to a life devoid of feeling, intensity: a life without pain, perhaps, but also lacking in vibrancy and joy.

She says, simply, 'The garden has been my refuge, Alex. It helped me sort out the turmoil our affair left me in. It does for me physically what poetry does for me spiritually, I suppose – calms me down, helps me make some sense out of the world.'

'And the poetry, Hester? I have all three of your collections. I keep them by my bedside and reread them often. You've come a long way as a poet, haven't you? Come a long way from that woman who announced at the school gathering the publication of her first poem.'

Hester looks at Alex fondly. He, more than anyone, knows how vital poetry is to her life. 'I've always wanted to thank you for that,' she says to him.

'What for?'

She hesitates; this is awkward for her, but she has wanted to say this to him for a long time. 'You helped make it happen, Alex. My poetry, the collections. All that confidence you had in me, in my writing. When the first collection came out, all I could think of was that I'd never get to tell you that, never get to say thank you.'

There. Done now. She is light-headed with having said it, said the things she has told Alex only in dreams, in fantasies, during the past years.

He is looking at her with such affection, such gentleness, that she cannot say any more. Oh, but it is easy being here with him, talking to him, drinking wine and watching the sea as they did all those years ago. But something grows in her as they relax together; something dormant is stirring and what is the use of that? Hester has written her poems of loss and grief and pain years ago – she wants now to write of the things poets of her age should concentrate on: approaching old age, death, memories of childhood perhaps, the intricate wonders of the world they will eventually be departing in this latter half of their lives. Alex, she is sure, is willing to forget the past, offer her a friendship she knows will be deep and lasting, but she isn't sure if it is possible for her. She would have to forget five years of being intensely in love, as well as all those years grieving over the loss of that love. She doesn't know if she can do it, sublimate that love into friendship.

So she is quiet this afternoon as she walks with Alex along the cliff-path around the harbour, sitting on golden granite rocks in the sun, watching small boats scurrying like mice around the bay and into the sea. And as it was years ago, it is all right still to be quiet around Alex; he lets her be, gives her space. Sometimes he talks himself, about his sons and grandchildren; or about the craftsman he has become, the love with which he makes his wooden horses. Mostly though he too is silent, and the afternoon drifts like clouds, easily and without jarring.

They are back in Pont-Plouay in time to have a shower and change before their dinner with Imogen and Bruno. Hester is looking forward to this; in spite of all her warnings to herself, she is remembering how happy, how contented, she always was in Alex's company.

But as they walk into the house Imogen, meeting them at the door, says, 'Alex, a friend of yours rang, a woman called

Ermi, just an hour or so ago. She said she is on her way south for her holiday—'

'Yes, yes, I knew she was leaving today. Is something wrong?'

'Oh no, she just said she was tired already of driving and has decided not to go as far as she intended the first night. She was going to take a hotel at Pont-Aven and wondered if you would like to meet her for dinner.'

'Oh, but—'

Imogen smiles beatifically at him, as if she is bestowing on him a wonderful favour. And perhaps she is, perhaps she is.

'I said, since she is a friend of yours, that she must join us tonight for dinner. And I also suggested that she stay here, instead of booking into a hotel. We have plenty of room, don't we, Mum?'

'Yes. Of course.'

'But—'

'There, it's all settled. She was delighted. In fact, we had a nice chat on the telephone. She said how refreshing it was to talk to English people who were so proficient in French.'

Alex, looking a bit annoyed, mutters to himself, 'What in the hell is wrong with *my* French?' but Hester is too distracted to pay attention. So the herbal hamster has not only followed him down here but has also been taken into the bosom of Hester's family. Great, she thinks sardonically, just great.

She tells herself she is over-reacting, that this Ermi is probably a real sweetheart, as they say in the American films and anyway – what difference does it make to her? If Alex and Hester are to become friends, then obviously she will have to get to know the woman with whom he is having a relationship.

'When is Ermi arriving?' Hester says as politely and welcomingly as she can.

Imogen says, 'Oh, she's already here. She's in the shower.'

Hester's heart suddenly cracks. 'Oh shit,' she says and then, furious at herself, runs for the garden, digging up non-existent weeds with bare hands as the house fills, or so she imagines, with the smell of rosemary and parsley as Ermi appears, radiant from her shower, and embraces Alex.

Chapter Ten

Imogen, followed by Alex and the Frenchwoman, comes elegantly down the lawn to where Hester is frantically digging in the hot brown earth and says, 'Mum, this is Ermi, Alex's friend. Oh, I'm sorry, Alex, I suppose I really should have left it up to you to introduce Ermi, but we have had such a long talk I feel I know her already.'

'*Mais oui!*' Ermi says smugly. 'Imogen is so kind, she gives me wonderful hot coffee and soft towels for the shower—'

'I believe Ermi and Hester have already met,' Alex says, somewhat flustered.

'Yes, of course,' Hester says amicably, remembering she is an English lady. 'You must excuse me for running off down the garden like this; I suddenly remembered the geranium must be moved at once, out of the hot sun. It is still small and delicate.' She transplants the plant into an earthenware pot, then finally stands up. 'We met at Roscoff,' she says to Ermi. 'At the ferry terminal.'

'But that was too brief,' Ermi says.

She looks Hester up and down inquisitively, and Hester wonders just how much Alex has told her. She seems not very impressed by what she sees and loses interest almost at once, which irritates Hester. She and Alex may be a thing of the past, but it is still annoying for his new woman to dismiss her as insignificant.

Imogen goes into the kitchen for drinks while the others sit down in the garden chairs. Hester watches Ermi as she chatters like a little squirrel about her holiday, how she left the children with her mother, how excited she is to be staying with some cousins in Biarritz.

'You haven't got very far, if you're going all the way down to Biarritz,' Hester says, her wide dark eyes all puzzled innocence.

Ermi looks at her with a trace of suspicion. 'Ah, I had the slight headache. And of course, such a coincidence, for I knew Alex was spending the night here nearby . . .'

And wanted to suss it all out, Hester thinks meanly. Make sure the old friend really *is* an old friend.

She chatters on and on. Hester notices against her will that the woman is not unattractive, as rodents go, despite the hamster teeth and chipmunk cheeks and tangly mouse-streaked hair. In fact on closer inspection Hester realizes that the hair is meant to be tousled like a rat's nest – subtle, that. She is wearing white cotton trousers gaily printed with some huge red flowers, and a white knitted sleeveless jumper with a scooped neck and no bra. She stands possessively close to Alex and after a while Hester says, breaking into the verbose chatter, 'Please excuse me, but I really must shower and change before we go out to dinner.'

Alone in her room Hester collapses on the bed before summoning up the energy to get herself ready. Outside the window the willow tree swishes benignly in the breeze from the sea and she suddenly wants to climb down the trunk and head for home, for her own garden and her dog and her cats. She feels distressed and out of harmony. She doesn't need this; she doesn't want it. It is too similar, in a more mild way of course, to the turmoil she was always in with Alex, and especially to the dark turmoil she floundered in when she knew she had to leave him. It is, in short, too much like losing him a second time, which is ridiculous. She knows this, for of course the reality is that she never had him a second time.

She lies on the bed and thinks: Sod it, I'll be late for dinner. I won't even go – plead a heachache, though I know in truth my pride will not let me do that. Groping towards some sort of rationality, she then tries to analyze why she is feeling this mixture of distress and anger, and yes, jealousy. After all, she knew about Ermi, knew from the very first day she was reunited with Alex.

Because she still loves Alex. At last, Hester admits it – and when indeed did she ever stop? If anything, she loved him most when she made the decision never to see him again, though God knows what Alex thought. They haven't discussed this at all yet, though Hester has been aware of the questions there, circling round in Alex's head like a buzzard waiting for the right time, the right moment, to swoop. Throughout their long lazy day, Hester had thought she was coming near to being able to talk about it, to tell him why she had to do what she did. She had hoped that perhaps, if they were able to talk alone long into the night, she would finally be able to speak of it. But now, thanks to Ermi, the moment is lost, and Hester wonders if it will ever come again. She wonders now if she will ever tell him what happened, why it was she wrote that letter, why she insisted they never see each other again . . .

'But please, can't you tell me why?' he wrote to the college where Hester worked, because of course he couldn't write to her at the rectory. *'What can have changed in the few days since your return from France? You beg me not to contact you, not to write, not ever; you insist we never see each other again, even when I return to England. I don't understand, Hester. What has changed, what has happened?'*

His letter, so full of love and bewilderment, only made Hester more determined. She wrote again, one more time, and her letter must have been both desperate and pleading; looking back, it was probably nearer hysteria. This time, if Alex replied, she was never to know. By then she had left her job at the college, had given implicit instructions that she did not want any mail, either personal or private, to be forwarded to her home.

Now, years later, Hester wonders if perhaps she did wrong not to tell him the truth, was wrong not to trust him enough. But she was afraid that if he knew, he would confront Angela, and so push her over the edge, which would ruin all their lives.

Angela. Even now Hester cannot think of her without a shudder. She knew Angela well, even before she knew Alex because she was, briefly, the nurse at the sixth-form college where Hester worked. Angela was bright, sparky, full of lively anecdotes which she told well and humorously. In the right mood she could wheedle, entice, fascinate; but the trouble was, her audience had to give the right responses or Angela's mood would change rapidly and she could become sharp-tongued, even vituperative. Hester supposed Alex hadn't seen this side of his wife until long after the honeymoon, for they hadn't known each other long before they married. Alex had just been accepted as a mature student and had to relocate; it seemed easy and natural at the time to marry Angela quickly and take her with him.

She was waiting for Hester on her return from France. Hester had gone back to the college to do a few days cover for another teacher and as she walked into the staff-room after her last lesson a voice said, 'Well, Hester. You are looking tanned and rested. I hear you've been abroad.'

Hester looked up, shocked to hear Angela, for long before Alex began to work at the college, she had left to take on a job at the city hospital. Occasionally she made a fleeting visit, for old time's sake (so she said) to the staff-room, but Hester had not seen the woman for almost a year, and she was unnerved. It was never easy being in Angela's company at the best of times. You were always on guard, even when she was happy and bubbly, for you never knew when a chance remark, an offhand observation, would in some way offend her, draw her in upon herself or out like a whiplash to snap the composure of the innocent person who was only trying to make conversation.

Trying to be calm, reminding herself that Angela knew nothing of her affair with Alex, that at any rate Alex and Angela had split up before the holiday in France, Hester said warily, 'Hello, Angie. How strange to see you here. Are you enjoying your job at the hospital?'

'It'll do,' Angie said, 'if you can cope with the inefficiency of most of the staff.'

So she was in her scathing mood, Hester thought. Not knowing what to say, she blurted, 'You've changed your hair.'

It was an inane remark, but the best Hester could do. Angela merely nodded. She had had her pale-blonde hair permed so that it curled innocently around her head. The effect was strangely unsettling, the soft lamb's-wool hair around that strong, rather severe face.

Angela said coldly, 'I'm not here accidentally, you know. I've been waiting for you. We'd better find some place to go where we can talk privately. I have a great deal to say to you.'

Meekly, Hester went with her. She knew, cravenly, that she had no choice. Angela's harsh, authoritative manner was intimidating even when one was innocent, and Hester, body and soul full of Alex, felt the trepidation of guilt.

They found, or rather Angela found, a small tea-house tucked away behind the park. They sat at a corner table with a tiny jug of freesias in the middle and china cups already laid out, ready to be used for a genteel afternoon tea. The two women seemed incongruous there, Hester with her dark hair tied gypsy-like in a bright silk scarf, and Angela with her frizzy blonde curls and her severe nursing sister uniform. All the other customers were old, clad in good wool or cord, and sweetly pink-cheeked.

'How are your sons?' Hester asked politely, because she could not bear the grim silence.

'Doing as well as can be expected, considering their father has put them through the trauma of a broken home this past year,' she replied briskly.

Hester felt put in her place, unable even to retort that actually both boys were safely away from home and settled at university before Alex made his break.

The waitress came and they ordered Earl Grey with milk, not lemon; and to this day Hester remembers, with a shudder, the delicate china teapot with the tiny yellow rosebuds. She remembers also how Angela paused until the waitress was out of hearing before she said abruptly, 'I know about you and Alex.'

There it was then, the banal scenario. Unprepared for this despite her forebodings when she saw Angela, Hester held her hands tightly in her lap to stop them trembling. But before she could ask how she had found out, the other woman went on smoothly, 'Alex told me, of course. Before we split up. Whatever he tells you, it is the real reason for the separation.'

The relief Hester felt was so great that she broke out in

dewdrops of perspiration. She fumbled for a handkerchief and wiped her face surrepitiously, trying to collect herself. She knew that Angela did not know, that she was only guessing, for Hester's faith in Alex was absolute. He would never tell Angela, knowing that she above all others would wreak havoc with the information.

Seeing that Hester was not going to respond, Angela went on: 'At first I thought I would go to Martin and tell him what his charming wife was doing behind his back.' She looked closely at Hester to gauge her reaction.

Hester stared back at the other woman impassively, not saying a word, so Angela continued: 'After thinking about it for a while, I decided poor Martin, with his angina – I see him often in out-patients, did you know that? – What would this do to him? Then I thought, Imogen and Abigail should know, they could protect their father.'

'You don't even know them,' Hester said stonily.

'Ah, but everyone knows the lovely Imogen. She's quite famous, isn't she, with all her modelling? The magazines are always carrying photos of her in one exquisite outfit after another.'

Hester ignored this. Keep calm, she told herself. She is only conjecturing. She knows nothing, nothing.

'And Abigail – she was at the college for the past two years, so of course I know her. I hear on the grapevine that she passed her exams brilliantly and is about to go off somewhere prestigious for further training as a musician.'

The jealousy in Angela's voice was clear as light on a crystal. The threat to Hester's children mobilized her and she said firmly, 'Angela, I honestly don't know what you are talking about. Alex is one of my colleagues, and of course I also know him through Martin, when Alex was at the comprehensive school. I have known your ex-husband for a long time now and we are friends, naturally. I hope we always will be.'

Angela actually smiled, took a few sips of her Earl Grey tea, saying, 'Hmm, delicious, I needed that,' before turning to Hester again. Her own tea had grown stone cold and was developing a skin in the pretty floral teacup.

'Hester,' Angela said almost kindly, 'I know. *Alex told me.*'

Hester began to gather up her things – her bag of books and notes, her old black raincoat. 'Angela, it's pointless to carry on with this conversation. I'm going.'

'Just you bloody well stay where you are.' Angela's voice hissed like snakes in a bad dream. Hester didn't move.

'I saw your husband at the hospital, when he came in for his check-up. Such a friendly man, we always have a nice chat. He said you were in France, visiting a friend. That you were actually taking time off from college to do so.'

Hester stared at the glaze forming on the tea in her cup. Angela went on, never taking her eyes from Hester's face, 'I knew Alex was in France, of course, and I figured out the rest for myself. One doesn't have to be very bright to realize you and he were together.'

She smiled complacently and poured herself another cup of tea. Hester used the time to think frantically. It was only supposition, she told herself. Angela was trying to trick her into admitting something.

She looked at the other woman coldly. Angela's hair, the perm tangled in their walk to the tea-shop, curled around her face haphazardly and looked even more at odds with her heavy, almost masculine features. 'This conversation is ridiculous,' she said. 'Come to the point, Angela.'

The other woman hardened; her face lost its superficial amiability and stiffened like glass, like cold steel. 'The point is this, Hester. I want my husband back, and I want you never to have anything to do with him again.'

Hester remained quiet, hearing her out. 'Believe me,' Angela went on, 'I'll know, you can bloody believe I'll know if there is any contact between you and Alex. If there is, I'll not only tell Martin, but also your two daughters.'

The silence between the two women was as deep as polluted rivers full of nasty things running with the current. That Angela would do as she threatened Hester had no doubt; her lack of evidence – for Hester knew Alex had not told her – would make no difference.

'You know it would kill Martin,' Angela said quietly.

'And it wouldn't bother me in the least. You're the one who would have to live with the guilt.'

Hester, shocked beyond measure, stared at the other woman with horror. Then she said, in a whisper which was all she could manage, 'Do you really want Alex back so badly? And do you think this is the way to do it?'

Angela's eyes were shrewd in that glass face, 'Yes, I do want my marriage back. And yes, I do think this is a fucking good way to do it.'

In the far corner of the tea-shop two sweet-cheeked geriatrics gathered their parcels and walked out through the door. Hester reached into her bag, found some coins and put them on the table for her undrunk tea. Then without looking at Angela she followed the old couple out.

Later, Hester remembered the wind. It had gathered force while they were in the tea-shop and now snarled and blew and grizzled with such ferocity as she walked blindly around the park, that Hester sometimes had trouble standing. Her silk scarf blew right out of her hair and went flying like a kite into the frenzied sky. She didn't even try to retrieve it, even though Alex had bought it for her in France; she only walked, on and on and on. Later she learned that there had been a hurricane that night, that the woodlands around Exeter where she and Alex had walked hand in hand were partially decimated. In weeks to come, when she walked there again, on her own this time and mourning his loss, the destruction she saw everywhere only seemed to mirror the destruction in her own heart, her own self.

But that afternoon, that dark and windy early spring evening, the wind seemed only to frame her turbulent thoughts, enhance them with special cruelty. Her first reaction was to get hold of Alex somehow, but the house in Kerrocher had no phone. Then, for a crazed half hour, she actually planned to run to him, abandon her family, return to France. What need did they have of her now, she thought. Imogen was twenty-seven and most successful in London. Abigail was well over seventeen and about to leave for her music college. And Martin? True, he had his aches and pains, his angina and his arthritis, but people had those things for years. Martin had learned to live with most of them, just as he would have to learn to live without her.

So the thoughts went flying like sparklers in Hester's head as she walked around and around the city, down by the canal and the river, along the footpaths, back into the centre of town, into the Cathedral – she didn't know where she was walking, what she was doing, and even the wind stopped bothering her, for the turmoil outside merely reflected her own tempest within.

She thought a great deal about Angela. Hester knew the woman would never have a marriage with Alex again whatever happened. Alex had left her once years ago, long before he met Hester; he would never go back to her now even if Hester had never existed. But Angela wouldn't believe that. She needed a scapegoat badly, for this time Alex, his sons grown, was not going back to her.

After walking for miles, numb and frozen from the cold and the wind, Hester finally began to calm down, to think rationally about the situation. Angela had no proof that they were in France together, only suspicions, just as she had no proof of their affair. Perhaps a student had once linked their names casually; perhaps they were seen together. Possibly one of their colleagues at the college had intuited something and mentioned it to Angela. But if anything, Hester and Alex had been over-cautious. They never met in Exeter, rarely spoke to each other alone at the college, and were totally circumspect in all their public behaviour. Hester would never know how Angela had first come upon her suspicions, but obviously they were reinforced by the lovers' simultaneous trip to France. It was enough for Angela to blame the whole collapse of her marriage on Hester.

As she finally made her way home that evening, Hester resolutely decided not to let Angela intimidate her. Alex would not be back from France for another two or three months and after all, he was separated from his wife: she would never know if he and Hester wrote to each other or communicated in any way. And when at last he did return, with any luck Angela would have accepted the fact that her marriage was over, and would forget about Hester, forget about Alex, and start making some kind of a new life for herself.

At last she came to a decision. Angela was bluffing: Hester was not going to fall for it. As long as she and Alex were careful when he returned, as long as they tried not to be too greedy, didn't see each other too often, everything would be all right. There was no way Hester could give him up now. Not now, not after five years, not after France, not after playing house with him for three whole weeks and learning to love him twenty-four hours a day instead of in brief clandestine mornings or the odd stolen evening. She loved him, and she had one of two choices: leave her husband and go to him, or continue meeting him secretly, however unsatisfying. Hester knew she could never leave Martin, who for all his faults loved her, nor could she leave Abigail, who at seventeen was still in many ways a child. The third option, putting an end to her long affair with Alex, could not even be contemplated. Simply, he was her life.

Satisfied with having made a decision, Hester drove wearily back to the rectory, to find Abigail waiting for her, white-faced and frantic. Martin was in hospital. He had been taken there an hour before with what appeared to be a heart attack.

It was a mild attack, no more than a warning, the doctors said. If Martin stayed calm and avoided stress, he would be fine in no time. And they were right; he lived five more years without a hint of trouble before his heart finally gave out on him. But that night, after Hester came home from the hospital, had soothed Abigail and seen her off to bed, and had phoned Imogen in London, she sat down and wrote the first letter to Alex.

It was short and precise. It said only that it was absolutely out of the question for Hester ever to see Alex again, or to keep in touch in any way. Hester didn't mention Angela, and perhaps this was wrong, she later wondered. Perhaps she should have told him everything, but she was afraid that if Alex knew the truth, he would return at once to England, confront Angela and provoke the scene which now Hester knew she must avoid whatever the cost.

For Angela, and of this Hester was deadly certain, would tell Martin if Alex confronted her, and whatever happened Hester knew it was a risk she could never take. She could not bear the guilt of Martin's death. She did not want him to die – she loved him, in an old companionable way she still cared for him and wanted to protect him. When his life was threatened Hester knew instinctively she had to save him, even if it meant ruthlessly sacrificing Alex. She was frightened – unhinged, perhaps. By then she even superstitiously suspected that Angela had, by some nefarious sorcery, caused Martin's heart attack, to show Hester she meant business. Crazy, yes. But Hester was crazy during that time.

And so, mad with grief and terror, she wrote the letter. And lost Alex.

Eight years ago. All water under the bridge, so they say, all unimportant now. But tonight as Hester sits quietly between Bruno and Imogen, with Ermi and Alex opposite, at a small restaurant just outside their village, she suddenly wants to explain to Alex, to say, 'Oh love, *je regrette, je regrette beaucoup*.'

'*Je regrette beaucoup*, Alex,' Hester says to him in her heart. 'I want to tell you about it now, how I was frightened and powerless and bewitched by Angela. I felt, as I sat in the hospital room with Martin, that she was right, that if I gave you up, your marriage would be whole and fine again, that Martin would survive his heart attack and live many more years, and that both my daughters and your sons would come out of all this unscathed. Perhaps they did, Alex, perhaps they did. But us? What did it do to us?

'I couldn't take that chance. No matter how careful we were, how circumspect, Angela would find out; by now I was endowing her with supernatural powers. She would tell Martin and he would have another, this time fatal, heart attack. And I couldn't tell you this, because I was a coward, Alex. I was afraid you'd ask me to come and live with you, you see, if our secret affair had to end. And what would I have said? To this day I'm not sure. But it was a no-win situation, you know that. Without you I was lost, destroyed; yet if I had gone with you, my guilt would have destroyed us both.'

Hester sits in the restaurant picking at her avocado, unable to concentrate on her food, which is most out of character. Deep in these useless thoughts she finds herself looking at Alex with such a sad, lost expression that he catches her eye and raises his glass slightly to her, looking perplexed and troubled.

'Oh Alex,' her pensive words continued in her head, 'how I would like to talk to you now! I am ready, at last, to explain things, to try and say what perhaps I should have said years ago.

'If I am honest with myself I have to admit it was my daughters who in the end stopped me from going to you. You said they were grown then, adults, but in some ways they were still such children, vying for their father's love, still bickering with each other whenever they were home together, still competing pointlessly for Martin's affection. For Martin was a hard father; he demanded from his children what he tried to demand from me – a willingness to agree that he knew best for the family, that what he decreed was right for all of us. The girls rebelled, of course, and Martin reacted by withdrawing his love. Not overtly, for he tried to be fair – I must give him his due – but subtly, which somehow was worse. It made the girls unsure of where they stood, and it provoked them to react by lashing out against each other, each blaming the other for their own fall from favour . . .'

'What, Imogen? You are going to do *what?*' Martin stared at his daughter with his pale, unblinking blue eyes. 'I cannot believe I am hearing you properly. For God's sake tell me this is a joke.'

Father and daughter were sitting at the long mahogany

table in the dining room at the rectory, having just finished dinner. They were alone, for Hester had taken Abigail, only six at the time, to a birthday party.

Imogen, dressed in a mini-skirt – they were only just beginning to come back at that time – and her hair sleekly and sophisticatedly tied at the back of her neck, sighed in a world-weary manner. She said, slowly as if to an idiot, 'I am quitting the sixth form. I am not doing A levels. I am going to London to become a model.'

Martin, controlling himself, gave Imogen a thin smile. His face was fine, aescetic, noble even; he had silver-white hair which fell smoothly over his forehead. He had the knack of looking beatific almost at will, which greatly enhanced his reputation as a headmaster, especially with the parents. At home he was more of a martyr, or so he saw himself.

'I'm sorry, Imogen, but you delude yourself. You are not going to London; you are staying here – *and completing your A levels*.'

'Dad, be reasonable.' She got up from the table and began pacing. She had bare legs under her mini-skirt and a halter top that was so skimpy Martin had forbidden her to wear it months ago. She had worn a shirt over it during dinner, but now, saying it was hot, she took the shirt off and threw it defiantly on one of the dining-room chairs.

Saint-like, her father ignored this childish display of rebellion. Imogen said, almost pleadingly now, 'Dad, you know I won that competition. You know one of the top modelling agencies in London is desperate to take me on. It's too bloody good to miss.'

'Don't swear, Imogen. I've told you often enough, yet you seem to be doing it more frequently. You're not a very good example for your younger sister—'

'Sod Abigail. Are you listening to me at all, Dad? Me, me, me, Imogen?'

'I always listen to you, Imogen,' Martin said mildly. 'Though sometimes you make it exceedingly difficult. I would now like a little walk after dinner; my digestion suffers when I don't. Please don't let me hear you mentioning modelling again. It is a profession for women who do not mind demeaning themselves for vast sums of money; it is a cheap way of making use of one's body when one's mind is not up to scratch. You have a good mind, Imogen. You have no need to sell your body.'

'Oh, you pompous – how can you say that? How can you come out with such things? And you never listen to me. I am telling you I am going to London—'

'It is *you* who doesn't listen, Imogen. I am telling you you are not. I would also appreciate your not flaunting your success in that puerile competition in front of Abigail. She's far too promising to be corrupted by your meretricious values.'

When Martin left Imogen threw a plate across the room. Later, it took all of Hester's persuasion to get her to talk to her father again. When Imogen finally left for London, there was an uneasy truce between them, though neither of them ever quite forgave the other.

Martin turned then to Abigail, pouring on the younger girl all the hopes and ambitions he had had for his aberrant older daughter.

'Come on Abby, let's hear that piece again.' Dutifully, in the study, her father sitting on the sofa where he could watch her fingers, Abigail played the Beethoven. When she had finished she turned to him shyly for approval.

'Wonderful, wonderful. You're going to be a most famous person when you are older.'

'Like Imogen?' Abigail said hopefully.

'I sincerely hope not, Abby. That is infamy, not fame.'

Abigail was silent, not knowing what her father was talking about, but not wanting to ask as his pale, fine face had clouded over. She waited quietly and finally he turned his attention again to her, saying, 'You know, Abby, if you are going to be a great musician, you have to be educated. I noticed your school report said you still have some trouble with your reading. I could hardly believe it – why, you're almost seven! Imogen could read fluently before she even started school.'

Abigail stared at her father's feet. Then she slowly turned

back to the piano and played the Beethoven all over again . . .

And so Martin took over Abigail, having failed so dismally with his other daughter or, as he preferred to see it, she having failed him. Being at home now, he had plenty of time to do this. On his retirement he had taken on the mantle of an invalid – he had arthritis, a touch of diabetes, and of course the angina – and this gave him back some of the power he had lost when he was no longer a headmaster. He needed someone on whom to exercise this power, and by then only Abigail was left. Luckily she was young and pliable enough to enjoy the attention, having always felt very much in Imogen's shadow during the latter's stormy adolescence.

This was a trying period for Hester. 'You stand in my way every time I try to discipline my daughters,' Martin said repeatedly.

'But I don't agree with your idea of discipline sometimes.'

'You undermine me.'

'How? Because I say what I think?'

'You are too lax with them. I won't have it, you know.'

'Oh stop it, Martin, just stop it,' Hester would say wearily, for he wore her out, shattered her spirit, with his constant criticism and disapproval.

But as she tried to stand firm against Martin, and not let him bully either her or the girls, she felt somehow that all she had managed to do was lose both of them. Though she had supported Imogen in her decision to try for success in the modelling world (thus incurring Martin's resentment for years to come), Imogen could not forgive her for not doing more, not breaking away herself from Martin when his behaviour became so intolerable. Like the young everywhere, Imogen could not understand the necessity, at times, for appeasement. She thought her mother should irrevocably confront Martin, abandon Abigail, and side with her to the exclusion of all the rest of the family.

And yet ironically, Hester felt she was losing Abigail also, so strongly and possessively did Martin dominate her. Bitter with the disappointment of Imogen's rejection of the academic path, he poured all his frustrated ambition for his children into Abigail, encouraging her music, listening to her play for hours, finding her the best and most expensive teachers in the county. The family muddled along like this for several years, Imogen becoming a very successful model, Abigail being promoted as an embryonic concert pianist, while Hester – Hester fell in love with Alex . . .

'Alex – *you* here?' she had asked incredulously, a few months after their first meeting at the rectory. By now she knew him slightly better; she had run into him several times since then, at various school functions. But today she was at her own college in Exeter and there he was, using the photocopy machine in the English Department office.

'Didn't Martin tell you? I've left the comprehensive and got a job here. I'm not in your department, of course, but our machine has broken and your secretary kindly let me use this one.'

'No, I didn't know. How nice to see you!'

'How's the poetry going?'

This endeared him to Hester at once; he had remembered their first meeting, when she had announced so confidently that she was a poet.

'I'm very excited,' she said, unable to stop herself. 'My first poem just came out – the magazine was in the post this morning.'

He made her take it out of her bag and show it to him, then and there. He read it twice, then said, sincerely, how much he liked it.

'I suppose I should be blasé about it,' she bubbled. 'But I've never seen a poem of mine in print before.'

'It's nothing to be blasé about, it's an important step for you. Look, it's lunch-time – can I take you for a pizza or something, to celebrate?'

She looked at him gratefully, glowing with success, joy, and the beginning of love, though she didn't realize it at the time. She had grown to like Alex, this slight gentle man with the soft dark hair and the yellow-green eyes like a tiger's. Though they met only infrequently, she was always pleased to see him. He considerably livened up the tedium of the obligatory functions she had to attend with Martin.

That first lunch lasted three hours, for by either chance or destiny, neither of them had a class until three-fifteen that afternoon. They had gone to a waterfront pub, sitting by the window and watching a canal boat go through the double locks outside. It was raining and cold, so they drank hot toddies, enjoying the open fire and noting the rain speckle the water with huge iridescent polka dots. At five past three they reluctantly went out into the rain and into Alex's car, rushing back to the college just in time for their last class.

'It was wonderful, thank you,' Hester said. 'A proper celebration.'

'We'll do it again.'

'When my next poem is published!'

He looked at her, seeing her hair tangled in the wind, her face translucent with rain, and said, 'Before that, I hope.'

In the next couple of months they met frequently, walking in the park next to the college if the weather was fine, or meeting at the pub by the canal when it was not. They were at ease together, happy, whether talking about college or themselves, or if they felt contemplative, not talking much at all but enjoying walking together through the streets of the city on such mundane errands as going to the bank, or looking for wedding presents for distant relatives. They walked for miles sometimes when the weather shifted from winter into early spring, along the many footpaths behind the city, finding quiet places to sit and talk, like the tiny old railway station, used only infrequently by local trains, tucked away behind the football stadium.

The station was at the end of an orchard through which ran a public footpath, and it was here that their relationship changed, shifted, on to the course for which it had been heading from the start. Classes that afternoon had been cancelled because of a student strike, but Alex and Hester were reluctant to go home on this sunny, blooming April day. All the fruit trees were in blossom, and as they walked along they were quiet, each intensely aware of the other.

They were silent for some time, until finally Alex said hesitantly, 'Hester, you do know, you *must* know, that something is happening between us?'

Hester felt great relief, and suddenly the spring day hurtled into focus, the blossom clearly defined on each tree, the flowers in the adjoining gardens exquisite in their intensity of colour.

'I know,' she said. 'I know,' though she really hadn't known, had only imagined, intuited, dreamed, until that moment.

'I need to know that you feel the same as I do. I can't ask anything of you, I know that, of course, but . . .' He trailed off, uncertain of how to go on.

'Oh, Alex! I feel the same. It's crazy.'

Now it was Alex who felt relief. A sudden giddiness made him realize just how important her reaction had been to him.

They walked along in a bewildered, joyous silence for a few moments, until they reached the railway station. Later they would feel the rest – guilt and despair, regret and pain – but now, for this one rare moment, only love and an incredible healthy well-being filled their bodies and souls. Sitting side by side on an old wooden bench on the almost defunct platform, they watched the local train chug slowly by, not even bothering to stop but heading out of the city on the single track bordered by wild hedgerows, newly coming into leaf.

He took her hand. 'It feels like that old movie, you know – *Brief Encounter*. Lovers in train stations, all that.'

'It's a sad movie. They part in the end.'

He took his hand away. 'This can only be . . . for this moment. There's no future, Hester.'

She nodded. 'Like spring – ephemeral. One breath and it's over, gone.'

'I didn't mean . . . my feelings aren't ephemeral, but neither of us is free,' he finished lamely.

'I know. It's all right, Alex, we both feel the same.'

'This is all we can have.'

'I know,' she repeated. She wrapped her little finger around his, for his hand was on the bench next to hers. A few straggly trees at the platform's edge had begun cautiously to burst their buds and expose vulnerable, pale-green leaves, and she thought it was the most beautiful thing she had ever seen.

'I told you it was a sad movie,' she said, and then he took her face, held it in his hands, and kissed her for a long time . . .

They didn't immediately go to bed together. At first, they didn't need to: it was sweet enough knowing their love was reciprocated, idyllic enough to find little hidden pubs outside of Exeter where they could hold hands under the table, or primrose-filled woodlands where they could hide under trees and indulge themselves in an illicit embrace. Neither one of them had had an affair before: both had believed, sometimes intolerantly, in fidelity. And so instead of jumping straight into that dark, deep and rather scary sea, they paddled, testing the water first, getting used to each new depth, going out a little further each time until suddenly, before they realized what was happening, they were in the deep, swimming for all they were worth.

'Oh Alex,' Hester cried the first time it happened. 'Oh, how I love you, how I love you.' And so it was. There was no guilt, only love, and for love and joy she clung to Alex and wept.

It was a late summer evening, hot and still, and they were lying on a bed of earth and leaves in a secluded woodland outside the city. Overhead the pines opened up to a clear twilit sky and as they lay there the stars began to appear, one by one.

'I never want to go home,' she whispered, and he held her close to him and slowly, gently, ran his hand down and around her body, tenderly, lovingly, stroking her as if she were rare precious silk, and indeed, so she felt to him. Then they lay still, entwined together like the limbs of the trees around them, until the night sky was full of stars, and slowly they began to make love again, and this time as she came she looked up and saw a shooting star high above the trees and knew, irrevocably, that she was either lost or found: whatever, she would never be the same again.

Once it began, their affair made up in intensity for that first hesitant beginning. All the passion they had held back was free to crash and break over the rocks of their new-found love, and the more the waves pounded them, the more enduringly those rocks stood. Like so many others before her, Hester had believed it could never happen to her. She was in her forties, settled into an austere, ordinary life, untroubled by any personal excess of passion. She would have said she loved Martin, even though he often grieved her in his handling of the children, and made her angry when he tried to subdue her own life.

'You're not going out again?' he said to her one evening, long before Alex had entered her life, as she hurried to clear the remains of dinner off the table.

'You know I am, I reminded you yesterday. There's a poetry reading at the Art Centre.'

'They're a waste of time, Hester, those readings you go to. Poetry should be read, not performed like a trained seal.'

'I don't agree with you. Do you mind doing the washing up? I have to pick Jennie up.'

'Who's Jennie?'

Hester was becoming irritated. 'Martin, you know very well that she's a colleague at work, and a friend.'

'Why haven't I met her, then?'

Hester chose her words carefully as she collected her coat, her bag, her car keys; she wanted to leave the house calm and unruffled, not angry and frustrated as she often did these days. 'You haven't met her because you haven't wanted to. You have talked to her several times on the phone and said she sounded vacuous.'

'Ah – that one. And so she is, from the sound of her conversation. You're demeaning yourself, keeping that sort of company.'

Before Hester could retort Abigail had walked in, so Hester just kissed her goodbye and left. 'Don't be late,' Martin called out after her. 'I can never get to sleep while you are still out, and I've got one of my headaches coming on.' And so, having ruined Hester's evening, scotching any plans she might have had for a quiet drink after the poetry reading, he went back inside the house.

These scenes were not infrequent, but Hester had learned how to deal with them. She ignored Martin's gibes (when possible), and got on with her own life whilst at the same time keeping some kind of harmony at home. And yet apart from these tensions within the family, Hester would have said she was fairly content. She had begun, tentatively, writing poetry again, having done so copiously and surreptiously in university, before abandoning it when life crowded in on her in the form of marriage and children and her job at the college. She was finding the poetry more than just satisfying. It was helping her to feel whole again, without having realized she was fragmented. She started to find peace, not having known she was at war with herself. The oppressive responsibility of a demanding family became easier to bear once she began writing again. It was as if since her marriage she had been taking small, shallow breaths: now at last she was beginning to breathe as she should, deeply and fully.

Did she ever love Martin? Looking back, long after he is dead, Hester thinks she did, hopes she did. Certainly she was attracted to him soon after she met him, at a school where she was a fledgling teacher and he was already a deputy head.

'Still working?' he would enquire solicitously, late in the day when Hester was still struggling to make sense out of barely-decipherable student exercise books.

'It seems never to end, all this marking.'

'You soon learn the tricks. Skim over it, or better yet, hand them back without reading any of it, and tell the kids the quality was so poor you didn't mark them.'

'You're not serious!' she exclaimed, shocked, for she was young, passionate, idealistic.

'Only half,' he said, for he had already become cynical, cloaking it with a dry humour that amused Hester, lightened the heaviness of this first difficult year of teaching. 'Come on, I'll buy you a drink.'

She began to grow quite fond of him, for he was not unattractive, and had a rather appealing worldliness that Hester, a sheltered only child who had never travelled far from home (even her university had been only two miles up the road), found quite lovable. He, sensing her lack of assurance, her vulnerability, took her under his wing. He helped her with lesson plans, and protected her from fractious students. She thought he was wise, wise and kind, and gratefully accepted what he offered her. Because he possessed tact and diplomacy – which was what had got him his Headship – he was soon able to convert Hester's gratitude into love, and despite the almost twenty-year age gap, it wasn't long before they were married.

The trouble began when Hester realized that Martin would never stop treating her as a student, and a recalcitrant one at that. He read her university poems tolerantly and gave them back to her, heavily marked with a thick red pen. 'Some promise here,' he said patronizingly, 'but you were right to give it up when you left university.'

'They are that bad, are they?' asked Hester, stung.

'No, not at all bad. It's just time you moved on to something else. Poetry is an exercise for those who are still wallowing in adolescence. Try prose, if you need to express yourself. Your prose is much better – you write a good letter.'

Had Hester been a little older, and a great deal more self-confident, perhaps she could have laughed at Martin. But instead, in those early days she saw herself as he saw her, and it was years before she began to take herself seriously as a poet and, she sometimes thought later, as a woman. The fact that both these things happened around the same time she met Alex was more than just a coincidence. He gave her assurance – he returned to her what Martin had taken away. Whatever else Alex did, he gave her that, for even after their love affair ended, Hester never lost that confidence in herself again.

And now as she sits in this restaurant in France drinking the wine that has been poured into her glass and oblivious to everyone talking around her, Hester thinks of Martin, asks herself if *he* ever really loved *her*. Trying to be honest she has to answer yes, but she knows it was the kind of love he felt for his daughters: the love of a creator for the things he has created. Hester was young enough to be malleable, unformed and unsure when she met Martin, and because of this he thought he could shape her. When he could not, when she grew rigid under his hand, he blamed her.

But he loved her, Hester accepts. And as she sips her wine, surrounded by people both new and old in her life, she tells herself she was right to stay with Martin, for as he guided and protected her as a young student teacher so it was right that she protected him later, gave him a peaceful old age by staying at his side, by giving up Alex.

Alex. Hester looks at him over her wine glass and finds he has been waiting for her to look up at him. When at last she does he raises his eyebrows in that funny, endearing way he used to, when he knew Hester was distressed, or confused, or just overwhelmed by their whole affair. Sometimes the look came in the staff restaurant when it was full of their colleagues, sometimes it came in a crowded pub. The look said: 'It will be okay, Hester. We'll get by. Things may be piling up on us and we don't know which way to go, which way to turn, but we'll manage somehow.'

She is suddenly grateful to him. For his concern for her, even though Ermi is here; for being patient with her and not asking her those questions he has every right to ask. For forgiving her – for being willing to become her friend again. For above all she must remember that they were friends first, before they became lovers, and they can be friends again now that they are not.

And then Ermi leans over towards him, her pointed little breasts poking through the thin material of her jumper, and asks him something, and puts her arm around his shoulder casually, like one does when one is staking a claim. And all Hester's calm analysis goes right out of the window as she perceives that for all her reasoning, she is not yet ready for this. She wonders with despair whether she ever will be.

Shaking away her thoughts like a puppy impatiently shaking off great drops of water after a bath, Hester makes herself concentrate on the present, on this evening which had promised to be so special, but has turned out so unbearable because of the unexpected presence of Ermi. And it gets worse. As the evening goes on the Frenchwoman becomes less and less inhibited; vivaciously she kisses Alex's ear, drapes her arms like shawls over his chest and shoulders; rests her hand lightly on his and lets it linger there when he is lighting her cigarette.

It gets to Hester. She tries not to let it but it does. She feels desolate and unsettled and grows waspish, finding consolation in the fact that after the meal Ermi has just eaten she'll be reeking copiously of garlic rather than smelling prettily of rosemary and lavender.

When finally the evening is over and they get home, Hester pleads a headache and says she must go straight to bed. 'Goodbye, Ermi, I shan't see you tomorrow, as I know you will have to make an early start since you are driving so far,' Hester says before she makes her exit. This slightly annoys Ermi, which satisfies Hester, wicked as she is. Ermi has Alex all the time back in Kerrocher; this is Hester's territory and she wants to be left in peace.

'Thank you for the lunch today, Alex,' she says breezily. 'Have a good journey back home.'

'I'm not in a hurry,' he says doggedly. 'I'll see you tomorrow morning.'

'I'm afraid not,' Hester says firmly. 'I am working on a new collection of poetry. I have promised my editor it will be ready at the end of summer, so I shall not come out of my room all day as I am right in the middle of a rather long poem I want to finish. I'm sure you'll be a dear, Imogen, and put a pot of your delicious coffee and perhaps a croissant or two outside my door some time in the morning? I really don't want to be disturbed until I have quite finished.'

There is an impressed silence; everyone is terribly in awe of creativity, except those who wrestle with it constantly and know what a hellish burden it is. Hester exits grandly, with what she hopes is dignity. When she is in bed she puts her pillow over her ears so that she doesn't have to hear Alex and Ermi come upstairs, so she doesn't have to spend the whole night wondering whether Imogen has put them in separate bedrooms or together.

'It doesn't matter in the slightest,' she says out loud, reaching for her pen and notebook. At least she has poetry. At least she will always have that.

Chapter Eleven

Like the oak, Hester does not bend. 'Sod off,' she says to the willow outside her window, which sways and curves in the soft morning breeze as if mocking her, as if whispering, 'See, it's easy, you can do it too: give a little, go with the flow, the sudden gust, the wind.'

Hester refuses, and remains unyielding. The next morning she wakes early after a restless night and tiptoes downstairs while everyone is asleep, making herself a pot of tea to take back to the bedroom. Later, Imogen tries to tempt her, knocking discreetly around nine o'clock and coming in with a tray of coffee and croissants. 'Alex went down to the *boulangerie* for these, especially for you. He said are you joining us for breakfast? He hopes you are, because it's beautiful in the garden. I quite agree, you must come down.'

'Has Ermi gone yet?' Hester asks, taking the tray and sniffing the aroma of coffee appreciatively.

'Why no, she's just gone out in the garden.'

'I thought she had to drive all the way to Biarritz?'

'She said last night that she wasn't in a hurry. Apparently it doesn't matter when she arrives. You haven't warmed to her, have you, Mum?' she states perceptively.

Hester sidetracks enigmatically. 'Oh, whatever makes you think that? Of course, she's . . . such a headache I had last night. Interesting profession the woman has, packing herbs. I'd get terribly hungry doing it, I'm sure. I'd keep thinking of a *ratatouille* or a *ragoût* or something. Anyway, I really must get on with this. I won't come down, if it's all right with you.'

Imogen smiles at Hester warmly. 'Of course it's all right. But are you sure you're not ill? You look rather wan, shall I call Bruno?'

She looks so eagerly at Hester that her mother almost

hates to tell her she feels fine, that a doctor's visit will not be necessary. 'Well, I'll leave you, then.' Imogen looks at her shrewdly. 'Ermi's not so bad, you know. Talks a bit too much, that's all. In fact we had a long talk before she arrived. She was telling me about her and Alex, how they met and—'

'Imo, if you don't mind, love, I really must get on.'

'Oh sorry, Mum. Of course you do, and I must too. I do waste time, these days. I don't know if it's France, or Bruno, but I'm more relaxed than I've ever been in my life. Will you be down for lunch?'

'No, no, no, no, I shan't be down at all. I really feel the muse, you know?' Hester gives a tinkling laugh to indicate that the goddesses of creativity are shining favourably on her today.

'Of course,' Imogen says reverentially. 'Shall I bring you something on a tray?'

'That would be wonderful. Thank you, Imo.'

At last she is gone and Hester is on her own. She wolfs down the croissants, drinks the coffee, and opens the novel she has been meaning to read since she arrived. The gusty breeze outside has, she sees with some satisfaction, dispensed with the beautiful morning the visitors are having in the garden and has brought on some black rain clouds which are threatening to spring leaks at any moment. A perfect day for staying in bed and reading a novel, Hester thinks without compunction, and anyway she was up until three o'clock the night before working on a poem about loss. *'Loss stalks the future like a cat,'* the poem ends, *'silently waiting in yesterday's dead grasses.'*

Re-reading the poem this morning, Hester sighs. She feels sad today, bleak and lonely. The rain starts, torrentially with no preliminaries. Hester is on the balcony when it begins, watching the bright pink and red geraniums in the pots below turning colour, darkening as the sky greys, then turns black. She thinks of Alex and Ermi in the back garden under the apple trees and wonders if they will leave once the rain starts, or whether Ermi will use the storm as an excuse to stay on at Pont-Plouay. Perhaps Alex will linger with her;

perhaps they will sightsee, go to Pont-Aven, maybe even visit Gérard's restaurant, for Alex did say he would like to see the man again. Alex could introduce Ermi, explain that she is now his new love—

Oh God, this will not do. Abruptly, Hester leaves the balcony, fastens the doors, and picks up her novel. Returning to bed she plumps the pillows, props herself up comfortably, and prepares to read. A little bit of occasional escapism never did anyone any harm, she tells herself as she determinedly opens the book.

The day passes far too slowly. It rains and it rains. Imogen knocks with some lunch for her, and Hester asks her to leave it outside the door. She has her radio on playing music softly so that she is not too aware of noises outside: cars driving away, voices murmuring goodbyes. She wants oblivion, until Alex and his wretched little rodent are far away from Pont-Plouay and she is left in some kind of peace.

It is late afternoon when Imogen knocks again. 'Mum, I brought you up some tea and *pain aux raisins*. Can I come in?'

It is a question, but she sounds obstinate. Hester senses that her daughter has begun to suspect this creativity lark and probably thinks her mother is becoming slightly eccentric – you never can tell with poets. So Hester says, hiding her novel and spuriously reaching for pen and notebook, 'Yes, of course. Come in, darling.'

They talk desultorily about the weather for a few minutes, then Hester says casually, 'Did our visitors both get safely away?'

'Yes, finally, though I must say neither of them seemed in a hurry. Ermi hung around until Alex said that he had to get back to Kerrocher, and she left when he did. What an awful day to drive too, and she's going such a long way. Anyway, she said to say goodbye and wish you luck with your collection. She also said you must come and visit her and Alex in Kerrocher.'

'How kind.'

'Alex said to tell you *au revoir.*'

'Oh?'

'Yes, that's exactly what he said, *au revoir*, and that he was most sorry not to see you today, but he quite understands the call of the muse.'

Tongue-in-cheek bastard, Hester thinks, but she has to smile. Alex always knew her far better than anyone. He would know she was running away, from him and from herself: he would also know why.

'Alex wanted to come upstairs and see you before he left,' Imogen goes on, 'but I stopped him. I said that you emphatically could not be disturbed.'

'Good.'

'He said he'd phone you, and thanked you for a lovely day yesterday.'

'Oh. Well, that's nice.'

'He's sweet, isn't he? How did you say you knew him?'

'Oh, he was a colleague of mine at the college.'

'He and Ermi seem a nice sort of couple.'

'Mm, yes.'

'He's older than her, of course, but that works fine, look at you and Dad. They don't live together, though. I don't think Alex wants to and Ermi says anyway it's handier this way. They don't get on each other's nerves. She said Alex—'

'This tea is just hitting the spot, Imogen,' Hester interrupts quickly, not wanting to know another thing that Ermi said about Alex. 'You are a darling to wait on me like this.'

Imogen starts to leave the room but turns, suddenly, and says, 'Oh, by the way, I almost forgot. Gérard rang – you know, from the restaurant in Pont-Aven. He said to tell you to go straight in the drive at the side of the restaurant, there's a tiny car park there. He says he is looking forward to tonight and has cooked you a meal you will never forget.'

Hester's dinner date with Gérard: it is this evening. She looks at her watch – five-thirty. 'Good God, Imogen, I totally forgot. Of course, it's tonight, it's Tuesday.'

Hester's first instinct is to ring and cancel. Her mood is as

believe him: for this moment at least she is beautiful. It is a long time since she has felt like this.

Gérard's cooking is superb. To please Hester it is a meal from the sea; she told him last week that she adores seafood and can never get enough of it in England. They have platefuls of fresh *langoustines*, pulling the meat out of the shell and dipping it in home-made garlic mayonnaise; then they eat scallops in an exquisite tarragon sauce with tiny succulent carrots and fresh local cauliflower. For dessert, Gérard has made light and tangy sorbet, which finishes the meal perfectly. Before they eat they have Champagne, laced with a soupçon of Cassis, then a Muscadet – for this is, after all, Brittany – then, with coffee, Hester has cognac.

After all this alcohol, which Hester is not used to, she dares not drive home, so she phones Imogen and explains that she is spending the night in Gérard's spare room.

Imogen is pleased that Hester has enjoyed her evening and ebulliently assures her mother that she will be fine on her own. As soon as she hangs up she turns to Bruno, with whom she is actually in bed at that very moment, and says, 'That was my mother. She's staying the night at Gérard's.'

'Hmmmm,' says Bruno, nibbling at her nipple.

'Because of the rain, you understand. She doesn't want to drive home in such a storm.'

'Aha. Your mother and Gérard Dupont, eh?'

'Oh Bruno, you're so French. It's my *mother*, for God's sake. I gather she's had too much Champagne and is crashing out on the sofa or something.'

'You are so naive, *mon petit bijou*. It is one of the things I adore about you.' He begins slowly massaging her belly.

'Naive, me? Oh Bruno, ohh, that's nice.' After a few moments Imogen, her voice thick and deep, says, 'Would you like to spend the night here tonight? Since Mum is away?'

'Ah yes, yes.'

Imogen is jubilant at this little bonus. Not that Bruno couldn't have spent other nights with her, for she knows that Hester would not mind, but the fact is that Imogen needs Hester, enjoys her company and does not want her to leave, not yet. She is afraid that if Bruno were to spend every night with her, Hester would feel superfluous, and tactfully return to England. And Imogen is not ready to be alone yet, nor is she ready to move in with Bruno. Though she knows she is in love, she is unprepared for the havoc love is wreaking in her life. She feels she has changed beyond measure, grown beyond measure, but it's all hard to handle, it's all come so suddenly.

Besides, there is another consideration. Imogen is planning to divorce Gordon on the grounds that he has abandoned her for another woman: if she were known to have another man in her bed, the settlement could be sticky, as she doesn't trust her husband not to make trouble. So Imogen is quite happy with the situation as it is; she has Bruno for long, loving hours in the privacy of his home, yet can return to her own territory alone, to get some breathing space from all that tumultuous emotion – not to mention physical exertions. Imogen is still shaken to the core by this new love of hers. For the first time ever she weeps over music, dawdles over poetry, finds her mind miles away whilst doing her accounts. She needs time and space to assimilate all this.

But right now is obviously not the time. Right now Bruno's hand is low on her belly and his tongue on hers and she lets herself go in the exquisite pleasure of it all. She is glad she found out what sex could really be like before she was too old to enjoy it. Clinging to Bruno she makes up for lost time.

And of course Hester does not sleep in the spare room, nor on a sofa somewhere. Somehow she finds herself in Gérard's bedroom, naked under the clean sweet-smelling sheets, and being made love to in the most delightful way by her very first Frenchman.

'*Ma chérie, tu est si belle,*' he says, and Hester believes him because the lights are dim and she knows he is seeing her with the powerful beacon of desire. Then she thinks, fuzzy from the Champagne and the heady lovemaking, it is not just the dim lights, it is not just the moment. 'Regain your pride in yourself, Hester,' she tells herself. 'You are a woman and beautiful because you have lived, experienced birth and death, grief and joy, passion and serenity. Time may have roughed you up a bit, but that doesn't make you less beautiful.'

These thoughts whirl around Hester's head like an aphrodisiac and she feels hot and uninhibited with a lust she had thought long dormant. Gerard's lovemaking is both skilled and tender; he takes time with her, draws the orgasm out of her slowly, patiently.

Later, they lie curled together like wood-shavings for quite some time, not talking, not even thinking: just enjoying the sensation of being comfortable and sated, their bodies slack with pleasure. Gérard finally stirs first, kissing Hester and saying, with great affection, 'That was wonderful, Hester. Thank you.'

Hester smiles at him and says, inanely, 'I don't usually do this sort of thing,' wondering if she will be shocked and horrified at herself the next morning when the heady effects of wine and passion have worn off.

But there is no point in worrying about that now, she thinks philosophically, pulling the duvet over herself in a rather late attempt at modesty. Gérard gets under it too and they talk a bit, nuzzle a bit, until he gets up, puts on a dressing gown, and goes to the kitchen to make coffee, since neither of them feel they will sleep.

Hester's head begins to clear and she thinks, with some wonder, about what has just happened. She decides she won't regret it tomorrow: the sex was good and it has been a long, long time. Gérard is a lovely man and was as thoughtful as he was passionate in bed. Hester confesses to herself that she enjoyed every lustful minute of it.

Yet here it comes. The sadness. The loneliness. The black pit, looming belligerently at her feet. For in the end she cannot help but compare this coupling to her lovemaking with Alex, and there is in the end no comparison. What happened with Gérard was a happy pleasuring of the body, not to be scorned, certainly, and already Hester knows she shall always look back on tonight fondly, with the most delightful memories.

But her lovemaking with Alex – how can she describe it, how does one find words? Not even poetry can do it. With Alex, their bodies also were pleasured, but oh, how sublimely, how rapturously. And in amongst the delights of the body were the emotional orgasms, the mental fusings, the ineffable feelings of oneness and unity.

Oh God, she thinks, in her ungrateful post-coital despair, so that is what love is all about!

And then Gèrard returns with a tray of coffee and an arrangement of chocolates. He looks so happy that Hester determinedly pulls herself together. Concentrating on Gérard, she accepts the hot black liquid, takes a chocolate, and together they munch contentedly, talking easily and naturally before finally, companionably, drifting off side by side into a deep, exhausted sleep.

The next morning is a bit of a shock. Hester has never in her whole life woken up in a strange bed beside a strange (well, fairly strange) man, and doesn't quite know the etiquette. But Gérard is so relaxed, so easy with her, that she soon feels as comfortable as if she had been doing this all her life. They have a long, leisurely breakfast together before he has to go down to his restaurant and Hester back to Pont-Plouay.

'An enchanting evening, my dear,' Gérard says as he sees Hester to her car. Last night's downpour has changed to a dull drizzle and the streets of Pont-Aven look wet and drab. 'You are an amazing woman. May I take you to dinner next Tuesday night? I know a restaurant which, although not quite as superb as mine, is still passable, and the owner is an old friend.'

Hester hesitates, but only briefly. What she feels for the Frenchman may not be sublime, but perhaps that only happens once in a lifetime – if at all, she thinks sombrely. *If at all.* Gérard is offering her a kind of love: a mature one perhaps, one based on mutual liking, amicability, respect. Despite last night's post-coital angst, Hester has to admit she feels quite good this morning: physically fit and mentally stable. She feels energetic, too, a far cry from yesterday, locked in her room mooning about Alex and remembering things past.

'Yes,' she says to Gérard as he opens her car door. 'Dinner next Tuesday would be lovely. Thank you.'

He smiles and his formidable silver moustache glistens with raindrops as he kisses Hester goodbye. He looks quite sparky himself, she thinks as she starts the engine and pulls slowly away, waving.

But as Hester drives through Pont-Aven she sees that it is market day here and so instead of taking the road home, she parks the car by the river and decides to buy some fresh vegetables, to cook herself and Imogen a *ragoût de légumes* for dinner. As she wanders around the stalls she ponders on plump aubergines, cheeky red peppers, courgettes green as forests. She investigates firm fat tomatoes with skins tight as girdles, and mushrooms pungent like moss. Finally she buys some of each, along with fresh garlic, chervil, basil and bay leaves.

This last purchase reminds her of Ermi, which makes her both cross and sad, and so she is delighted to be distracted by Colette, Bruno's vibrant mother, swooping upon her like an elegant rare bird as Hester considers life by the cauliflowers. Colette asks Hester to join her in the gallery for coffee and she accepts with alacrity.

'Ah, Hester, what a joy to see you on this grey day!' Colette says as she unlocks the door and they go in amongst the paintings. 'Luc is away in Paris, and I long for company.'

As usual she looks elegant in wide grey silk trousers with a matching tunic top, her ash-blonde hair frizzing artistically around her baby face. Her skin is amazing for a woman in her seventies, and Hester makes a mental note to get back to the moisturizer. Maybe devoting oneself exclusively to poetry and gardening when one is not even sixty is not such a brilliant idea, after all.

Colette takes Hester to a room behind the gallery which turns out to be a combination of office and small sitting room. It is full of plants: huge ferns lunging and drooping from every corner, great red geraniums on a shelf under the window. Two of Colette's paintings are hanging there – street scenes, one of which Hester recognizes as market day at Pont-Plouay. They remind her of happy summer sunsets, or early spring trees and wild flowers, when the colours are so new, so fresh, you know that you must stop and look at once for the next day everything will be slightly older, slightly dimmed. Hester resolves to check her finances before returning to England, to see if she can afford one of Colette's paintings.

'My favourites,' Colette says offhandedly when Hester praises the canvases. The other is also of Pont-Plouay, only of the small harbour bustling with boats and fishermen and wives and sweethearts waving off their men. 'They are not for sale. When I die, they will go to Bruno. He says he likes them, and of course Pont-Plouay is his village now.'

Colette puts water to boil in a red enamel saucepan as she says, 'Shall we have tea instead of coffee? You see how English I can be. A man from London who bought three of Luc's paintings sent us over all these teas. Assam? Lapsang? Darjeeling? You can have your choice.'

When the tea is made they settle down to talk, Colette in a wicker chair and Hester, easing off the strappy black sandals she had first put on last night on her way to Gérard's, sitting comfortably on a huge, soft chocolate-brown cushion on the floor.

'Ah Hester,' Colette says, '*Je suis désolée*! You were shopping in Pont-Aven this morning and were not even going to stop and see us at the gallery?'

'Oh no! That is, I was only on my way home. I actually didn't intend to stop at all.'

'Ah.' Colette's plump lips widen into a smile. 'Of course, last night you had your dinner with Gérard, he was so looking forward to it. How nice that you stayed over. Gérard is such a lonely man despite his *bonhomie*. He needs the company of *les femmes*, or shall I say one special *femme*.'

'Oh, Gérard is such an attractive man and so pleasant to be with, that I'm sure he has plenty of women friends,' Hester says uncomfortably.

'No, not so many, not for years and years. He is

extremely busy with his restaurant, you know. As he says, cooking is his first love.'

'And he does it superbly.' Colette looks at Hester with amusement and the Englishwoman adds, squirming, 'Cooking, I mean. He cooks like an angel.'

'Nevertheless, a little feminine diversion is excellent, excellent. You will do him good, Hester.'

Hester tries a lighthearted laugh. 'Colette, we have had only one dinner together.' She omits to mention the night, but Colette knows, she knows.

The Frenchwoman reaches over and pats Hester's cheek, and Hester gets a whiff of a delicate perfume. 'Don't worry, I am not trying to be the matchmaker, nor do I want to pry. You are an attractive woman, Gérard is a charming man, and if you can make each other happy occasionally – *voilà* – what could be better?' She leans back and sips her coffee contentedly. Even in repose she seems vital, full of the same energy that glows from her paintings.

'Colette,' Hester says impetuously. 'Thank you for keeping my secret, that day at Gérard's restaurant. You understood I had something to hide, that I did not want him to talk about Le Café de la Mer in Kerrocher and the . . . the man I was with then.'

'But Hester, of course I understood at once what the situation was. Am I not a woman? Have I not myself some little secrets?'

'It was mostly Imogen, you see. My daughter. I wouldn't want her to know . . .'

'It shall never be mentioned again: not by Gérard, not by myself. We French are nothing if not discreet.'

Hester nods gratefully. They drink more tea and talk eagerly, easily, as women can do, about themselves and their lives. Colette finds a soft black lamb's-wool cardigan for Hester to wear, for the rainy day is chilly and Hester is still wearing Imogen's skimpy black dress. Then she goes next door to buy some pastries: 'Ah, you are like me, I see, needing food constantly. It is the creativity, *chérie*, it makes the hunger' – and as they eat they discuss painting and poetry, their own and others. Later, Hester will go home and write a poem about her morning with Colette, about the ease with which they got to know each other as the mist drizzled against the window and the day became grey and languid:

'Accommodated by rain
and a fulsome melancholy
the day was wistful
as those China teas we sipped
cross-legged on the carpet. . .'

Colette mentions a friend of theirs – a young French poet who has also done some English translations, and says she would like him to see Hester's work for a possible French collection. Hester invites her and Luc for lunch next week, and promises to pass on her three published collections to them to lend him.

And then, finally, the two women talk about their children. Leaning towards Hester, Colette says with a sparkle, 'My Bruno, I think he adores your Imogen, *n'est-ce pas*?'

'I know Imogen adores him. She is truly in love, Colette. I have never seen her like this before.'

'She is good for him, and I am pleased. He feels protective of her because of what her husband did.'

'I think Imogen is taking great delight in being protected. She always had to be tough, abrasive even, in the business she was in. It is so lovely to see her relaxing, unwinding, letting go.'

'Yes, I too can see this happening, even though of course I do not know Imogen well.'

'She seems so much less volatile now,' Hester says thoughtfully. Except where her sister and Gordon are concerned, she adds silently. 'Imogen was forced, by her profession, to grow up too quickly, and in many ways she wasn't ready. She thought herself so sophisticated, but the reality was different. Emotionally she was in many ways a child, and a stubborn child at that. But each day now, with Bruno, I see her beginning to change.'

'He has great patience, my Bruno. He can be almost too understanding, too relaxed about things. Imogen is good in that she keeps him on the toes.'

The two women smile, thinking of their grown children.

'Ahh, Hester,' Colette sighs. 'Would it not be superb to see them settled together? Married, even? Do you have grandchildren?'

'No. I only have the two daughters, Imogen and Abigail, and neither of them has children.' Hester hesitates. 'You know, of course, of Abigail and Imogen's husband?'

'Yes, Bruno has told me all. Silly foolish girl. But you mustn't be too hard on her, Hester, when all this is in the past. She has freed your Imogen for my Bruno—'

'Yes, but her own sister?'

Colette shrugs, purses her fat lips. 'It is not honourable, I agree. But we all know what the power of love can do.'

They are silent, thinking about it, then Colette says delicately, 'Your daughter, Imogen – she most likely does not want children, am I right? With her career of such importance . . .'

'Antiques are not really her career. She was a model, then ran a modelling agency, but gave it all up in the end. She enjoys the antique business, of course, but only took it up because of Gordon. She's certainly not adverse to having children, she told me that the other day. It was just that she'd never wanted Gordon's children. I think she must have known from the early days that the marriage was not going to be a good one.'

Colette smiles so radiantly that Hester could swear the grey day outside seems to brighten. She really is an extraordinary woman.

'Ah,' Colette beams. 'So there *is* hope for us yet, Hester. Bruno is our only child, you know. I was forty-two when I had him, such a delightful surprise that was. How old is your Imogen?'

'She will be thirty-six before very long.'

Colette beams again. 'Splendid! Bruno is thirty, just the right age. A woman should always be slightly older than a man, she ages so much more gracefully. Ah Hester, if only you knew how I long for grandchildren.'

They sit dreaming together. Grandchildren . . . Hester hadn't given them much thought, probably because she didn't fancy the idea of Gordon being the father of her grandchildren. Now it seems rather a pleasant idea.

The two women talk idly for a little longer and then Hester gets up to go. Colette kisses her twice on each cheek and they confirm the time for next week's lunch.

The rain has at last stopped as Hester walks jauntily to the car. She feels rather pleased with her life at the moment, glad to have had a chance to get to know Colette, glad to be on her way to Pont-Plouay to share a delectable lunch with her daughter, and glad too – yes, she readily admits it to herself – that she had her night with Gérard. She feels both sated and alive today, and never mind that the act was pure pleasure rather than transcendent bliss – just be grateful that you enjoyed it, woman, she tells herself sternly.

Don't be greedy, she thinks as she gets into the car and drives out of the town towards home. Ineffable bliss, sublimity, is not a day-to-day occurrence: be glad of what you have. If there is no more transcendence, no more of that mysticism which maybe love is, at least there is peace and tranquility: with some pretty good sex besides!

And furthermore, she adds as she goes into the house and finds Imogen taking out the fresh bread and salad and cheese and pâté for their lunch, I may have lost the magic but at least there will be no pain. And this of course is no small advantage, the absence of pain.

Hester joins Imogen and eats a huge lunch, describing to her in detail all the magnificent food that Gérard prepared for them last night. As for the rest, Hester is silent and Imogen does not ask. She suspects, for her mother is looking smug and assured, but then she thinks this is her mother – her English mother for God's sake – and dismisses her suspicions.

As they eat they eye each other speculatively. One day, Hester has no doubt, they will be able to talk about these things together. But there is no rush, no rush at all. With a great sigh of contentment, she spreads pâté thickly on her bread and begins, sensuously, to eat.

Chapter Twelve

June passes by slowly, indolently, with a rather breathless feeling as though it is waiting for something. And although Imogen and Hester have settled into a placid routine, Hester can't shake off the sensation that they too are waiting for something.

There is still no word from Gordon or Abigail. Imogen rarely mentions them; it is as if they have ceased to exist. Hester notices that one of the spare bedrooms is accumulating boxes of clothes, books and papers, and she assumes it is the débris of living that the two left behind when they had to scurry away so ignominiously. Imogen is trying to spring-clean her husband and sister away, tidying up her house and her life simultaneously. She thinks that she can wipe them right out of existence, like cobwebs. Hester wants to tell her that eventually they will have to be faced, but Imogen will not hear their names mentioned.

The relationship between Imogen and Bruno is thriving. Hester brings up the subject of her return again, but Imogen dissuades her. She loves Bruno and hopes one day to live with him, marry him even, but it is too soon, for her if not for Bruno, who would be ready at a moment's notice to install her permanently in his house and in his bed.

Hester is helping her daughter out now in the antique shop and showroom, for which Imogen is most grateful. Summer is, of course, her busiest time, and there is a great deal of work for one person. Hester at least is able to show customers around, thus freeing Imogen to travel across the country on her necessary purchasing expeditions, and to go through the massive amount of paperwork and correspondence that always seems to be piling up. Hester has been frantically, but enjoyably, learning about the stock from Imogen and Gérard, and from various books she has found in the house. She feels more at ease with the customers once she is able to knowledgeably discuss the pieces.

Colette and Luc came for lunch, and then on another occasion with Gérard for dinner, when Hester, tongue-in-cheek, cooked a steak and kidney pie. In return she has visited the French couple's home, and an easy friendship has developed between all of them.

The young poet and translator has read Hester's work and is rapturous about it; with her permission, he has begun work on the poems and his own publisher is interested in the completed translation. Hester finds all this very exciting; it is the first time she has been translated into another language. She looks forward to meeting the young man, whose name is Valéry Baye, but he is in Paris at the moment. Colette says he is coming to stay with them some time this summer and would like to collaborate with Hester: being a poet himself, he understands how delicate these matters of translation are.

Hester sees Colette often. On market day in Pont-Aven she frequently buys her vegetables there, always stopping to take coffee with Colette and Luc at their gallery. Sometimes Colette goes for a stroll around the town with her while Luc stays behind to deal with customers, or if the day is fine they sit by the river and talk. Hester finds the older woman easy company, for she is intelligent but gentle, kind but never cloying. Colette has an inquisitive attitude toward life; even now, in her seventies, she is still interested in new ideas, new experiences. And yet she is not restless; in the centre of her exuberance is a steady calm that Hester finds soothing.

Hester is also thoroughly enjoying the company of Gérard Dupont. Though she may not feel the vibrant tingling of every nerve-ending that she felt when she was passionately in love with Alex; she is old enough and wise enough to recognize that for the madness it was. Now, through the Frenchman, she is seeing life as something enjoyable, pleasurable. Gérard knows a great deal about antiques and his loving lessons on the subject are both fun and helpful; Hester is starting to feel quite confident as

Imogen's assistant. Together they visit antique shops, go to house sales, and drive miles in the pleasant countryside looking for the odd bargain.

Gérard buys an antique if it is beautiful, and if he falls in love with it. He never bargains but accepts the going price, and if he cannot fit the piece in his own house or restaurant, he offers it to one of his many friends or acquaintances at the same price he paid for it. He loves old things, old and beautiful hand-made things; sometimes Hester observes him looking at a cherrywood table for a half-hour, touching it lightly, meditating on it. His enthusiasm makes these outings sheer joy for Hester, and of course he also helps her to choose with a practised eye the best bargains for Imogen's shop.

Hester and Gérard see each other once or twice a week and it suits them both. She is busy, and he has his restaurant. They make love when they can and enjoy it; Hester has stopped herself wanting something more, from longing for the sublime.

Alex has not phoned her. This troubles Hester more than she likes to admit. It plays on her mind like an old, sad tune, a melody she cannot get out of her head. Was their reunion, she thinks, of such little importance to him that already it has receded from his mind and his heart like the sea when the tide ebbs? It distresses her, to think it may be so, but she reminds herself that it was she who let Alex go, and, more recently, she who backed away from the friendship he seemed to be offering.

She has received a postcard from him, from Kerrocher, thanking her and Imogen for letting him stay the night, and saying how much he enjoyed his day in Concarneau with Hester. He says he will be in touch, and asks Hester not to return to England without planning a stay at his house. Then he says he will phone her when he winds up some business that is occupying him at the moment.

But he doesn't phone. The weeks pass, and he doesn't phone. Hester tries to tell herself it doesn't matter, but to her dismay it does, it does. And so she struggles, trying to put her old lover into some kind of perspective. It helps that her days are full, crowded; it helps to have Gérard. She tells herself that life should be sweet in this blissfully hot summer, that the sharp acid tang of a hopeless regret is out of place, an anachronism. But it seeps into her days, it erodes her nights, when her restless dreams are all of loss, of partings, of tears.

Summer escalates; the high-tourist season begins, visitors to the little village multiply each week. Although the antique showroom is not theoretically a shop for tourists, people on holiday are always ready to pick up what they think is a bargain: an exquisite bit of porcelain, an old cut-glass vase, a nineteenth-century embroidered panel. Hester finds she has a knack of dealing with the customers; she is helpful but not overpowering, accommodating without being unctuous. The days are indeed busy, but she seems to thrive on it, finding she still has so much energy left in the long summer evenings that she can return to her poetry, especially when Imogen is with Bruno and the house is still and quiet.

Hester hardly goes to Pont-Aven these days because the town has altered beyond recognition. As July passes and August begins there is hardly a French person in sight in this famous town of the painters; there are Germans, English, Belgians, Dutch, Japanese, Americans and a spattering of nearly every other nationality, but the French keep well away. It is so crowded one often cannot walk along the pavements but must risk life and limb dodging the many cars going down the main street through town. And now it is Colette who mostly visits Hester in the quieter village of Pont-Plouay: the two women sit in the garden listening to the blackbird which still delights Hester with its indefatigable singing.

'It goes well, do you not think?' Colette says to Hester on one of these days. She has brought a selection of Gérard's delicious pâtés for their lunch, as well as three or four different salads of every variety and content: *cous-cous* with tomatoes and chives and shrimps; mushrooms in a delicately herbed sauce; pasta with avocado and fresh mayonnaise. 'The children, I am talking about.'

They are alone in the garden. Imogen is having her lunch at Bruno's house in the village, the shutters conveniently drawn against the hot sun as the lovers take advantage of the long French midday break.

'Yes, it seems to be going very well,' Hester replies. 'Imogen is with Bruno now, I believe.'

Colette smiles indulgently. 'Yes. I stopped by his house just now with a small painting of his father's which he wanted for his waiting room, but the shutters were tightly closed even though his car was outside. I did not even knock; I shall see him another time.'

Hester thinks about Gérard, wondering if she would forego this delicious lunch to romp with him deliriously under the sheets, as obviously Imogen and Bruno are doing. She decides probably not: even though the sex has continued to be very good indeed.

'It's all to do with being young,' she muses out loud. 'Right at this moment I'd rather be in the garden eating pâté, listening to the blackbird.'

'No, *ma chérie*, it's all to do with love. You do not love Gérard, that is why you prefer the pâté at lunch.'

Hester feels discomfited. This is after all one of Gérard's loyal friends, and she does not want Colette to think she is treating him lightly. So she says, 'I do not love him, you are right, Colette. But I am fond of him. I treasure him – do you understand?'

'Of course, Hester, and that was by no means a criticism, my observation. You are two adults who take great pleasure in each other's company. That is all, and it is quite sufficient if you both agree that it is what you want.'

Perhaps it is the wine, perhaps it is the sun, perhaps it is Colette herself dressed all in white, thin loose cotton trousers and layers of flimsy silky stuff draped kaftan-style over the trousers, Colette with the beautiful skin that the fine baby wrinkles only seem to enhance, Colette with the plump lips and the harvest-gathering smile. Whatever it is, Hester finds herself saying words that come straight from her heart. 'No, Colette. That's the trouble – it *isn't* sufficient. I thought it was. I thought it would be, but I keep remembering how it was when, like Bruno and Imogen, I burned to be with the person I loved, when every cell in my body ached for him, when satiation was never reached because the more I was with him, the more I wanted to be with him forever . . .'

Colette nods. 'The man in Le Café de la Mer, *n'est-ce pas?*'

'Yes. I had an affair with him for five years and I loved him beyond description.'

And then Hester tells her. For the first time ever she talks to someone about Alex – about their affair and how it began, about their three weeks in France . . . about Angela and her threats – and finally, about the two letters she wrote him, letters which finished their affair irrevocably. The only thing she does not mention is that she has met Alex again, that he is at this moment only a three-hour drive away in the same house where they loved so frantically for such a very short time.

'This wife of his, this Angela,' Colette says finally, 'did she do what she wanted, make a life again with her husband?'

'No. She tried – even went to see him in France.' Alex had told Hester this on their day out in Concarneau. 'He made her finally understand that their marriage was over, that he was not returning to England. He stayed in France, you see.' Because of my letters, Hester thinks sadly. Because he said he could not face England without me.

Colette says, 'His wife, she was very distressed?'

'Mostly angry. She liked being married – it was cosy, secure. Her house and possessions meant a great deal to her, and she didn't like the idea of splitting it all up. And when she and Alex had that first separation, she found out that there weren't many people around who would put up with her moods the way he did.'

'She was difficult, then?'

'Yes, very. I know, I worked in the same college with her for years.'

'So they parted for good?'

'Yes. Finally.'

They are quiet for a short time, thinking their own thoughts. The garden is still except for the humming of bees, a sudden birdsong. After a time Colette says, 'Did you not ever think of leaving your husband? Staying with your lover?'

'A thousand times. Constantly. Alex wanted me to, of course. He wanted me never to go back to England. But I couldn't do it, couldn't hurt Martin. He was a good man, you see. Or so everyone said.'

The last sentence froths out uncontrollably with the bubbles in the sparkling wine they are drinking; it surprises Hester more than it does Colette. She finds herself continuing, 'It's not easy, living with a good man, a perfect man. Martin always did the right thing, always ingratiated himself with everyone. Maybe you have to do that if you are a headmaster in England.'

Colette smiles. 'I never did understand your educational system.'

'He knew how to please everyone, did Martin. He always reasoned with his students before doling out punishment, and with their parents he was so understanding that it bordered on insincerity.' Hester sighs, remembering, then goes on: 'He was perfect with his staff, too – always reasonable, always polite. He never demanded, always asked. The school was, he liked to say, run democratically.'

'And yet, what was wrong, Hester?'

'You realize this bubbly stuff is going to my head, Colette? I have never spoken of this to anyone, except perhaps to Alex, but the fact of the matter is, this gentle, liberal "good" man had the makings of a tyrant at home. Perhaps he needed to be, perhaps this was his safety valve.'

'But you suffered for it.'

'We all suffered. Oh, suffering is the wrong word . . . it was just sometimes stifling, you know? Never being able to tell him he was wrong about something because he would lose his temper or worse, sulk for hours. Never having a say in the running of the house, the family . . .'

'That is difficult.'

'The thing is, you could never win because later, as he got

older, he was not a well man, you see. He made the most of his illnesses: when the girls or I tried to get our own way in anything, he would take a turn for the worse. Then we would become frightened, and feel guilty, and back down.' Hester smiles wryly. 'Or I would. The girls had more stamina than me. Or more to lose, perhaps.'

Hester closes her eyes in the sun, remembering how, when Abigail was around twelve, she wanted to take her younger daughter to London for the half-term. Imogen had actually invited all three of them – Hester, Martin and Abigail. She had just moved into a new flat, with a new boyfriend, and wanted to show them both off. She was twenty-two.

Martin flatly refused to go, as Hester thought he would. He had only visited his daughter once in London and the visit was not a success. Martin was sullen and disapproving, Imogen volatile and angry. So Hester made plans to go with Abigail, who was immensely looking forward to it.

Martin was against it, but Hester planned to go regardless. 'Go if you must,' he said several days before half-term, 'but I don't want you to take Abigail.'

'Martin, it'll do her the world of good, *and* Imogen. God knows there has been enough acrimony, enough misunderstanding, between them—'

'That's nothing to do with us, Hester. More importantly, what about this boy?'

'Martin, what are you talking about?'

'This young man with whom Imogen is now living.'

'He's quite nice, actually, as I told you. I met him the last time I visited Imo.'

'But they weren't living together then.'

'No, but—'

'I'm not having Abigail stay at that flat, she's still a child.'

'Oh Martin, how can you be so old-fashioned?' Hester wailed. 'So they are living together! Would you rather they got married?'

'God forbid, a rock musician? No, of course I wouldn't. What I object to is Abigail staying there, imbibing their values, their lifestyle – that of a fashion model and a rock star. I want at least one of my daughters to aspire to higher than that.'

Hester was so incensed she had walked out of the room. For two days Martin did not speak to either of them, much to Abigail's confusion. Then, the night before they were to catch their train, he had such an acute attack of sciatica that the doctor had to be called in to administer an injection. Martin, his saintly face even more pallid, writhed and groaned on the sofa all night, unable even to walk upstairs to his bed. In spite of the injection, as well as the tablets that the doctor had left, he was in such pain he passed out whilst trying to get to the bathroom.

Of course Hester couldn't leave him. She and Abigail cancelled their train reservations and spent the entire half-term ministering to him: Abigail playing concertos and serenades to soothe him, and Hester constantly on the telephone fending off Imogen who was vowing never to speak to her father again. Abigail, intercepting one of these phone calls, said loftily to her sister, 'You have no sympathy, Imo, no compassion, carrying on against Dad that way. He's really in a lot of pain, and I need to be here to look after him, not running around London with you. Mum was right to put off our visit, so stop moaning to her about it.'

Overhearing this, Martin said to Abigail: 'You are my angel, Abby. What would I do without you? Come now and play me that Mozart piece you've been working on.'

Hester, despairing, found refuge with Alex, for their affair was just beginning. Then Imogen, in a surprise turn of heart, sent her father several huge bouquets of hothouse flowers, three or four hardback books by the latest literary giants, and a short note wishing him well.

'How thoughtful!' Martin cried, and in turn wrote her a loving, forgiving letter saying he wished she would abandon London and come home, he missed and needed her. Imogen, gleeful, phoned home and read the letter to Abigail. All in all it was a horrid week, and the memory still sears Hester even now.

She shakes her head despondently, looking at Colette, so

elegant and cool under the shade of the apple tree. 'I don't know why I am telling you all this. Martin had his faults, but he was . . .' She falters.

'He was a good man,' Colette says sardonically.

'Oh yes, that's the trouble, everyone kept telling me what a good man he was, how lucky I was. He was generous, he was always buying the girls and me presents. He did charity work, and never grudgingly; and he opened the gloomy old house and gardens to the village two or three times a year for Church fêtes and bazaars. Those who knew him through school – he hadn't any friends outside his profession – found him kind and thoughtful.'

'And yet he was not so good in the family, it seems.'

'No.' Hester closes her eyes for a moment. When she opens them she says, 'Perhaps he was too old when he had children. He was almost twenty years older than me, you know, and resigned to being without a family. When Imo arrived, and later Abby, he couldn't seem to separate himself from them: they were his, he had waited a long time for them.'

Colette nods sympathetically. 'I can understand how that can be. Luc and I were in our forties when we had Bruno, and we had to teach ourselves not to be possessive, not to suffocate him. If anything, I sometimes think we erred the other way, giving him too much independence.'

Hester smiles. 'It hasn't harmed him, if that is so.'

'But to return to your husband: did you love him, Hester?'

'Yes, I did once. That is, I thought so. Until I met Alex. And even then, I remained fond of Martin. I knew in spite of his petty tyrannies that he didn't mean to be cruel. Worse, I knew he loved me.'

'Worse?'

'Oh Colette, how do you leave someone who loves you? How?'

Colette is quiet. 'You don't, of course.'

Something in the way she says this makes Hester look at her sharply. But Colette's plump lips are pressed very firmly together; she is miles away and not about to disclose what she is thinking, though of course Hester speculates. She wonders if Colette too loved someone once, and if he was as lively and appealing as her husband Luc, with his bright manic scarves and boldly-coloured Italian shoes and deep, gloomy subterranean paintings. That Luc and Colette still love each other is obvious, whatever happened in some distant past; and Hester is glad that they are together, still enriching the lives of those who know them.

And then, Gordon comes back. One Tuesday in the early evening Hester returns from a day out with Gérard to find her son-in-law in the garden with Imogen. He is seated calmly on one of the chairs but Imogen is obviously distraught; she is walking round and round the little courtyard like a demented seagull searching for scraps from a picnic lunch.

'Gordon, you here?' Hester says. 'Where is Abigail?'

Her words are greeted in silence. Gordon looks uncomfortable, Imogen distracted and angry.

'I'm intruding, I'm sorry,' Hester says. 'I'll leave you.'

She starts to go inside the house but Imogen stops her. 'Please stay, Mum. I want you to hear this. I don't believe it, I really don't.'

Tentatively Hester walks into the garden and sits down on the edge of the other chair. She's not sure she can face this without a cup of tea or, better still, a stiff brandy, but she resignedly waits to give it a try.

Still no one speaks so she says, 'What exactly is going on, then? What is it you want me to hear, Imogen? And Gordon – I take it Abigail is not with you?'

Gordon flashes Hester his instant smile, then kisses her on the cheek. Bastard, thinks Hester. 'Hello, Mother,' he says audaciously. 'You're looking well, better than I've ever seen you. France obviously suits you.' He says this with apparent sincerity.

Hester, though loathing as usual his use of the word 'Mother' (sure that he does it maliciously), has to admit the scabious charmer has got his act together beautifully. He is so smooth you can almost believe him. Almost. Hester has known him too long to give him any benefit of the doubt now.

'How lucky for Imogen that you're here,' he says earnestly. Hester has forgotten how handsome he can be when he sets his mind to it – all that curly fair hair and glossy teeth. And he has obviously set his mind to it: he's shaved off his moustache and looks clean-cut and golden with a new tan and dazzling white shorts.

Hester ignores his remark and he continues, 'I've been worried about Imogen, you know.'

This is just too much. 'Oh come now, Gordon – you bloody well ran off with her sister,' Hester says snappishly.

Gordon remains unperturbed. 'Do you think I don't know what a fool I've been? It was the biggest mistake I've ever made. I've already told Imogen how much I regret it, how sorry I am.'

Imogen looks at her mother with not a little despair. 'Mum, you won't credit this, but he actually believes that he's coming back to me!'

There is an ominous silence as Hester struggles with this new shock. Then she gathers her wits and hisses, 'For God's sake, Gordon! Do you think that's all it takes, a brief apology and you can undo all you've done to both my daughters?'

Imogen is obviously distressed. 'I've told him it's just not on. He's mad to even think of it!'

'And I've told her that if we just talk this over rationally, like two sensible adults, we can work it out.'

'God, Gordon, you're mad!' Imogen explodes.

Hester sees that she is beginning to lose her temper, something she has not done for weeks. She interjects quickly, 'Aren't you forgetting something, Gordon? It's not just for you and Imogen to discuss. I'm sure Abigail must have something to say about all this. Where is she, anyway? Why isn't she here?'

'She's at the house where we've been staying, perfectly happy. She's sent you a note, I left it inside on the kitchen table.'

'Perfectly happy!' Now it is Hester who explodes.

'Gordon, are you completely insane? You've fornicated with her, torn her away from her family, run off with her then abandoned her, and you say she is perfectly happy?'

At this Gordon has the grace to look sheepish, though on him, Hester thinks, it looks suspiciously sly. 'Well . . . the fact is, she doesn't know. I haven't told her yet.'

'Haven't told her what, for God's sake?'

'That I, um, want to make a go of my marriage.'

Imogen stares at him. 'For fuck's sake, Gordon, you shit,' she whispers, almost unable to speak with the rage she is feeling. 'You bloody sod, how I ever married you—'

'Gordon, let me get this very clear. You have asked Imogen to take you back, yet you have not informed Abigail of this rather important bit of news. Is this correct?'

Gordon is actually sweating; he's got up out of the chair and is pacing about like a rat in a cage. 'You don't understand. Just stay calm and listen. Please, will both of you just listen? Abigail knows I am here, she knows I need to see about the business—'

'It's running better than ever without you, it always has.'

'And we have to talk, Imo. For Christ's sake, eventually we have to sit down and talk seriously. I told Abigail I needed to see you and settle things, and she understood.'

'I see,' Hester says through clenched teeth. She really would like to hit this man. 'You didn't tell Abigail the truth because you wanted to keep your options open. If Imogen refused to have you, you could go merrily back to the other sister without having burned any of your bridges.'

This is so obviously the truth that Gordon is silent for a few moments, desperately casting around for what to say next. 'I was only thinking of Abigail,' he finally manages. And then, gaining confidence, 'I wanted to break it to her gently, after I had talked to Imogen.'

'Gordon,' Imogen begins warningly, but he is back on form now and interrupts her with glib assurance.

'I'll talk to Abigail as soon as I get back, convince her that this is all for the best. She's an understanding person, she'll soon accept that it's right for Imogen and me to get back together again. I'm sure she'll come around to wishing us well.'

There is a stunned silence. Finally Hester manages to say, 'Gordon, you pratt. You utter and complete pratt.'

She is so angry and upset at her son-in-law's mendacity, that she storms down to the bottom of the garden for a few minutes to restore some equilibrium. Above the sweet beauty of birdsong and the cooing of doves she can hear Gordon's voice droning away at Imogen.

'I'm sorry, Imo, I've made a fine mess of things.'

'I don't want to hear any more, Gordon.'

'I'm not all to blame, you know. You haven't had much time for anything other than the business since we moved here.'

'You never minded before. You were glad I worked non-stop so that you had time to play.'

'You were quite happy to play, in the early days in London.'

'I grew up, Gordon. There comes a time when you have to start being at least a little responsible.'

'Come on, Imo, you're starting to sound pompous.'

'Besides, whatever I did, I made sure my business didn't go under. Which is more than you did.'

'Does it matter? We've got one even better, more lucrative, set up here.'

Imogen stares at him distastefully. 'That's just like you, isn't it? You make a fucking mess of things, and who cares how many others you bloody ruin along the way. There's always someone like me around to set things right again. Or there *was*, Gordon. Not any longer.'

He is ready with an angry retort but suddenly checks himself. Going up to Imogen he puts a tentative arm around her, saying softly, 'Let's not squabble, darling. We've done too much of this kind of bickering over the years. Whatever's happened, I've never stopped loving you, you know.'

Imogen walks away from him. 'Gordon,' she says wearily, 'no more. It's far too late for that.'

He follows her. 'It was all a stupid mistake. How many times do I have to say I'm sorry?'

'My sister, Gordon – did it have to be my sister? Couldn't you have had just a bit more sensitivity than that?'

'She was just there, Imo—'

'That's enough now. Please shut up.'

'It was just – it wasn't important.'

'Oh God. Have you told that to Abby?'

'I had no intention of leaving you, Imo. I never wanted our marriage to break up, I didn't mean—'

'You didn't mean to be caught out, that's all,' Imogen snaps.

'Oh, for Christ's sake!'

'How nice, how convenient it would have been for you, had things gone the way you meant them to. Why, you could have lived happily ever after, bonking my sister and enjoying the luxuries provided with my money.'

'*Our* money, Imogen.' Gordon's face has hardened.

'No, Gordon, not quite. The money *I* earn while *you* fuck Abigail on the Blessed Shrine of Sainte Barbe.'

'You bitch.' Gordon steps quickly towards Imogen, his hand raised as if he is about to hit her. But Hester, aware of the mounting anger and tension has, unnoticed by the other two, walked back up the garden and now stands squarely in front of her son-in-law.

'Imogen has made it perfectly clear how she feels, Gordon,' she says firmly. 'I think you should go now.'

He looks coldly at them both. 'No, Hester, I'm afraid I'm not going. I'm not leaving until Imogen and I have got something settled. This is, after all, my house and my business.'

'Wrong, Gordon,' Imogen says. 'This is half your house and half your business. You wouldn't even have that if I hadn't paid off all your debts.'

'That's history, Imo,' he retorts curtly. 'I'm interested in *now*. If you think you're getting this house—'

'It was bought with my money. So was the business.'

'Nonetheless they are still also in my name. Nothing you can say or do will alter that.' He looks at her calculatingly. 'We'd both do better to stay together,' he says softly.

Imogen, also softly, replies, 'You're a devious, scheming bastard, and if I lost every penny I've ever earned I would accept it gladly to be rid of you.'

They look at each other; then away. And so it ends, Hester thinks sadly. All those years of living together, being married – only to end like this.

Imogen breaks the silence. 'I've already discussed all this with our *notaire* in Pont-Aven,' she says dully. 'I'm prepared to buy you out of the business for a very generous price. I'm also prepared to be more than fair in making you an offer for your half of the house.'

Gordon, rallying, says, 'I might want this house myself, as a matter of fact.'

'Too bad. You left.'

'I'm back now.'

'You can't come back.'

'I already have, and I'm not going again.'

'Just get out of here, Gordon.'

'Why should I go just to please you?' He smiles nastily. 'I don't feel like pleasing you right at the moment, Imogen.'

'Get out.'

'Go to hell. You can't throw me out of my own house.'

'I can, Gordon. If you choose to fight me, I'll win. You were the one who left *me*, remember? I'm the injured party, I'm the innocent one. Don't you ever forget that.'

They stand face to face, the years' injuries, both real and imagined, swarming around them like vindictive wasps. And then, as happens every evening at this time, there is a roar of a Citroën screeching to a stop outside the house, and in comes Bruno, sunglasses securely in place, jeans squeaky clean and faded and clinging erotically to his crotch, his dark hair gleaming and almost touching the shoulders of his black cotton shirt.

'*Bonsoir*,' he says breezily, before he stops and takes in exactly who is there.

There is an audible groan from Hester. There goes Imogen's innocence, her status as injured party, she is thinking frantically, blown right out over the trees and disintegrating into the balmy French skies. For if Gordon even suspects Imo's relationship with the doctor he will use it to his advantage, accusing his wife of fornicating with Bruno long before he himself bedded Abigail.

There is a frozen moment while Imogen looks panicked, Gordon dumb, and Bruno, the situation dawning, incredibly fierce. But before Bruno can rush to Imogen and stake his claim on her, Hester cries, 'Oh, thank God you've come, Bruno,' and falls to the grass in what is not quite a dishonest swoon because she is indeed beginning to feel quite shaky.

As everyone rushes to her she says, groggily but loud enough for everyone to hear plainly, 'Thank God Imogen called you out for me, Dr Lambert. I was in Pont-Aven but had to phone to my daughter that I was coming home. I have had this headache, you see, and today such dizzy spells . . .' Hester trails off in a not-entirely simulated collapse.

Imogen understands, and falls right into it, exclaiming dramatically how worried she's been about her mother's health, and how kind Bruno is to come like this, before his supper even, and isn't it comforting to know that the doctors in France still come out to visit at a moment's notice. As she waffles, she and Hester are watching Bruno anxiously, Hester through half-closed lids, wondering if he will get the rather blatant message.

Suddenly, to their great relief, he does. 'Madame,' he says to Hester in his best doctor's voice, 'you are lucky I am on call. I came at once. Now let me take your pulse.'

Hester slumps back in a more genuine collapse this time, being so relieved she actually does feel quite weak. She wonders fleetingly if Gordon has noticed Bruno is not carrying his medical bag, but Gordon is too angry to notice anything. Without saying another word he tears out of the house, knocking over a kitchen chair in his furious exit. Hester holds her breath until, mercifully, she hears his car door slam and the angry screeching of his tyres as he roars off down the hill.

'Now,' says Bruno, taking off his sunglasses. 'What exactly is going on? Are you really ill, Hester? I think not.'

Hester opens her eyes cautiously. Bruno is looking at her sternly, and she thinks irreverently what lovely eyes he has, rather vulnerable and innocent, not in the least like a rock star's. She wonders if that's why he always wears sunglasses.

Imogen is standing over them, and before Hester can answer she too sits down on the grass and hugs her mother impulsively. 'Oh Mum, you are a genius. What a performance!'

And then she begins to laugh shakily, perhaps a trifle hysterically, but laughter it is, and then Hester joins in because she too is an emotional wreck after that scene with Gordon and she'd much rather laugh right now than burst into tears.

And Bruno, dear wonderful Bruno. He doesn't ask for explanations, not then, not yet: he throws back his gorgeous dark head and laughs with them. Because that's the kind of person he is, Hester thinks – like his parents, willing to find the fun and the laughter in the most trying situations.

Hester, suddenly, decides she could love this young man. In her heart in the midst of her laughter, she gives him silently, with all her blessings, to her daughter.

Chapter Thirteen

Hester, Imogen and Bruno, collapsed in the grass under the apple tree, giggly and weak with laughter, do not at first notice that there is another visitor in their idyllic garden. Hester looks up suddenly to see something black and predatory flapping over her, and for one distorted moment she thinks it is the blackbird grown like Alice in Wonderland, hopping under the trees like a blown-up raven.

The beak of this great crow is opening and shutting in amazement, and some odd croaks come out of it. It is not a beak, of course, but the pointy mouth of the priest, Father Bonté, who is standing like Sin itself, murky and dark, in the middle of the courtyard.

The three fractious children, for this is how they feel, abruptly stop their laughter and get up quickly. Since the incident at the Blessed Shrine of Sainte Barbe, the good priest has been a frequent visitor to this house. He seems to have taken Imogen's plight to heart and made her an honorary member of his flock. Besides, he likes her coffee.

Rather agitatedly now, he says to Imogen, 'Madame, was that not your husband I just saw in the car leaving your house? He has returned?'

'He tried,' Imogen says shortly. 'He had the nerve to say he wants to come back to me.'

Bruno swears. He wishes he had known this when Gordon was still there; he'd have shown that preposterous arrogant swine exactly who was now the only man in Imogen's life.

'But my dear Imogen!' the priest exclaims joyously. 'It is a miracle! Your husband has given up his sin and desires to return to the fold of Holy Matrimony.'

Bruno swears again, under his breath so the priest doesn't hear, and puts on his sunglasses, the better to brood and glower, Hester supposes. Poor lad, she thinks, it must be a shock to know Gordon has been trying to worm his way back into Imogen's affections.

Imogen says, 'I sent him straight away, of course. Told him I never wanted to see him again.'

Bruno breaks into radiant smiles and kisses her possessively while the priest nearly has apoplexy. 'You what?' he shouts. 'Have I lost my hearing, have I lost my wits? You refused your husband?'

Imogen is taken aback. 'Why yes, of course I did.'

'You are sending him back into sin?'

'I only—'

'But you are dishonouring the sacred bonds of marriage!'

'Me? No. No!'

'Tell me it is not true. Bruno, tell me at once, quickly.'

Bruno looks discomfited but says, '*C'est vrai, Monsieur le Curé*. It is entirely true.'

The priest flaps his arms, hits his forehead with both hands, and points a shaky claw-like finger at Imogen, who scurries to Bruno for protection. 'God will punish you, Madame,' he roars, his voice awesome with righteous fury. 'I swear by the Shrine of the Blessed Sainte Barbe, God will have His vengeance.'

Everyone freezes at these words, too stunned to react. Wildly the good father circles the garden, gesticulating ominously, spouting a torrent of words that neither Imogen nor her mother can understand.

Hester is glad Bruno is here. The priest is red-faced and trembling, and his eyes seem to blend into one accusing torch in his anger: he looks quite intimidating. His voice, loud and strident, is gaining both volume and strength as he warms to his subject.

'*Monsieur le Curé*,' Bruno says suddenly. 'Perhaps you should not say these things.'

The priest ignores him and carries on in his unique blend of Breton and archaic French, shouting at Bruno now. On second thoughts, Hester reflects, perhaps Bruno's presence is not a good thing; the young man is scowling, listening to the priest who is obviously reviling Imogen.

'Père Bonté,' the young doctor interrupts again. 'I'm afraid I must ask you to stop this abuse—'

The priest takes no notice. Bruno's fists clench, his mouth sets like concrete, he takes off his sunglasses. Hester begins to worry: if the priest goes on like this, Bruno might flatten him. She wonders whether she ought to faint again, especially as Bruno now is shouting: '*Monsieur le Curé*! This is enough!'

Suddenly, there is a rustle of graceful silk and a waft of exquisite perfume and like a miracle in walks Colette. 'Ah, my friends! Here you all are, and together, too – how fortunate for me.'

The priest, cut off in mid-torrent, is immobile as stone, staring at this beautiful vision who is going from person to person and kissing them four times, twice on each cheek as is the Breton way.

When she gets to the priest she says, in her gentle warm voice which reminds the Father of the sea breezes when he was a boy growing up near Carnac, 'Ah, *Monsieur le Curé*, I have long been wanting to meet you. My son is one of your flock and speaks highly of you. I have never had the good fortune to attend one of your Masses, even though we live such a short distance away.' She introduces herself and shakes his hand warmly, and he is lost, entranced; his anger disappears like dirty bath-water down a drain and he is clean, emptied, ready to be enchanted by this lovely apparition in opalescent silk.

'Ah, Madame Lambert, of course I know your son the doctor very well, a credit to our small village. And of course I know you through your wonderful paintings, and your husband's also . . .'

He splutters on in this vein for rather a long time but no one minds. Colette is naturally sympathetic and interested in people and listens intently; Imogen and Hester are so relieved they collapse into the chairs as limp as dead spaghetti. When there is a lull in the priest's monologue Colette says, 'Now listen, everyone, I have come to collect you in my car and take you to a most magnificent ancient château near the sea, not very far from here. Luc has already gone ahead with a picnic meal and Champagne; there is to be music in the castle grounds, a festival of some sort, and you must all come with us.'

She turns her full smile on to the priest and cries, 'And you, *mon père*, must join us – I insist! My husband, I know, will be delighted to meet you. The music is reputed to be excellent, some vocal works by Bach and Handel, and some Scarlatti with, I believe, a Telemann cantata.'

She takes his arm and slowly guides him, a man temporarily blinded by her sunlight, out of the garden and into the car. Like acolytes the others follow meekly, and gratefully, behind.

The next day, Imogen and Hester try to decide what to do about Abigail. 'We should tell her, Mum,' Imogen says. 'Gordon never will. She should know exactly how devious he is.'

'I'm not so sure, Imo. For a start, she probably won't believe us. She's totally infatuated with him, and you know how convincing he can be when he puts on the charm. He'll just say we've made it all up to divide them.'

'What about the letter – didn't Gordon say he had a letter for you, from Abigail?'

'Yes, I found it in the kitchen after he left. She didn't write much, just that she's sorry she hurt so many people, but she and Gordon have been in love for ages—'

'Huh!'

'—And that one day you'll forgive her.'

'Never. She must be mad if she thinks I'll ever forgive or forget this sordid episode.'

In the end Hester persuades Imogen that it is pointless to write to Abigail about Gordon. By now he will have twisted the story so expertly to suit himself that Abigail would only think Imogen was being vindictive if she wrote. Hester thinks they should both remain silent until they can see Abigail again, and finally Imogen agrees, though not gracefully. Hester wonders about Imogen's motives in wanting to tell Abby, whether it is to genuinely warn her against Gordon, or whether there is some spite there, an understandable desire to get a little of her own back over this whole unfortunate affair. That old sibling rivalry creeping over everything like mould in damp cellars, Hester thinks gloomily.

She grows pensive, thinking about Abigail and Imogen, about their relationship with Martin. Since Abigail went off with Gordon, Hester has had to confront many old memories which she had obliterated from her consciousness, of the girls, of their difficult relationship with each other, but mostly memories of Martin, of how, in the name of love, he compounded the rivalry and exacerbated it . . .

It became quite noticeably worse when Imogen, having got her way despite her father, had gone to London and achieved almost overnight the success for which she craved. Soon, her face was on the cover of almost every glossy magazine in England. Yet success wasn't enough: perversely, Imogen now tried to secure her father's approval, but in vain. He had been her first love, before her younger sister was born, and though she tried to tell herself now that he was a pompous, intolerant and silly old man, something in her secretly longed for his praise, for his favour.

'Can't he once, just once, say I've done well?' Imogen, in an unguarded moment, cried to Hester. 'I'm one of the top models in the business, I'm good at what I do, conscientious at my job, and everyone recognizes it, respects me for it – except him! Can't he ever, even once, give me credit for anything?'

Repeating this to Martin, Hester said, 'Haven't you made your point, Martin? About how Imogen has failed you? Isn't it time you recognized that she wanted to live *her* life, not yours, and that she has done it extremely well, far better than anyone anticipated?'

'Her life is comprised of glitter and glamour, tinsel,' Martin replied. 'She chose it, and that's her affair. I'm certainly not going to give her my blessing, not now, not ever.'

Failing to win her father's approval, Imogen then sought his attention with pointless acts of rebellion, such as threatening to pose nude for a national magazine or, on another occasion, packing her bags to run off to the West Indies (when she was seventeen) with a cricketer she had met only once at a party. There were various other episodes also, and although Imogen never actually carried out any of her threats, she came close enough to cause complete turmoil in the household, thus assuring herself that she wasn't forgotten.

When not in a rage over each new bizarre scheme of Imogen's, Martin tried to ignore the fact that he had an older daughter and turned to Abigail.

It was no easier for this second child, this quiet meek girl with the blazing ginger hair and the docile blue eyes. Although her father apparently doted on her, as he had on Imogen so long ago, he never seemed to forget his older daughter, never stopped making comparisons.

'Abby, your handwriting is atrocious,' he would say. 'Look at these old exercise books of your sister's when she was your age and try to copy her writing – it's exquisite.'

Or: 'Only a "C+" for your history project, Abby? I expect you to get straight "A's" in history, like your sister did. After all, it's my subject.'

Sometimes Abby would rebel, though not often. 'I'm not Imo, I'm *me*,' she once said petulantly.

'And thank God you are,' Martin replied smoothly. 'I'm relying on you not to waste your life like Imogen is doing, not to disappoint me like she did. I had such hopes for her, I was so proud of her as a child. I thought she'd go on to university, follow some worthwhile career – all pipe-dreams, I'm afraid.'

And so, though basking throughout her sunny childhood on the warm sands of her father's affection, Abigail never quite forgot that she was number two, that her father's first surge of parental love had been for his eldest daughter. For Martin had been proud, once, of that wayward firstborn of his. In her bright sharp mind, in her fine bones, her long lanky body, he saw himself mirrored. Though his disillusionment had been rank and bitter, he couldn't help but remember nostalgically what it had been like before, when Imogen was still a child, and like most people who reminisce, the memory was somewhat oblique with wishful-thinking. And so a picture was formed in the child Abigail's mind of another child so overwhelmingly perfect in every way that it made her at first uncomfortable, then uneasy, and later discouraged. Of course she grew to resent her sister, for it never occurred to her to resent her father. He was good to her. He loved her, took her on all the same outings to the zoo, to museums, to children's theatre productions, to which he had taken Imogen. But always, try as she might to ignore it, was this shadow following behind, of a perfect child, lurking behind doors, in ice-cream vans, in the hushed darkness of a theatre before the lights went on and the clowns ran in.

It didn't help that Imogen became, with indecent swiftness, so overwhelmingly successful. By the time Abigail was an adolescent, her schoolmates were begging her to get her sister's autograph, her female friends were all having their hair cut like Imogen's, and her male friends clamoured like mad dogs to have a look at this gorgeous celebrity on her occasional visits home. Even if there had been no rivalry for their father's affection, this would have been hard to take. As it was, the rift deepened like a fissure after an earthquake, and it never, even when the girls were grown and had left home, fused again.

What a mess, Hester thinks sadly: what a woeful little mess it all was. Suddenly she longs to see Abigail, to talk to her alone, to ask her how she feels, how she sees the outcome of all this confusion. But there is no phone at the house where her daughter is living with Gordon, and Hester cannot contact her. Abigail has not rung her, and obviously does not want to talk to her mother, which saddens Hester somewhat. She realizes that Abigail will see her mother as taking sides, staying with Imogen. All her married life people have been trying to force Hester into taking sides, she thinks disconsolately. First there was Martin, wanting her to side with him against one daughter or the other; then there were Imogen and Abigail, each wanting her to stand against the other. She tried to be fair, to spread her love and loyalty equally amongst all three of them, but she knows she must often have failed.

Depressed, Hester suddenly wonders if perhaps she should leave France, go home. The great white Michaelmas daises she loves so much will be in flower, and there are many things to do in the garden as summer starts to come quietly to an end. Her cats, over-indulged by the neighbours, will no doubt have grown sleek and fat, and Simnel, her labrador who looks like a golden Easter cake, will have forgotten her, romping with all those children on her friends' sprawling farm.

And Alex hasn't rung. Though she tries not to think of that, it's there daily, enveloping her like an old forgotten scent. Hester had the postcard, but that was all, and it has been a long time since their day out together. That day preys on Hester's mind: the warmth of it, the pleasure, the peace she felt with Alex until Ermi's unexpected arrival which Hester still resents. It niggles her, a tiny splinter in the mind.

She tries to be honest, tries to face it: Alex will never be part of her life again. It was a mistake to force friendship on a relationship that was based on rapture and intensity. She cannot cope with being friends anyway; she cringes with embarrassment when she thinks how churlishly she behaved to Ermi when the tangled-haired mouse appeared to chew her way into Hester's one day with Alex.

But Ermi had every right to appear like that, Hester tells herself severely. She is Alex's partner; she has a right to seek him out, be with him, munch on his ear if that's the sort of thing he likes. She was a fool to be jealous, to lock herself in her room like a sulky child. God knows what Ermi thought of her. Alex, too, for that matter.

Oh hell, she says to herself wearily, forget it. Luckily she is seeing Gérard this evening, having a meal with him at Colette and Luc's house in Pont-Aven, then going back to his place later.

Gérard. Another problem. As Hester slowly showers and dresses she lets surface the bubbles of uncertainty that have been sitting dormantly at the bottom of her mind. Thinking about Alex has stirred them up – they threaten to fizz everywhere.

Gérard, then. On the surface everything is fine, just fine. They have been seeing each other regularly for almost three months now, and Hester likes him more and more each time they are together. He not only makes her feel attractive and sexy, he also makes her laugh, not a bad combination. Loving life, he shares this passion with Hester. So many things give him pleasure – the sea at sunset, a good *soupe de poissons*, the tinkle of Colette's long silver earrings as she lifts her head quickly to laugh. Best of all, he doesn't pressurize Hester. Whatever it is she is giving him, he seems to find it satisfying. He doesn't ask for more, he doesn't ask for the future. Now seems quite sufficient for him, just as it is for her.

But . . . Why am I becoming uneasy, Hester thinks. Why do I feel the occasional quivers, more and more often these days, that underneath the ramparts of this solid healthy relationship something is moving, shifting? She doesn't know, can't analyze it. Increasingly she wonders whether she shouldn't return home.

Luc and Colette's home is as welcoming as always, with masses of multicoloured candles in every corner, plants and interesting bits of scuplture everywhere, and paintings on every available wall space. The furniture is old, unremarkable but wonderfully comfortable, with printed shawls and mammoth scarves in variegated colours draped here and there where the upholstery has worn. They have lived here since the early days of their marriage, have taken root here like the house itself, large and rambling and digging securely into the hillside overlooking the river and harbour.

Hester has been invited to dinner, along with Gérard and another young man, a Frenchman in his late twenties with short cropped hair, a square pleasant face, and large round tortoiseshell glasses.

'Ah, Hester, at last you can meet Valéry Baye the poet and also, of course, your translator.'

Valéry shakes her hand warmly, speaks to her in impeccable English. 'I have wanted to meet you for so long, but I have been away in Paris. I am very taken with your poetry; it is expressive and lively and polished, yet so simple too in many ways. What more can I say?'

Hester smiles, pleased but embarrassed, and says that she is honoured that he is translating her work. 'I have not had the pleasure of reading your poetry,' she tells him, 'though I look forward very much to doing so.'

'I have taken the liberty of bringing some of my work for you to peruse. I hope you find it acceptable.'

'Valéry is making quite a name for himself in the literary world,' Luc says, handing her an apéritif. 'We are all very proud of him. He is my godson, you see, so I have a special interest in him.'

The conversation becomes more general and it isn't until after dinner that Valéry and Hester have a chance to talk again. From a briefcase in the hallway Valéry produces his own books, his two published collections of poetry, and begs Hester to accept them as a gift and to read them with kindness. He really is quite a nice young man, Hester thinks, terribly serious and intense, more like an academic than the poets she knows.

Valéry has several questions he would like to discuss about Hester's earlier poems from her first collection, which he is working on now. Though they have set a date for next week, when they will meet and go through the ones he has already begun to translate, Valéry is eager to clear up one or two points this evening.

'By all means we will excuse you for half an hour. Do go into the study,' Colette says. 'Luc and Gérard and I will digest our dinner companionably in the living room, listening to Mozart.'

Hester and Valéry go into the study and he takes out a notebook, showing her the translations of two of her poems. She likes his work; it is lyrical, and though the lines are now in French the rhythm is still her rhythm, the essence still her essence.

'These are good,' she tells him approvingly.

'Your poems are good! But it is in this one here, the poem about the forest, that I have a problem. You see, there are two different ways we can begin it, and to be truthful, I don't know quite which is the best way. You have a good knowledge of French, perhaps you could advise me?'

This is a very early poem, one Hester wrote after she had finished with Alex and had returned, weeks later, to the woodland near Exeter where they had so often escaped to be alone. The hurricane that had begun the night of Martin's heart attack had devastated the trees, and Hester stared with horror at the decimation around her. Returning in tears to her car, she got out her notebook and wrote a poem for the first time since she had broken off her relationship with Alex. She called it, simply, *End of the Affair*.

Guilt would have done it:
there was no need to send a cyclone,
hurtling trees around the forest
like a god demented, like one
who has lost all sense of order.

Time would have done it also:
the lack of it, the cramming of quiet
moments with muddy necessities,
the sepia water of life filling our hollows
like rain in those craters where
once trees dug fiercely into their earth.

It would have ended. There was
no need, I think, to uproot oaks
we once lay under and strew them
carelessly like confetti
across paths we walked on.

You over-reacted. There are no
paths now, no trees.
There isn't even love.

Hester closes her eyes, remembering the bitterness and despair she felt as she sat in the car at the edge of the woodlands, the trees splintered all around her, her affair with Alex splintered like the trees. She hasn't re-read the poem for years; she hasn't looked properly at that first collection since it was published, other than skimming briefly through Alex's copy when she met him on the ferry.

She leafs through it now. Nearly every poem is written for Alex though of course not all are obviously so: most are cloaked in metaphor and imagery, though some are starkly simple and swim nakedly in front of her on the white pages. Here is the poem about the dolphins she saw shimmering in the moonlight the night she left Alex in France; here is the one she wrote one early spring when she was so full of love she felt plumped up like the buds on the trees, sleek and smooth as the fat breasts of the robins.

And then she sees her very first poem about Alex, the one that was written before their affair, before they had even spoken of their growing attachment to each other. Then, they were still only colleagues, in different departments but sometimes sharing their offices to work side by side long after everyone else had gone. The poem evokes those late afternoons, the haunted quiet of the building after all the students have gone, the weariness at the end of a day's teaching, the comfort derived from a shared sympathy, a shared understanding. *'There is in the end only this,'* she wrote of that moment: Alex's hand on her shoulder and the silent echoes of the vanished students in the empty building.

Hester reads, sensing something stirring inside her: her poems are talking, telling her things she should have listened to long ago. *'There is in the end only this . . .'*

She reads on. Here is the one she wrote after the first night she and Alex made love, in the sheltered woodland with the pines overhead parting to reveal the stars slowly coming out as they lay together on the soft grass and moss:

We lay as if we were at home there,
ordinary flotsam of the forest
entwined like vines, threaded like needles
in our need of each other . . .

Hester reads and her throat contracts. So long ago, so very long ago.

Valéry is discussing the poetry, dispassionately and professionally. He has a query about the last line in the college poem, about a phrase in the forest poem. One part of her is listening, answering, helping him come to a decision; another, deeper part of herself is responding to the poems, and remembering.

That night when Gérard takes her back to his house, for she has left her car there and the two went together to Luc and Colette's place, she accepts a coffee from him but tells him she cannot stay the night.

'But why, Hester?' he asks, full of concern. 'Are you not well?'

'I'm perfectly well, my dear friend, and I am going to find this very difficult, but there are things I must say to you.'

Gérard moves to an armchair facing her, giving her his complete attention.

'I've had some very happy times with you, and I hope we can still have many more. You are a most attractive man, very sexy, and our nights have been as pleasurable and enjoyable as our days together.' Hester stops, not knowing how to go on.

'But?' says Gérard kindly. 'For of course there is a "but" in this somewhere. Just tell me honestly and plainly. Nothing is that difficult to say between friends.'

Hester looks at him gratefully. 'I shall have to say this next thing in English, I'm afraid, because the words are so important. I know you will understand.'

Gérard smiles. 'I lived several years in England, so there will be no misunderstanding between us.'

'The "but" is, my dear, that I don't love you. I like you enormously, I have a tremendous fondness and affection for you. I also have taken great pleasure in you physically. But . . .'

'But.'

'It's odd, Gérard, but shouldn't that be what love is? A great affection, combined with physical enjoyment? What more do we want?'

'What more do *you* want, Hester?' he says gently.

'I'm foolish, I know. I'm too old to long for such things as the ineffable, as the sublime. But you see, Gérard – I remember it. I remember it too well to settle for anything less, even if it means I do without.'

There is silence for a few moments. Hester looks at Gérard and he is looking away, contemplatively. After a while he says, 'I am not like you, Hester. I do not want to do without, even if it means accepting something less. Perhaps "less" is the wrong word – something different, I should say. But I understand your meaning. And I understand what you mean by love. There is only one woman I have ever felt that way about, and I still do, to this day.'

Hester looks at him compassionately. 'Yet you aren't together,' she says. 'I'm sorry.'

'She won't have me, I'm afraid. Many years ago we had a love affair but she gave me up. She was married, you see. It was entirely my fault. I was becoming too intense, too demanding. She loved her husband also, and he too was a dear friend of mine.'

'How sad.'

'That was why I so well understood your friend, Alex, at Le Café de la Mer. We were both weeping for women we had lost.'

'Where is she now, Gérard? Do you ever see her?'

Gérard suddenly smiles. 'But of course, every day if I can. She is right now with her husband Luc in their house where you have just had dinner.'

Hester stares at him, stunned. 'Colette – of course! I guessed she had a lover in her past, someone who meant a great deal to her, but she never told me it was you, even when I confided in her about Alex.'

'She would not; she is totally discreet, and you must remember that you and I were just embarking on our relationship. She would in no way have spoiled it for either of us.'

'My, my. Colette. Does Luc know?'

'We have never talked about it, but Luc is a generous, open-hearted man of great compassion and understanding.

I often suspect he knows, or at least guesses. It does not prevent us from being the best of friends.'

'How . . . how very French,' Hester says lamely.

'Perhaps. So I understand you, Hester. I understand because even today, after all these years, the magic, the sublime as you call it, is there when I look at Colette, and nothing has ever been quite like it ever since. If Luc was ever to leave her – and I am sincere in wishing him a long life because I love him too – I would ask her to have me back. Even now, even after all these years.'

They part in affection – with love, yes, and understanding – and agree to be friends, to meet for the dinners, the outings to which they have become accustomed, but it is understood that Hester will no longer share his bed. Driving back to Pont-Plouay she wonders if she will regret this, but now all she can feel is a great sense of relief that the restless uncertainty inside her has at last been stilled.

As she drives along the dark, empty road she thinks of Alex, and of those long-ago poems to him which tonight crystallized her unease over her relationship with Gérard. For in the end, as she sat over those translations with Valéry Baye, only half-listening to him, reading instead those early, primitive poems of hers, she knew that she would never in a thousand years be moved to write such poetry for Gérard.

So that's what was missing, she muses as she drives through the little village and up the hill to home: poetry. With Alex it was poetry – mystical, earthy and exalted, and though she never has it again she will remember it firmly, gratefully.

The house is quiet. Imogen, thinking her mother is staying over at Pont-Aven, is spending the night at Bruno's. Hester goes into her bedroom, opens the French doors on to the balcony, and by the light of an almost-full moon, writes the best poem she has written all summer.

It is to Alex, of course. It is a poem of remembrance.

Chapter Fourteen

August is a crowded month, and the next couple of weeks go quickly for Hester, for the shop and showroom are still inundated with people. During the rare quiet times, Hester scribbles poetry at Imogen's huge desk in the back office, or writes letters to England, to friends and neighbours, explaining that she is staying on longer than expected. The pensioner tending her garden sends her a photo of it, in all its summer splendour, with her two cats sleekly dozing under the marigolds. Clearly he is delighted that she is not yet returning and so, obviously, are the friends who have Hester's dog. They hint in their letters that the family would like to keep Simnel: the children adore him, and will be heartbroken when she comes to claim him. Hester's editor phones, and stops fretting when he hears that her new collection is near completion. And so there is nothing to prevent her from staying on, nothing to compel her to return to a future about which, for the moment, she is refusing to think.

And then, at last, Alex rings. As she answers the phone one balmy evening and hears his voice she knows that she has been waiting for this, that she has lingered in this addictive country for more than just her daughters, or the flow of her poetry, or the new friends she has made. She has stayed because of something still unresolved, still troubling her, and though she can't pinpoint exactly what this is, she knows that it has to do with Alex.

He seems tense, not wanting to talk much after the preliminary exchanges of pleasantries. 'Look, Hester,' he says, almost abruptly, 'I can't talk to you on the phone, there's too much to say. Will you come to Kerrocher this week and stay with me at my house for a few days?'

Hester says, without thinking, 'It took you long enough to phone.' She has been wounded by his silence.

She can hear a smile in his voice as he responds, 'Now who was it who locked herself in her room the last time I was there, refusing even to say goodbye?'

'I was working.'

'If you say so.' Again, that unseen smile. 'I didn't get in touch sooner because, as I told you, I had to wind up some business first. It was important to get that out of the way.'

'And now you want to see me.' She knows she sounds petulant, but can't seem to help it. Oh God, she thinks despairingly, why can't I behave like an adult? Why do old feelings that should be long dead claw at me, make it difficult for me even to talk to him now?

But Alex knows her; of course he knows her. 'Hester,' he says gently, 'will you come to see me?'

Hester thinks of the house on the sea with the sun on the stone, the house where she and Alex were lovers, and knows she cannot face it, cannot ever go there, not now. 'Alex,' she says, as gently as he did, 'I can't cope with it. I'm sorry, but I can't cope.'

'Hester—'

She cuts him off, for she can sense the tenderness in his voice, and even more than the house, she cannot cope with his affection, his understanding. 'Look,' she says briskly, 'I know this is probably an inadequacy on my part, but I don't seem to be very good at converting old lovers into dear friends. I'm sorry, but I can't seem to help it.'

'But this is ridiculous – we've *got* to talk. If you won't come to Kerrocher, I'll come to you.'

'You can't this week. Imogen has clients from England staying in the house with us and I have to help entertain them. We'd hardly see each other.'

'Oh hell, and I'm off after that to London, delivering another horse. You're definitely staying here for some time longer?'

'Yes, I'm not leaving yet. But I'm not sure it's a good idea, Alex – seeing each other again.'

'We haven't talked, Hester. Not about what happened, not about why it happened. I have to know; if nothing else, we have to talk about that.'

Knowing he is right, Hester capitulates. 'All right then, you can come here. Look, I'll phone some time after you've got back, and we'll arrange something then.'

Hester is distraught when she hangs up the telephone. She has been lulled by these calm French summer days and now Alex has upset them, churned them up like froth on the sea. She will see him once more, she tells herself, and explain what happened eight years ago: she owes him that. And then no more, she decides. She wants to return to England with some kind of peace of mind, to face a winter that she somehow knows will be bleaker than normal after this French summer.

The next couple of weeks are crammed with activity, for which Hester is thankful. She is wined and dined by Imogen's house-guests, and when they leave, she sees Gérard a couple of times. They are totally at ease now and are able to enjoy each other's company. Gérard is philosophical about Hester and though he delighted in her in his bed, and would have liked the relationship to continue, he is a romantic and understands love, and so forgives her. Besides, he has his restaurant which is receiving great acclaim these days and is busier than ever in these summer months. And of course there is Colette. Living in such close proximity he sees her daily, sometimes with Luc, sometimes alone, and though they rarely speak of the past it still lives with them, still colours their most mundane conversations.

Hester observes him with Colette sometimes and wonders how she did not see it before: the way his hand lingers on hers during the most casual conversations; the way his kiss of greeting or farewell lingers also. Hester watches Luc, too, but if he notices, he seems not to mind. The look he gives to Colette and Gérard when they are together is always one of benevolence.

From Abigail and Gordon, there is not a word. Gordon has not tried again to get in touch with Imogen, though she, through her solicitor, has begun legal proceedings. She wants a quick divorce, wishes to be free of him as soon as possible. The priest is, of course, scandalized, while Hester worries constantly about Abigail. She has written to her daughter, as tactfully and positively as she can, asking her to get in touch so they can talk, but so far there has been no reply.

Colette, a mother also, worries with Hester. One day the two women lunch together at Gérard's restaurant and Hester finds herself pouring out all her anxieties about her youngest daughter to her French friend.

'Ah, Hester, I understand only too well the worries one has with one's children. One cannot rest, cannot think properly, until one knows the youngsters are at peace. I myself worry constantly about Bruno, in spite of my painting, my full life here.'

'I hope you're not worried about him now?' Hester smiles.

At that moment Gérard himself brings them each a bowl of his *soupe de poissons*. He smiles at them both but Hester notices that while the smile for her is full of warmth and fondness, the one for Colette reveals an emotion far beyond mere affection. Colette returns it, and their eyes reflect their feelings for each other like ponds reflecting sunsets. Hester is moved, and turns away, giving them their private moment.

'No, Hester, no longer am I worried about my darling son.' Colette turns back to their conversation when Gérard has walked away. 'Your Imogen is perfect for him. He has become alive again; he was in too much of a dull routine before your daughter.'

'I'm so glad, because I feel Bruno has been equally good for her. She's changed, you know. She was very much two people before – the successful, ambitious model and career woman, and the immature, insecure child who never grew up – not emotionally, at any rate.'

'Difficult to merge those two things together,' Colette says.

'She never could. But since Bruno she is calmer, more balanced. They talk for hours, I've noticed, seem so easy together.'

'Yes, I have noticed this also. Your Imogen doesn't seem so eager to return to work as she used to be. She is more ready to linger after a good lunch, or to close the showroom at a fairly decent hour.'

Hester agrees with this. Then, as she sprinkles more grated cheese into her soup, Colette adds, 'But to go back to your other daughter, Abigail. I have not met her, but Bruno of course knows her from the months she stayed with her sister before she and Gordon did this most foolish thing together. Bruno says Abigail is quiet but most pleasant. He was very shocked and surprised at what happened, though of course as he says now, he cannot help but be glad of it, because it gave him Imogen.'

'Yes, I can't blame him for that. Abigail *is* pleasant, a lovely young woman in her own right, but she has always had this lack of self-confidence, probably because of this age-old competition with her sister. But I've told you all about that.'

'Bruno told me that Gordon wanted to come back to Imogen. My son was so angry!'

'I'm sure he was. So was Imogen. Of course there was no way she would even consider it, and I'm glad, but the whole thing doesn't bode well for Abigail.'

'She doesn't know, then?'

'Gordon won't tell her, and I don't see the point in informing her of it myself. She would not believe me – she would think it was all a plot to undermine her confidence in Gordon. But it worries me dreadfully. The man seems incapable of any kind of love or commitment to either of my daughters.'

They finish the discussion as Luc joins them for coffee. 'I have sold my favourite new painting,' he says mournfully, looking quite cheery in deep-blue cotton trousers and a dazzling bright shirt of blue and red stripes.

'But how wonderful!' Colette exclaims. 'Did you come down on the price?'

'No, that was the point. I made it high because I could not bear to part with it yet. But the customer never even tried to haggle. It is going to a home in Amsterdam and I shall never see it again.'

Colette commiserates; she understands exactly what Luc is going through. Hester thinks how lucky she is that when she has written a poem, she does not have to part with it even though it is published and sold a hundred times over. She would not like to never see a poem again after it has been written, and so she too clucks sympathetically with Luc until his spirits are quite restored. By then the restaurant has cleared and Gérard joins them, and they drink strong black coffee happily together for another half-hour before breaking up and returning to their various commitments.

And then a few days later the phone rings and it is Abigail. 'Mum, I'd like to see you,' she says without preliminary.

'Of course. Where are you – still in the south?'

'No, I'm . . . I'm actually in Pont-Aven. I just arrived yesterday. I hitchhiked.'

'Good God!' Hester exclaims, for this is completely out of character for her rather timid younger child. 'Abby, how could you?'

'Sheer desperation, Mum,' she said cheerfully. 'Did me good, I think.'

'Where's Gordon, is he with you?'

'No, no, he's still down south. I'm staying at the house of one of my pupils. Ages ago, before Gordon and I . . . well, you know . . . before that, when I was giving their daughter piano lessons, they asked if I would stay in their house for two weeks towards the end of summer, when they went on their holiday – to look after their cats and plants and poodle. I wrote to them after Gordon and I went away to say I'd still do it.'

'That was rather cool and prudent of you, Abby,' Hester says, just a touch sardonically.

'Well, I didn't know how long Gordon and I had his friend's place, and I thought we could maybe both move into the house in Pont-Aven while Gordon was, well, you know, sorting things out with Imogen. But it hasn't worked out like that.'

'I see. Actually, no, I don't really see.'

'Look, Mum, I can't explain on the phone, but I need to talk to you alone. Can you come here?'

So Hester says she will come at once. Luckily it is Sunday; the shop is shut and Imogen has gone off for the day with Bruno. Hester was out in the garden when the phone rang, so she changes into a clean pair of jeans and a long white cotton shirt and is shortly in her car driving into Pont-Aven.

The house where Abigail is staying is just outside the town and Hester finds it easily. It is a new house, spacious and austere with floors that look like marble and the furniture modern and sparse. As Hester goes up the long steps to the front door she hears some strands of Brahms coming out of the open window and can see it is Abigail, playing with great concentration on a beautiful baby grand piano in the living room.

Mother and daughter embrace emotionally. Hester's heart stirs for this mixed-up daughter of hers, who has surprised everyone so much this summer. Abigail appears tired, and her eyes look bruised, with great dark circles underneath. Her bright ginger hair has been cut again and is slicked back behind her ears. It will suit her, Hester thinks, when she is not so absolutely exhausted: it makes her eyes look enormous, her face piquant.

Abigail utters inanities while she makes tea, talking disjointedly about the weather, the house, the poodle she is looking after. She says laughingly that she ran out and bought some tea when she knew her mother was coming. 'I know you like tea in the afternoon, Mum,' she says, prattling on to cover her agitation. 'I know you're addicted to your tea.'

Hester doesn't tell her that she only occasionally drinks tea now, that she loves the coffee in France, its strength and aroma. Hester doesn't say much, as a matter of fact, but rather lets Abigail ramble on a bit to combat her nervousness, for her child is as taut as a violin string.

Finally they settle in the enclosed patio at the back of the house. This is as lush and crowded as the rest of the house is bare and stark. A grape-vine laden with fruit twists capriciously all around them, and the air is heavily scented with honeysuckle. There are pots of hibiscus plants everywhere, bright reds and yellows, fresh and shiny from the watering Abigail has just given them. A white poodle, named (Hester cannot believe it) Fifi, jumps up and sits contentedly in her lap, slightly spilling the cup of tea she is holding.

When they have settled down again after mopping up the mess Abigail says, 'You probably realize that I've left Gordon.'

Hester hadn't realized anything of the sort. In her gloomiest of speculations she had thought Gordon might kick Abigail out, leaving her totally devastated, and in her most hopeful ones, she envisaged Gordon remaining behind in the south while Abigail came up to sort things out with her sister. It would have been just like Gordon to send Abigail on her own, to try and placate Imogen into keeping him in the business.

So Hester says, cautiously, 'What exactly has happened, Abby?'

Abby sighs and stands up again, too restless to sit still. She is wearing a dress full of blue cornflowers on a paler blue background; it is short and child-like but very becoming on her slight frame.

Fifi jumps off Hester's lap and follows Abigail as she circles around and around the patio. Hester tries not to let the two of them, bobbing around like apples in a tub, agitate her, for they are each as nervy as the other and it makes her feel jumpy too. If only her daughter and that ridiculous dog would sit still, she could concentrate, but as they don't, she takes a deep breath and prepares to listen.

'Well, you know a few weeks ago Gordon went back up to Pont-Plouay to see Imogen and sort out the business?'

'Yes,' Hester says warily. 'I knew he had come up to see Imogen.' Surely he hadn't told her his real reason for going there, to try for a reconciliation?

But no, not at all. Abigail goes on, 'When he returned he was full of bitterness. All he wanted to see Imogen about was to come to some sort of friendly arrangement about splitting up everything fairly, parting amicably. But apparently Imogen said that she was going to screw him for everything he was worth in both the business and the house, that she was going to make sure he came out with nothing. He was furious, as you can imagine.'

So is Hester. This is so outrageously untrue that she wants to shout at her daughter, shake her. But Abigail is continuing, lost in her own thoughts, unaware of her mother's reaction.

'Gordon went on and on about it. I sympathized, of course, but after a few days of this I started to wonder a bit. I felt quite treacherous, doubting Gordon's veracity, but I couldn't help remembering that of all Imogen's faults – and God knows she has more than most – greed and avarice are not part of them. In fact, I have to be fair to her: she has always been generous with her money.'

Hester sits back in her chair, relieved. This is, of course, quite true. As soon as Imogen began to make money, she was eager to bring it home, buying the family lavish presents and always generous with gifts or loans.

Abigail continues, 'So finally I said something to Gordon. Oh, nothing inflammatory, I only rather timidly suggested that perhaps he had misunderstood her, that I didn't really think money was all that important to her and I couldn't believe she would really want to leave him penniless.'

'Good for you,' Hester says with a slight smile.

'Oh Mum, it was dreadful! He turned on me, really turned on me, said I was as bad as she was, said – God, I don't want to repeat what he said, but we had our first real quarrel. He was like a vengeful fury, he swore and—'

She breaks off, obviously distressed. Hell hath no fury as a man scorned, Hester thinks, and is sorely tempted to say it aloud. Instead, she says gently, 'What a terrible thing for you, Abby. It must have been quite a shock.'

Abigail sits down and absent-mindedly strokes the poodle which has jumped on to her lap. 'We argued all day about it, and then – then he just stopped speaking to me. I mean, can you believe it, he didn't say a word. We both pottered around the house, I went shopping, he went out somewhere or other; we ate a meal together in the same kitchen but he didn't say a word for forty-eight hours. I was frantic!'

'I'm sure you were. Despicable man,' Hester mutters.

'In the end, we made it up. He woke up one morning and was all nice and sunny, as if nothing had happened, but I . . . I don't know, something was wrong, only with me this time. In one way I was so happy, so relieved that everything was all right with us again, but in another way I felt so nervous – frightened, really. Like, in the back of my mind was, could it happen again? He's quite violent when he gets angry, you know.'

'No,' Hester says faintly. 'I didn't know.'

Abigail starts to pace again, but this time Fifi, fed up with all the leaping up and down, ensconces herself firmly on Hester's lap and goes to sleep. 'I tried to put it out of my mind, but it just wouldn't go. It nagged at me, Gordon going on about Imo having been mean and stingy with him all through their marriage, especially when he lost all his money and had to live off her. I knew that this just simply wasn't true, that Imogen shared all her money equally with Gordon, and I kept thinking that either he was lying or totally crazy. And then the thoughts went on that if he was lying about that, he could be lying about so many other things, like how unhappy Imogen had made him, how cruel and terrible and heartless she was to him throughout their marriage.'

'Oh God,' Hester explodes. 'Did he really say all that?'

Abigail looks rather sheepish. 'Well, Mum,' she says defensively, 'I know Imogen has always been your favourite—'

'Abigail, don't you dare—'

'But we all know she can be quite heartless sometimes, quite selfish.'

'Oh, Abigail, so can most of us!'

'And anyway, I was hopelessly in love with Gordon and you know how convincing he can be, how persuasive . . .'

'*Was*, Abby?'

'Oh Mum, yes I was, completely. I was totally taken in by him. You wouldn't know, you couldn't understand what it's like, not being able to live, to breathe, to exist without the person you love passionately there at your side.'

'Abigail, you may be surprised to hear this, but I—'

'And so I left him. I knew I had to make a quick decision, because the people who own this house were expecting me. Did I go with Gordon, or on my own? In the end I just walked out, one morning when Gordon was off with some people he'd met who own a boat. I left a note, took some clothes, and hitchhiked here because I hadn't a penny by then.'

'Oh, Abby,' Hester groans, horrified.

'Mum, I was so misguided. He's not even a very nice person. Oh God, this is hard to say, but I've been such a complete and utter fool! He's not even good in bed.'

She looks so dejected, so pathetic, that Hester takes her in her arms and holds her tightly, much to the annoyance of the poodle, which jumps off her lap and goes to sulk in a corner. 'Oh darling, you poor child,' she says, soothing her as she did when Abigail was little. She says no more but lets her daughter find some release from her tension and despair in tears.

After a while Abigail raises her head and says, sniffling, 'I don't know why I did it, I really don't. When I got to France my life was in a mess. I felt a failure as a teacher, my music was going nowhere. I hadn't even had a decent relationship in my life, nothing meaningful or even important.'

'You're young, love. There's plenty of time.'

'So I came to France feeling totally inadequate in every way – and there was Imogen. Successful, perfect, assured . . .'

'Oh, Abby . . .'

'And there was Gordon.' Abigail involuntarily sighs. 'He overwhelmed me with attention from the start. He told me about his marriage – oh, I know I was a fool, but I believed him. I saw how Imogen was completely wrapped up in the business.'

'She had to be,' Hester says gently.

'Look, I loved him, and you don't think straight at the time. He said he loved me, hadn't loved Imo for years. And there she was, my sister. Beautiful, efficient, capable – and so bloody smug about herself, about her marriage, everything. She didn't even care how much Gordon and I were together, she was so sure of him, so sure that he wouldn't look twice at her plain, boring little sister.'

'Abby, I'm sure Imo never thought—'

'It made me so angry, I cannot tell you how angry.' Abigail runs her hand distractedly through her hair, shakes her head sadly, and finally looks at Hester. 'I can't make any excuses for myself, Mum. I don't want to make excuses – except that I loved him, and I really believed he felt the same way about me. He told me he did, told me so many things—'

Abigail breaks off, beginning to cry again. Hester holds her tightly, not saying anything. 'I did love him, Mum. I was obsessed by him, wanted him so badly – oh God, how can I explain? I *can't* explain. You don't know, can't know, until you've been through it.'

Hester strokes her hair, kisses her cheek. 'I know this is hard for you to believe,' she says finally. 'But I do understand. I really and truly do.'

Later that evening Imogen says to her mother, 'And then she said *what*? I can't believe I'm hearing this.'

'Abigail then said, "I want you to go back to Imogen and tell her from me that I'm sorry I took Gordon away, but I've realized I was wrong to do it and she can have him back now." She then went on to explain at great length how she was blinded by love at the time and maybe one day you will be able to understand and forgive.'

Hester doesn't try to cloak the words in a colour that would be acceptable to Imogen, because she knows Abigail is writing her a letter which will say more or less the same thing. Imogen explodes. 'That is the most pompous, the most condescending thing I've ever heard!'

'She doesn't mean to be, Imo,' Hester says mildly. 'I think she is genuinely sorry.'

'And she doesn't know, you never told her, that Gordon has already been here, begging me to have him back?'

'No, of course I didn't tell her! What's the point?'

'The point is, it would stop her gloating like this. The bloody nerve, saying she's giving him back to me, just because she now understands she made the biggest mistake of her life.'

'She'd be devastated, Imo, if she knew about Gordon doing that behind her back. She is pretty shattered by it all as it is.'

'So you want me to keep quiet, to protect her. Oh God, all my life I've had to defer to my sister, sweet cuddly adorable Abby—'

'You're getting sidetracked, Imo. The point is, it would destroy Abigail's confidence completely if you tell her Gordon wanted to leave her and go back to you.'

'Oh, I see, so we build up her fragile self-image at the expense of making me look a fool.'

Hester sighs in despair. Reasoning with her two daughters is like following a maze when you have had too much to drink. 'How can you see it like that?' she asks wearily. 'You have the satisfaction, if that's what you want, of knowing that Gordon came back to you, willing to jilt Abigail if you'd have him again. You also have the love and devotion of one of the most attractive and eligible men in Brittany. What does Abigail have?'

'She took my husband,' Imogen says stubbornly. 'And you want me to keep quiet, hide the truth, so that her feelings won't be hurt, that her confidence won't be shattered.'

Hester can see her point. 'Oh Imogen,' she says, giving up. 'Of course I have no right to interfere, or to say anything, and of course I won't blame you if you want to tell Abigail everything. You must do what you think is right, say what you need to say.'

Imogen slumps into the elegant, cream velvet sofa opposite the fireplace in the living room. It is quite late at night, Bruno has gone, and the two women have been talking for about an hour. Imogen looks troubled and distraught, and Hester is upset for her, as she was upset for Abigail earlier on in the afternoon. So she does the only thing she can: she goes to Imogen and puts her arms around her, just as she did with her other daughter a few hours ago.

But it is not enough, just as it wasn't enough with Abigail. Hester's heart aches for the babies she once was able to soothe and make happy just by rocking them, or loving them, or keeping them warm and dry and well-fed.

She could weep for those days. It is searing, this, knowing one is powerless to curb the distress of one's children. Pain seeps into her like a cat, warming itself on the hearth of her heart, and the fact that it isn't her own pain but her children's makes it infinitely harder to bear.

Chapter Fifteen

It is not until the next evening that Abigail and Imogen meet. The time is after ten and it's pouring with rain, and Imogen and Hester are sitting in the living room watching a film on television. Bruno is working at the hospital and Imo has just had a shower and washed her hair, and is curled up on the sofa wrapped in her red silk dressing gown.

Hester answers the door when the bell rings, wondering who it can be at this hour, on such an unpleasant night. To her surprise, Abigail is standing there, dressed in jeans and a dark green jumper and looking quite wet and forlorn.

'For God's sake, Abby, you're soaking! Come in quickly and get those clothes off. I'll find something for you to change into.'

Her daughter is shivering. The evening has turned cold for August and she only has on a thin cotton jacket, which is soaked through.

'How did you get here? Has something happened?'

Hester had phoned Abigail earlier that day, to see if she was all right, and to ask whether she wanted her to come over. Hester could not invite her to the house because of Imogen, who said that the only reason she'd want to see her sister was to tell her in full detail the extent of Gordon's treachery. But Abigail said on the telephone that she was fine, enjoying being on her own, and made arrangements to meet her mother again in a day or so.

Hester helps her peel off her tight jeans and her sweater. Even her underwear is soaked, so her mother grabs a towel from the downstairs bathroom and hands it to her as she strips to the skin. Hester is just on her way upstairs to get a warm dressing gown for Abigail when Imogen, hearing her sister's voice, comes flying into the hallway, looking like a flame of fire in her shiny red dressing gown. Her hair, still wet, is wrapped in a scarlet towel, turban-like. She looks majestic and quite formidable.

'Abigail, what is going on? I thought I made it quite clear I want nothing to do with you again.'

Abigail is at a decided disadvantage, being stark naked except for the rather small towel she is trying without success to wrap around herself.

'You don't make it easier, do you,' she says peevishly, rainwater dripping from her saturated hair. 'I'm sure our mother has told you that I have left Gordon, that I am sorry for going off with him. I came here because I realized it was cowardly not to face you myself.'

'So? I'm supposed to say, "Oh, that's all right then, come in and have a cup of tea"? You're more of a fool than I thought you were, Abigail, if that's what you expected.'

'God, you don't change, do you, Imogen! I said I'm fucking sorry, didn't I? I hitchhiked in this shitty weather all the way from Pont-Aven because I couldn't leave it any longer, not making my peace with you, and I thought it cowardly just to write you a letter. I should have known you'd show me your usual sympathy and understanding. Sod it, I'm going.'

This proves to be difficult because she is standing there without any clothes. Exasperated, she begins picking up her wet things which are lying on the floor, and starts trying to get into them. This turns out to be practically impossible since she is still clutching the towel and trying to hide her shivering, goose-bumpy body from the stormy and scornful gaze of her older sister.

For a moment or two Hester is incapable of either speech or action. She doesn't know whether to run upstairs quickly and get a dressing gown for her naked shivering child; or to stay put to intervene in case they start to pull each other's hair out (which they tried to do once or twice as children). She is also rather stunned at her younger daughter, who never swore (she left that to Imogen); who always played it safe (and here she was hitchhiking all over France); and who was always totally predictable – until she ran off with her sister's husband. All these things are flying through her head as she stands on the stairs irresolute and immobile.

'God, you've got a nerve!' Imogen says, stepping threateningly closer to her sister who is having trouble getting into her wet underpants. 'You abuse me, abuse my hospitality, you hurt and humiliate me – then when you've done just about everything you can to ruin my life and betray me, you think all you have to do is say you're sorry and we'll be one big happy family again. To hell with that, Abby. And to hell with you.'

Abigail gives up on the underpants and stands up straight, indignant, letting the towel fall to the ground in her fury. Her short wet hair clings so tenaciously to her scalp that she looks even more naked.

'What a hard, unforgiving bitch you are,' she says stridently. 'I should have known, should have remembered, what you're like, what you've always been like – cold and frigid and unfeeling.'

Imogen shakes her head as if she cannot believe what she is hearing. As she does so the towel on her hair falls off and her hair too lies wetly against her scalp. Going up to her sister she takes her by the shoulders, gives her a good shake, and snarls, 'You shit, Abigail. You little shit. Get out of my house.'

At that moment Hester throws off her paralysis and comes flying down the stairs to land rather shakily between them. 'Stop it! Stop it at once, both of you, do you hear?' she shouts imperiously. 'Abigail cannot possibly leave now; she is soaked through and when she is dry and dressed in other clothes I will drive her back to Pont-Aven. Abby, go upstairs to the airing cupboard and get a bath towel to dry yourself properly, then go into my room next to it and I will find some clothes for you. Imo, I suggest you dry your hair and then perhaps you will be kind enough to put on the kettle. If you don't stop verbally abusing each other and calm down, I shall leave this house myself, this very minute, and never come back.'

Her daughters stare hatefully at each other for another second or two, then they hesitatingly – and rather sheepishly – look at Hester to see if she means it. When they see that she does, they reluctantly begin to do what she asked.

But before Imogen disappears off to the kitchen, she says ominously, 'Perhaps it's just as well we talk, Abigail. Perhaps there are some things I need to say to you, some home truths you appear to be unaware of.'

Before Abigail can retort Hester hustles her up to the bedroom. 'What a crazy idea, coming without warning,' she chides her daughter gently when they are out of Imogen's hearing. 'You must have known how your sister would react. And for God's sake, will you stop hitchhiking? It's terribly dangerous, especially at this late hour. Promise me.'

'Mum—'

'Promise, Abby. I know you will soon be twenty-six and I am an overcautious fool of a mother, but that's the way it is. And besides, you have given me enough heartache and worry just lately. I don't need also to have to worry about you being attacked in a deserted lay-by somewhere.'

Abigail mutters what sounds like a promise and Hester has to be content with that. Will it never break, she thinks, this invisible umbilical cord binding her to her daughters, making her well-being dependent on theirs? She has never felt it so strongly as she does now, as she runs around the house finding clothes for Abigail, helping Imogen make coffee, trying to soothe them both out of the anger that consumes them, just as she used to do when they were children. Will it never end, she thinks despairingly, fearing it won't, and suddenly saddened and wearied by it all.

In about twenty minutes the three of them are sitting cosily – or at least superficially so – in the living room. The television has been shut off and Hester has stoked up the wood fire in the open grate, the first they have had all summer. A pot of coffee is on a small side table and the three women are sitting in silence, a rather heavy one, in front of the fire. Abigail is wearing Hester's dressing gown and a pair of woolly socks and her hair is fluffing around her ears as it dries by the fire; Imogen also still wears her red dressing gown. They look like an idyllic scene from the novel *Little Women*, Hester thinks, and the irony is not lost on her.

'Now that you two have decided to at least talk to each other, and to listen to what the other has to say, I'll leave you alone,' Hester says, getting up to go.

They both protest simultaneously and with alacrity that they want Hester there, that they have nothing to say to each other that cannot be said in their mother's presence. Unwillingly, Hester resigns herself to the unwanted role of mediator. She would much rather go up to her bedroom and let them get on with it.

'All right, I'll stay,' she says reluctantly. 'But I'm not going to say anything, I'm not going to get involved. I shall not be taking sides, either, is that clear? You are both my daughters, and I love you equally, as you know. Nothing has changed that.'

Imogen snorts. 'All this business about loving us equally is bullshit, Mum, if you don't mind my saying so.'

Hester is shocked and hurt. 'Imogen, how can you?'

'Oh, I don't mean you, I guess you've always tried anyway to treat us equally. But Dad never even tried – it was always obvious who his favourite was.'

Before Hester can answer that Abigail says bitterly, 'You really are going to rub it in, aren't you? You're really not going to let me forget it, even now after he's been dead three years.'

'What the hell are you talking about?' Imogen snaps.

'The same thing you are. About you being Dad's number one favourite, the golden girl who could do and say the most outrageous, horrendous things, and still be forgiven. Talk about the bloody black sheep syndrome, you were the classic.'

Imogen looks totally bewildered. 'You're crazy, Abigail, you're talking rubbish. Just ask Mum, she must know – everyone did – how *you* were the golden girl, the favourite daughter, the little darling.'

Hester shakes her head slightly and sips her coffee, saying nothing. She is not going to be drawn into this.

Abigail protests. 'You can't believe that, Imogen. Why,

the whole time I was growing up, Dad kept holding you up as an example, how you learned to read and write quicker than I did, how bright you were when you were my age. He was so wounded when you went off to do modelling that I thought he'd never get over it. No matter how much I tried to love him, to make it up to him, it was never enough. He always yearned for you.'

Imogen stares at her sister. 'You must be joking, Abby! I can't believe I'm hearing this. He hated me, I was nothing but trouble for him, wanting to be a model, wanting to do all the things he detested. You were the goodie-goodie, and not only that, you were the talented one too who could sing and play the piano and the violin . . .'

'That only came later. Anyway, it was pretty obvious that he turned to me to get his own back on you because you were being so rebellious and difficult. I think that bothered me more than anything, knowing that though he was making a fuss over me, all you had to do was snap your fingers and he'd go running back to you.'

Imogen looks astounded. She stares into the fire for a few moments before shaking her head and saying, 'I don't know where you're getting all this.'

'It's true, you know it's true.'

Imogen looks up at her sister. 'Abby, you can't remember what it was like when you were a baby, a toddler. Everyone adored you. You were not only beautiful and cuddly but a perfect baby, hardly ever cried or made a fuss like I had, just sat in your bloody pram and smiled all day, for Christ's sake.'

'God, Imo, I can't help what I was like as a baby!'

'No, I suppose not. But there I was, in that awkward, ugly pre-adolescent stage—'

'Not you, never.'

'I *felt* ugly. I was far too skinny, my skin was spotty, and there you were, round and rosy and beautiful.'

Now Abigail looks confused. 'Look, it's you who is crazy. I always used to think Dad loved you best not only because you were so clever, but because you were so beautiful and I wasn't. I . . . I still think that.'

The two sisters stare at each other in bewilderment. Hester, silent in a big apricot-coloured armchair at the side of the fire, sighs and wonders why it is that parents can never get it right no matter how much they love their children.

Imogen speaks first. 'My God. I'm stunned, Abby. I thought the same about you, you know. Ever since the day you were born I envied your hair, all that wonderful colour—'

'I've always hated it!'

'And you were so good, that was the hardest to bear. Everyone talked about what a wonderful happy baby you were, so sunny and placid, and there was I having sulks and tantrums that I couldn't seem to control. I hated myself for it, and then I hated you for making me seem so much more awful by comparison. I couldn't bear the fact that it seemed so easy for you to be good, while I was such a bad-tempered child.'

'It was only easy because I wasn't as bright as you. Everyone always said you were the clever one. I had a talent for making music, that's all.'

Imogen sighs. 'That's all,' she repeats sardonically. 'Abby, you played the piano like an angel, everyone said so, everyone raved about that talent of yours. You looked like an angel too, playing away so contentedly, looking so sweet with that amazingly-coloured hair and your big blue eyes.'

Abigail makes a deprecatory remark but Imogen insists, 'That's why I was so stubborn about modelling, why I gave up my A levels and ran off to London. I wanted to prove I could be just as famous as you, because by then Dad was going on and on about the marvellous career you would have as a musician.'

'Imo, no!'

'Honest. Oh, there were other reasons, of course, but that played a large part in my final decision. Dad was always on about how you were destined for great things, even when you were only six and seven, so I was determined to make it before you did. Modelling was the only thing I could think of where being skinny, all bones and angles, was an advantage.'

The two are quiet for a moment. Then Abigail says slowly, 'All my life I was always aware of you, of someone better than I was. Dad at first kept telling me to listen to you, look up to you, be like you because you were so bright, passed exams, were sparkly and full of life. Then, when you and he fell out, I always knew I was second-best, I always knew that when the black sheep came home I'd lose my position as favourite. I lived in dread of that, I think, until the day he died. I worshipped him, you see. My earliest memory is crying myself to sleep because I knew he would never love me the way he loved you.'

Imogen looks at Abigail for the first time with real compassion. 'I never knew, Abby. Never even suspected it.'

But Abigail is not looking at her sister. Rather she is staring at the fire as she says, with difficulty, 'I think – I'm sure now, it's been going around and around my head for the past twenty-four hours – it's why I . . . why I had the affair with Gordon.'

Imogen stiffens, loses her soft expression, but Abigail goes bravely on. 'Oh, I fancied him, of course. I didn't do it deliberately, calculatingly. I didn't actually coax him into bed to get even with you. I really was infatuated with him, really thought I loved him.'

She pauses. No one says a word and the only sound is the hiss of the fire, the sound of the rain on the old tiled roof.

'But even so,' she finally goes on, as if talking to the fire, 'even so, even though I loved him quite irrationally, I hope I would have stayed away, hope I would have said no to him, if I didn't have these mixed feelings about you, Imo, and this burning, hopeless jealousy of your relationship with Dad. I remember even thinking, once, after . . . after Gordon and I had finished making love, that I wished Dad were alive, to see that I had done something better than my older sister, to show him that I could be one up on her, that I could have something she couldn't.'

She hesitates, then goes on. 'I guess I wanted Dad to know that there was a man who loved me more than he loved you, Imo. A man who, when having the choice between you and me, chose me.'

She is silent and the fire hisses and hisses; there is a wet log on it somewhere. When at last Abigail turns to her sister she says, with tears brimming from her eyes, 'I'm sorry, Imogen. I am really and truly sorry. And I know that is not enough, just to be sorry, and I know you can't forgive, but that's all right. I don't blame you. It was a dreadful, wicked thing to do. I never knew I was capable of such things.'

She is distressed and crying but she intrepidly keeps her eyes on her sister's face as she says all this. The two look at each other for a moment, and perhaps it is the first time they have ever really looked at each other.

Then Imogen says, 'Oh, Abby,' and goes to her and takes her in her arms and they cling and cling, and cry and cry. Hester, unnoticed, tiptoes slowly out of the room and sits at the kitchen table with her head in her arms and cries too for all those wasted years, for all the misunderstandings and heartache that even with love she could not prevent.

Some time later she goes to bed, stopping in the living room first, to say goodnight to her daughters. They are deep in conversation, and though they kiss her warmly, and invite her to stay, she leaves them alone, knowing they have a great deal to say to each other.

When she is in bed she cannot sleep. She is thinking of Martin – the concerned family man and responsible husband, respected and well-liked both in the community and at his work. She is thinking also of herself, searching her conscience for times when she could have stood up to him with greater determination, times when she could have interceded for her daughters more than she did, when she should have been able to smooth things over, explain. She had thought she did all she could; now she realizes it wasn't enough, she failed. It is a troubling thought and her sleep, when it comes, is broken, haunted by nightmares.

The next morning when Abigail is still in bed in her old room upstairs and Imogen and Hester meet over breakfast in the kitchen, Hester says to her older daughter, 'I feel terribly guilty, Imogen. I feel sad and guilty that I didn't do more to soften your father's attitude to you both, and to help both you girls to understand why he acted the way he did. Perhaps, for him, children came too late. He had become resigned to childlessness, and this chance, when he had given up hope, was too much for him. He became possessed by you, possessed with loving you too much, wanting to mould you into what he thought children should be.'

But Imogen will have none of it. 'Mum,' she says in her brisk sensible voice, 'Abby and I know all that. We discussed everything last night, we stayed up for hours. We talked about you and Dad a lot, and as we did we remembered all the times you talked to us, tried to smooth things over, tried to explain about Dad, how he was. We both agreed that we never listened, or if we did we never believed you. We were too busy competing for Dad's attention, and making war on each other, to take much notice of you.'

Hester can see there is some truth in this, but she still wonders if she could have done more, still feels the nagging whine of guilt and doubt. She tells herself that at any rate it is all over and done with now, and regrets for what might have been are always futile.

Then she says, as her daughter pours her some coffee, 'Imo, did you tell Abigail?'

'What about?'

'About Gordon. Coming here a few weeks ago and wanting you back. Before Abigail left him.'

'Oh, that. No. I didn't think it would do her any good, Mum, and anyway, it's not important any more.'

'I'm so glad. You are a good person, Imogen.'

Imogen is gratified but embarrassed by this praise. She pours herself more coffee, then sits down at the table next to her mother and they both drink in silence for a few moments. At last she says, smiling, 'You know, Mum, what one of the perks of all this has been for me?'

'Bruno?' Hester says.

'Ah yes, Bruno, that goes without saying. As do a good many other things: Abigail and I sorting all that childhood stuff out, giving us a second chance to get to know each other. And, of course, my getting out of a loveless marriage with Gordon.'

'What else, then?'

She grins. 'The thing that delights me no end is the fact that my sweet baby sister, my goodie-goodie angelic little sister, was quite capable of doing something horrid and wicked – that she is, after all, human like the rest of us! It makes me quite warm to her, for the first time ever!'

Hester laughs, and tucks into her breakfast with a great deal of relish. Although it is still raining and cold, the croissants are as fresh as ever and the baguette still warm from the bakery where Imogen collected it not long ago. France is still most satisfying, Hester thinks, even in the rain.

Soon Abigail wakes and her mother drives her back to Pont-Aven, for there is the poodle and the cats to tend to. Imogen is busy in her office at the back of the shop and Hester notes with satisfaction that she gets up and gives Abigail a warm kiss and embrace as they say goodbye.

In the car Abigail says, 'Imogen told me about Bruno, Mum, about their relationship. What a surprise! I don't know him very well, but he seems nice. I'm pleased for her.'

'Abigail,' Hester says, taking her eyes off the wet road for a moment and looking at her, 'you won't tell Gordon, will you? Not yet, anyway. I assume he'll be phoning you up, getting in touch. It could make the divorce settlement tricky. Gordon could use the knowledge to be difficult.'

'I know that, and of course I wouldn't tell him. Mum, I know this sounds crazy, but I really am over him. The sheen, the sort of glowing halo I saw him in has suddenly disappeared, and all I feel is a great deal of embarrassment about it all.'

'I'm glad.'

They ride in silence for another mile or so and then Abigail says, 'You know, it makes it so much easier that Imo told me about Bruno. When I left Gordon I felt such guilt – I'll always feel guilt about the whole episode – but she has made it a lot easier for me by confessing that she hasn't loved Gordon for ages. He used to say she didn't love him, but I know he never believed it – he's too vain to think anyone could ever stop loving him. I can't tell you how relieved I am, Mum, that the whole awful thing is over.'

'What will you do now?' Hester says. 'After your house-sitting in Pont-Aven, that is. Do you want to go back to England? You are always welcome to stay with me, and if you want to return now, you can use the house. I'll have to leave France eventually, I suppose, though I shall do so with regret.'

Abigail stares out at the wet road, the summer gardens flattened by the rain.

'I don't know,' she says finally. 'Imogen said I could stay with her. She knows you'll be gone by autumn, as you have your classes and workshops and poetry readings, and Imo says though she and Bruno plan to marry eventually, it's still far too early even to live together. She says she needs space – to get the divorce, sort things out – before jumping into another live-in relationship, much as she loves him. Apparently Bruno quite understands.'

'Will you do that? Stay in France?'

'I'm not sure. I think I'd like to. I was just beginning to get known as a piano-teacher when . . . when all that happened. Also, shortly after I got here, I was asked to be soloist for an excellent ensemble based in Brittany, not far from here actually. They do a lot of touring apparently. They heard me play somewhere and said they will be needing another pianist soon. They really are good, and it would be quite fun to do some concert work again.'

Hester is delighted, and says so. Abigail brightens at her mother's encouragement and promises to seriously consider the offer.

'I shall come over especially to be in the audience at your début,' Hester announces proudly, pleased with these tentative plans. She has always felt that Abigail was wrong to abandon her own piano playing and turn instead to teaching, and perhaps this will be a way for her to start again. *If* that is what she wants, Hester thinks hastily, determined never to try and push either of her daughters into anything.

'Imogen has also said I can help in the shop like I used to, until I can get my piano-teaching sorted out once more,' Abigail adds.

'Yes, she does need someone, with Gordon gone and my time here coming to an end,' Hester replies. She thinks about Abby staying on in France, living with Imogen for a while. It might just work: she hopes it does.

Turning the corner from the main street of the town, Hester heads towards the house where Abigail is staying. 'Well, you have plenty of time to decide what you want to do,' she says as she lets Abigail off. 'Don't rush into anything.'

They kiss and Abigail is gone, and Hester slowly turns the car around to go back to Pont-Plouay. It's too wet and windy to visit Colette and Luc or Gérard, and besides, she is suddenly feeling exhausted. The euphoria brought on by her daughters' reconciliation is gone now, blown away by the unseasonal wind from the sea, by her own broken night, by the sudden intimations of autumn, and her obligations back in England which are insidiously crawling around her like ants at a picnic.

The house feels damp and chilly. Imogen is busy in the shop with a customer and doesn't seem to need help for the moment. Hester shivers a little; she is still dressed for summer and it seems to have disappeared somewhere. She thinks about her poetry, knows she should use this wet dreary day to polish off a poem she has been working on for ages, one she wants to include in her new collection which is almost ready to be sent to her publisher.

But this is one of the rare times poetry cannot tempt her. The garden also holds no appeal; even if it were sunny Hester knows she would not want to be out there. What she really wants is someone to talk to – not a daughter, not family, not new friends either, no matter how dear or how sympathetic, but someone she has known for a long time, someone who knows her inside out, someone with whom she can be her floppy worn-out self. She briefly contemplates phoning up one of her old friends in England, but the enthusiasm for that soon wanes as she admits that she doesn't know quite what she wants to say to them.

What Hester really wants, she realizes, is to be with the one person she has felt the closest to in her whole life; the person who was her soul-mate, her friend, her lover for five years, the person to whom she was able to talk with more honesty, more passion, with more mutual understanding, than anyone else before or since. She wants to speak to him again, about so many things. About Abigail and Imogen, about her time here in France, about her future in England. About her poetry, yes – that too. There is so much to say, so much to catch up on.

She goes to the phone and looks up a number. Soon it is ringing and ringing and when he answers Hester says, without preamble, 'Alex, it's me, Hester. I've had second thoughts about friendship. I'd like to have a try at coping with it. Am I still invited to stay a few days at your cottage? I'd like to come soon, if Imogen can spare me from the shop for a day or two.'

The next morning Hester is on her way. The rain has stopped and although there is still a cloud or two lingering, the sun is beating them away and drying the sodden earth with an intensity that more than makes up for the cold of the last few days. Summer, she notices joyfully, as she drives through the Brittany countryside, has not after all totally vanished.

Chapter Sixteen

Hester sees the hydrangeas first. There are even more than she remembers, growing in profusion around the sides of the house: pink and blue and white, the huge bushes heavy with the last of the summer's flowers. As she drives slowly down the tiny lane she takes it all in – the fields of corn to the left, the shady woodlands to the right. And in front of her the house, on its own at the end of the track, and behind it, the sea.

She stops the car and just sits for a moment, overwhelmed, remembering. The cottage has not changed, not at all. The hydrangeas are more blatant, strident almost with colour, but the stone of the house is still golden, the shutters and the front door still painted white. And the sun that she remembers so well is still shining hot and sensuously above it.

'We used the sun wisely,
like an aphrodisiac, letting it filter
drop by drop through the cracks in the shutters,
you following with your lips
the patterns on my body . . .'

Hester sighs. She will never write poems like that again about Alex, but never mind, never mind. She gets out of the car, determined to distil some kind of harmony for herself and for Alex from that long-ago passion.

And then he is there, embracing her warmly, kissing her affectionately. 'I never thought you'd come,' he says. 'Until I heard your car I was sure you'd change your mind.'

They go into the house. And here, of course, there *are* changes. Eight years ago it was only a summer house; what pieces of furniture there were, were ugly, functional, sparse. The wallpaper was old and faded, peeling apologetically in corners:

'We decorated it with laughter,
and promises we were never able to honour . . .'

Enough, Hester. She forces herself back to the present and sees that the house has been furnished with care, and with love. A woodburning stove stands in the grate where they used to burn logs, and the bare wooden floor has been sanded and polished. The furniture too is old, not antique but solid, comfortable. On the wall are maps: old maps of Brittany, Celtic maps, shipping maps. It is an attractive, pleasant room. A masculine one also, Hester is happy to see.

She shakes this unworthy thought from her mind. When she decided yesterday to see Alex, to see if they could indeed become friends after all those years of being lovers, she knew she would have to accept him the way he is now, and that of course includes Ermi, his herb lady. Still, Hester is human enough to be glad there is no sign of her, not in this living room, nor in the kitchen where Alex takes her next.

This too has changed; instead of the two-burner camping stove where Hester and Alex boiled water in an old saucepan for tea and coffee, there is a modest electric cooker. The table Hester remembers is still there, the old oak one she loved, but the shelves above and below the sink are new.

'Did you put these in?' she asks admiringly.

'Yes. And the cupboards in the corner.'

'You've done a good job. They're very fine, and fit perfectly in here.'

And then she turns. Alex has opened the French doors that go from the kitchen on to the tiny balcony and there it is, the estuary right below them, with the full tide deep under the balcony and in the distance the sea, throbbing and glinting with a dozen little boats and the sun shining on everything – on the estuary as it narrows below them, with the woods and hills on either side, on the dazzling water as it widens its banks towards the sea, and on a kingfisher that suddenly, magically, chooses this moment to fly from one side of the narrow estuary to the other, right in front of the balcony.

'Oh,' Hester says foolishly. 'Oh my, Alex. It's still so very beautiful.'

He puts his hand lightly on her shoulder. 'It is, Hester, it truly is. Welcome back, my dear.'

That night Hester sits in the kitchen, at the old oak table, and watches Alex prepare a meal – a lamb casserole, he tells her.

'I thought about taking you to Le Café de la Mer at Kerrocher,' he says with a grin.

'Is it still there?'

'Oh yes, but nothing like it was when Gérard owned it. Very touristy now, full of our fellow countrymen killing time before their ferry leaves from Roscoff.'

'I'm glad we stayed in. It's so peaceful here.'

Alex and Hester had spent the afternoon walking in the woodlands along the side of the estuary, picking blackberries and emerging often from the cool of the forest to sit on the rocks at the sea's edge. They talked endlessly, just as they used to, as if the years had never intervened, never severed their continuous dialogue.

She told him all about Imogen and Abigail, and how she hoped they had at last resolved their childhood antagonism. 'For the first time, there seems to be peace between them, Alex. After all those years of friction. Yet I still feel so guilty. I feel I should have done more somehow.'

They were sitting on a huge granite rock facing the sea as they talked, the sun hot on their bodies, the blackberries ripe in the woodlands behind them. Alex said, 'We all feel that about our children, Hester. But you did so much, believe me. I remember you spending hours talking to the girls, both together and separately. You were always taking one or the other out for lunch, or staying in to talk to them.'

'Did I, Alex? You're not just saying that?'

'Not at all. I remember it especially because there were days and days that you refused to see me, either because Imogen was home and you wanted to stay around to make sure all ran smoothly, or because you needed to be with Abigail, to reassure her about something or other. I used to resent it sometimes.'

'Did you? I never knew, you never showed it.'

Alex got up, skimmed a stone into the calm sea and watched as it touched the surface and bounced up again, and then again, and again. 'I had no right to be resentful, and I knew it. Your daughters always came first with you, but it had to be that way. I learned to accept it.'

'Oh, Alex.' Hester stared at the spot where the stone finally sank and said, after a moment, 'I'm so glad you told me that. It has always been a secret worry of mine, a terrible nagging remorse, that our affair blinded me to their needs, took up time that should have been given to them. I thought that if I hadn't loved you so much I'd have seen more clearly what was going on, prevented it all from getting so out of hand.'

Alex shook his head. 'I don't think so, Hester. If either of of the girls needed you, if there was ever a problem, you always cancelled our meetings, always. I'm sure our affair never came between you and your daughters, believe me.'

Standing there at the edge of the sea, watching Alex skimming stones and listening to him talk, Hester felt, for the first time in years, a lightening of the spirit, and realized how heavy this burden had been: the guilt she had carried around with her, afraid that by loving Alex, she had somehow failed her children. As she walked with him back through the woodland, picking more blackberries and eating them in the cool of the thick, dusty summer trees, she laid yet another ghost to rest. Perhaps, as a mother, she would always wonder what she could have done differently for her daughters, but she would no longer blame any real or imagined failings on her affair with Alex. If anything, he helped her survive those years: soothing her when she was fraught, giving her the calm and courage and love to go back into the fray again.

Oh, he *is* a good friend! Hester thought as Alex picked an especially fat blackberry and popped it gently into her mouth. Oh Alex, I had forgotten what a dear good friend you always were.

And now they sit in the kitchen, the French doors open to the balcony and the sea, and Alex is chopping the lamb, then some onions, then some green and red peppers.

'Can I help?' Hester says.

'No. I'll just get this going, then we'll sit out on the balcony with a drink and watch the sun go down.'

They are comfortably silent while Alex peels and chops. He puts it all into a heavy iron casserole and from an open shelf takes some jars of herbs, opens them, sprinkles them into the pot.

'Ermi's?' Hester can't help asking.

'Yes.'

'She must keep you well stocked.'

'Yes. Yes, she does.'

He obviously does not want to say any more, and suddenly neither does Hester, not about Ermi, at any rate. But as the lamb starts to cook and bubble she is there, here, everywhere, in the smell of rosemary permeating the whole kitchen, in the tang of bay leaves and tarragon. Hester suddenly feels, inexplicably, saddened. She is still not very good at this friendship thing, she chides herself, and she wonders if this will yet prove to be a mistake she has made, coming here again. The memory of this day, this house, the sun on the sea, and Alex calmly chopping garlic and onions may bring her pain on a cold winter's day when she sits alone in her house in England.

Alex turns the electric cooker down to simmer and they take a bottle of chilled white wine out on the balcony. The sun is hovering just above the woodland, where the trees end and the sea begins. The boats all seem to have vanished;

there is no one in the world out there, only a vast, but somehow comforting, emptiness.

They drink the wine silently. The sun goes down and Alex refills their glasses.

'Is the dinner all right?' Hester asks, breaking the spell. She can smell the aromatic herbs, the garlic, and instead of the breathtaking sunset, the superb wine, the companionship with Alex, she is thinking miserably of that woman who smells like rosemary, the woman with whom Alex must now be in love. Suddenly she is cross with herself. Why can't she let go, forget the past? If she is not careful she will ruin this new, tenuous relationship on which she is embarking with her old lover.

But she has forgotten how Alex can read her thoughts, her moods. 'About Ermi,' he begins.

'It's all right, Alex. I quite understand. Explanations are not necessary between friends.'

Hester feels this is hitting the right note: properly cool but still matey. Hard work, this friendship thing, she thinks bitterly.

But Alex is smiling and shaking his head. 'Oh Hester, my dear lovely Hester, I can read you like a book, like your beautiful poetry. Of course explanations are necessary, and if you will listen carefully to me, I will tell you all about Ermi.'

This isn't what Hester wants, not now with the stars out, the dinner cooking, the wine making her light-headed. But Alex listened patiently to her all afternoon and now it is his turn to talk.

'Ermi came into my life about three years ago,' he says slowly. 'As you know, she and her two young sons live with her mother and father in the village. She moved back to her family home when she and her husband separated.'

Hester is silent. She cannot think of anything to say, even though Alex has paused, and eventually he goes on.

'I met her one day in the village, I can't remember exactly where, in a shop I suppose, or perhaps at a mutual friend's house. She knew I was a carpenter and needed some conversions done to her parents' barn, which they said she could use to package her herbs.'

Alex breaks off what he is saying to go into the kitchen and stir his casserole. Suddenly Hester is starving, famished. She doesn't want to listen to Alex's love story; she wants to eat, stuff herself with food, be comforted.

But he comes back out and sits down again, saying, 'Not quite ready yet.'

'Oh. I'm hungry.'

'It won't be long. Anyway, to continue. Naturally I saw a great deal of Ermi, working in her barn every day. I wasn't much interested in finding a woman, starting a relationship again. In fact, after you left I took rather a grim pleasure in seeing myself as a crusty old bachelor for the rest of my days.' He grins. 'Or divorcé, I should say. Whatever, I certainly had no intention of ever getting myself tangled up with a woman again.'

'Oh. But then . . .' Hester trails off.

'But then – and you must remember that it was a good five years after you and I parted – somehow Ermi and I got together. I don't even remember how; these things just happen sometimes.'

Hester thinks of Gérard and has to agree.

'I'm sure Ermi was attracted to me less for my ageing charms, than for the fact that there was a definite lack of eligible men in the village. Somehow we found ourselves in bed, and from there we rather haphazardly drifted into a relationship.'

'I see. Of course.'

'It was an easy relationship, pleasant but prosaic, for both of us, I think. At one time she tried to pressure me into letting her and the boys move in here, more to get out of her parents' house than because of any great love for me, but I was still crusty enough and bachelor enough to make it clear it would never work. And so we drifted amiably along.'

'I see,' Hester says again, stupidly. 'Alex, I'm very interested, but I'm really so hungry, could we eat now?'

Alex laughs, he actually laughs out loud. 'Hester, you are wonderful, you never change. You always want to eat when you don't want to face things.'

Hester bristles at this. 'I have changed more than you

know,' she says mysteriously, thinking of how she jumped into bed with Gérard the first time he wined and dined her. She hasn't told Alex about it yet, and wonders if she ever will. It certainly isn't the time now, she thinks impatiently: if they both indulged themselves with talking about their love affairs, they'd never get dinner.

'Well, go on,' she says, a bit snappishly. 'If you will insist upon telling me about your love-life right before dinner, I will listen, but grudgingly.'

To Hester's surprise, Alex kisses her boisterously. 'This is much better, Hester. I like you when you are feisty, and not trying to be all understanding when really you are furious with me for not waiting patiently for you all these years.'

Hester starts to protest but he is helping her up, leading her towards the kitchen. 'I'll take pity on you. We'll eat first before you hear the rest of my romantic saga.'

The dinner is delicious, and Hester has three helpings. While they are eating they don't mention Ermi, and Hester hopes the subject is done with.

But when they have finished their meal Alex brings up another difficult topic, one Hester knows must be faced some time before this visit is over. Looking up at her across the table he says, 'I have wanted to ask you this since I first saw you again, Hester, but I kept quiet, waiting for you to begin. But you never did, and now I have to know.'

She senses what is coming, and of course he is right, he has to know.

Alex continues, 'Why did you break everything off so finally? Why did you never reply to all my letters? Why did you refuse so totally ever to see me again?'

And so, at last, Hester tells him. About her meeting with Angela, about the woman's threats, about her own fears. Then she explains about Martin's heart attack, coming suddenly as it did, and how she panicked, was afraid that if their affair continued, Angela would know, tell Martin, cause a second and fatal heart attack. She tells him everything, and when she is finished she wishes she had told him years ago.

Alex is silent for a very long time. Then he says, 'I am so, so sorry, Hester. For all you had to cope with.'

'I was terrified, Alex. I wasn't thinking straight at all. I knew she couldn't have known for sure about us—'

'She didn't. I never even mentioned you. But people talk, I suppose. Our colleagues at the college – we were careful I know, but people watch, gossip. Yet no one could have known for sure.'

'I knew that rationally, but if you could have heard her – threatening me, saying that if I ever saw you again, she'd warn Martin, and if it killed him it couldn't be helped . . . God, it was chilling.'

'I wish you had told me. I was frantic, not knowing what had happened.'

'I know. But I was too frightened, you see. Not for myself, but for my family.'

And then Hester tells him all the things she has wanted to for years, the things that have been going around and around her head, especially after their day in Concarneau, when she wanted to explain everything and Ermi interrupted. Alex listens quietly while she unburdens herself, describing her fears for Martin, for her daughters, of her irrational terror of Angela, the guilt the woman instilled in her . . . Hester talks and talks and when she finishes, she says what she should have said the first time they met again, on the ferry to Roscoff.

She tells Alex she is sorry. For the pain she caused him, for not trusting him enough to write to him about what happened. 'I was wrong not to tell you. I cannot say how much I regret it now. And how I despaired at the time, how I agonized over letting you go. I was going against all my instincts, my emotions. But I thought, I honestly thought, that it was my only option.'

Hester doesn't know if any of this is relevant now, but that's not important. What is important is to let him know these things.

And then Alex talks. He tells Hester of his confusion, his desolation after her letters. He tells her of his own letters, which he wrote later, and which Hester never received because of course she had left the college, had told the secretary not to forward anything after that initial batch.

'When my letters were returned I rang the college and tried to find out what had happened to you. Once, I even rang the rectory. I knew you had begged me not to, but I had to find out. Martin answered, and I boldly asked for you, said I was an old colleague of yours – he never recognized my voice, because of course I never saw him again after I left the comprehensive.'

'I never knew that. Martin didn't tell me.'

'I gave no name. He said you were out, and would I call again later.'

'Martin was always bad at giving me messages. He must have forgotten as soon as he put down the phone.'

Alex looks distressed. 'After that I gave up. It had been in my head that Martin could be seriously ill or worse, that *you* were ill, and that was why you wrote and ended everything. When Martin answered the phone sounding hale and hearty, saying you were out somewhere, I told myself I had better face the truth – you just wanted me out of your life, and I had better resign myself to it.'

Hester reaches out across the table, across the years, and touches his hand. 'I caused you all that pain, and yet I loved you so much,' she says sadly.

He holds her outstretched hand. 'I caused you pain, too, loving you when you were so tightly committed to your family.'

They are both quiet, remembering the past, remembering the pain. Finally Alex says, 'Shall we go out on to the balcony again? It's a lovely evening.'

He opens the cupboard, takes out a bottle of brandy and some glasses which they carry out to the balcony. As they sit and sip their drinks the moon, yellow and new and crescent, appears as if on cue from behind a small cloud and lies on its back over the ocean. They watch it for a long time, silent but at ease with each other.

'Ermi,' Alex states, breaking the spell. 'I was telling you about Ermi.'

'Oh Alex,' Hester sighs inadvertently. 'Do you have to?'

And spoil such a lovely meal, she thinks, but once again she controls her tongue. I'm getting better at this, she tells herself. Maybe I'll make a good mate after all.

'Hester, please just listen to what I am saying. I don't love Ermi, I didn't love Ermi, ever. I was fond of her, I still am, and feel great affection for her children, but I don't love her.'

'Well, no matter,' Hester says politely. 'As long as she understands that. One can have a very satisfying relationship without love.' Once again she thinks of Gérard.

'Ermi has always understood that, for she feels the same about me, though at times she has spells of thinking she loves me because she'd like to get married again, have a father for her children.'

'So why don't you marry her?' Hester says breezily.

'Oh, Hester, I've told you. I don't want to, have never wanted to.'

'Well, that's fine. You can just carry on the way you are.'

Alex goes into the kitchen for the brandy bottle and pours himself another drink. 'No, we can't carry on the way we are. I've finished that.'

'What? Why?'

'I haven't done it lightly. I've thought about it for weeks and weeks, ever since I saw you again on the ferry. I don't know about you, Hester, but that meeting totally disorientated me.'

'I know,' Hester says, reaching for the brandy. 'You were seasick for the first time in your life.'

'Hester, don't be flippant. Please.'

'I'm sorry, Alex. This is hard for me.'

'It's hard for me too.'

They are quiet for a minute and look at the moon, which beams splendidly on the water. Alex finally goes on, 'I came back to Kerrocher, after seeing you again the next day at Imogen's house, completely bemused. I wasn't sure then how I felt about you. I was as confused and uncertain as you must have been. But seeing you again reminded me of something, something I thought I had long ago forgotten.'

'Alex—'

'And gradually, as the days went on, as I talked to you once more, first on the phone and then seeing you again on that lovely day out we had, I gradually realized that whatever it is that I want in this life, whatever I need to be truly content and at ease with myself, it isn't what I had with Ermi.'

'Oh, Alex.'

'And I thought, if that was the case, what was the point of continuing the relationship?'

'Just like that?' Hester says weakly, trying to clear her head.

'It wasn't just like that, Hester. I thought about it all summer, that's why I didn't get in touch with you for a while. That was the business I kept telling you I was trying to wind up.'

'Oh.' Hester decides not to have any more brandy. Her heart is lurching about wildly, doing terribly daring things.

'I thought it better not to see you, not until I had sorted out in my own mind what I felt. Then when I was sure about my feelings, I had to resolve things with Ermi. I wanted to be fair to her, you see, and not see you until she and I had finished our relationship.'

Ermi, that poor dear herbal hamster. She has lost Alex, and Hester's heart goes out to her. For a second or two.

'How . . . did she take it?' Hester asks.

'In some ways I think she was relieved. She really does want to be married, you know. Hanging around with me was preventing her from becoming attached to anyone else. It would have ended anyway, because of that if nothing else. You appearing on the scene only precipitated it.'

Somewhere out on the water a light beams. Somewhere inside Hester lights are exploding. She blames it on the brandy. Neither one of them says anything for what seems like a long time. The light on the water flashes again in the dark.

'Hester, I don't know how you feel about me now – maybe you will never want to see me again after these few days. But I feel we have so much unfinished business left, so much we need to find out about each other before we let each other go a second time.'

Once again the light flashes. After a pause Alex adds quietly, 'Not that I want to let you go again.'

Hester turns to him. He is looking at her with such tenderness, such love, that she is not quite sure if she can bear it. She closes her eyes. This is her moment: and not the moon, nor the stars, nor the vast splendour of the sky at night can compete with what is happening inside her.

When she opens them Alex is looking at her. 'Don't cry,' he says gently.

'I'm not,' she lies.

When she can speak again Hester says, 'Please don't – ever let me go a second time. Please.'

He takes her hand and kisses the palm, the tips of her fingers, her wrist. 'Oh, Hester,' he says at last, 'I've been in such a turmoil since I met you on that ferry. Have you?'

'Me?' Hester says. 'Me?' She begins to giggle.

'Hester, are you laughing at me?' he asks, smiling.

'Oh Alex, no. No, I'm not laughing at you. I'm laughing because suddenly for the first time since I've seen you again, I'm *not* in a turmoil.' She stops, touches his face.

He says, only half teasingly, 'Do you want to write a poem about it?'

How well he knows her!

'Not yet,' Hester says. 'One day I will, but not yet. You know me, Alex – life comes first.'

He folds her hand between both of his and draws it to his chest, holds it there so that she feels his heartbeat through the cotton of his shirt.

'Or at least it is beginning to do so again,' she says softly. 'After all these years, life is taking over again.'

Alex winds his fingers tightly through hers. Across the darkness the lone light flashes off and on, off and on, into the sea.